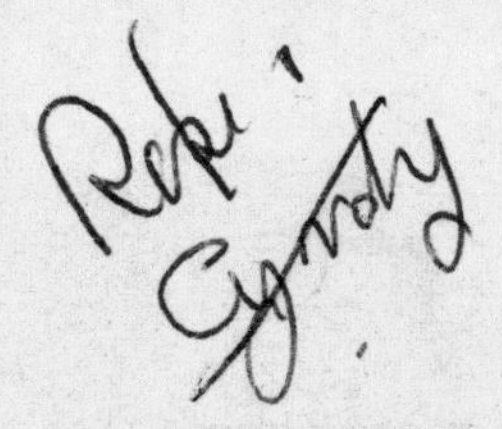

END GAME

Anna Smith was a frontline journalist for more than twenty years and is a former chief reporter for the *Daily Record* in Glasgow. She has covered wars across the world as well as major investigations and news stories from Dunblane to Kosovo to 9/11. Many of Anna's novels are set in different locations, such as Spain, Bosnia and Romania, as well as Glasgow and London. She lives mostly in Ireland and sometimes travels for research across Spain.

Also by Anna Smith

THE ROSIE GILMOUR SERIES

The Dead Won't Sleep

To Tell the Truth

Screams in the Dark

Betrayed

A Cold Killing

Rough Cut

Kill Me Twice

Death Trap

The Hit

THE KERRY CASEY SERIES

Blood Feud

Fight Back

END GAME

ANNA SMITH

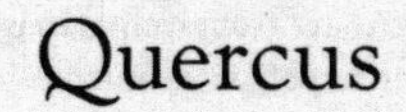

First published in Great Britain in 2020 by Quercus
This paperback edition published in 2020 by

Quercus Editions Ltd
Carmelite House
50 Victoria Embankment
London EC4Y 0DZ

An Hachette UK company

A CIP catalogue record for this book is available from the British Library

PB 978 1 78747 400 0
EB 978 1 78747 398 0

10 9 8 7 6 5 4 3 2 1

Typeset by Jouve (UK), Milton Keynes

Printed and bound in Great Britain by Clays Ltd, Elcograf S.p.A.

Papers used by Quercus are from well-managed forests and other responsible sources.

For Ross, who has always been there,
to listen, to talk and most of all to laugh!

'No one you love is ever truly lost'
Ernest Hemingway

PROLOGUE

He was screaming, but behind the duct tape it was no more than a muffled choking sound. Only his crimson, sweating face and the fear in his bulging eyes told of the terror. His ankles were bound tight, and they'd taped his hands across his chest and secured them fast to his body. Like the corpse the sick psychos planned to make him. Wolfie struggled and thrashed as much as he could inside the white satin-lined coffin, but all that happened was that his heart pounded so hard it felt about to burst in his chest. He saw them coming towards him with the coffin lid. They were actually going to fucking screw it down. He could hear the whispers and sniggers. He looked up at their faces so he would remember every single one of them. The whispering stopped, and all he could hear was the blood rushing in his ears as the lid was placed over the coffin. Pitch black. Then the sound of the screws being turned, and he tried to gulp in a breath of air. But there was none.

Wolfie had had no idea where he was at first when he'd come to after being clobbered on the head in the multi-storey car park earlier. But he'd swiftly realised he was in some fucking funeral parlour. And he wasn't one of the mourners. His head had been thumping from the blow on the temple that had brought him to his knees, and from the corner of his eye he had seen it was already swollen. Not that it seemed to matter now. He closed his eyes, and for a moment he could see himself as a young man, a girl on his arm, the free, happy charmer that he'd been all his life. And the grief that had overwhelmed him when he'd lost her. Christ! His life really was flashing in front of him like they said it did. Then the face of his darling daughter, Hannah, the beauty she had turned into, and his sadness that the last time he had seen her she had been sitting opposite him in a prison visiting hall, her face thinner, but her eyes as dancing with rage and determination as ever. She was getting out this morning and they'd been going to disappear, the two of them, far away, for a new life. They were rich beyond belief. This shouldn't be happening.

The diamond heist had been his fucking idea in the first place. He was the guy who had masterminded the whole operation. He was the man who had put himself on the line, working away inside the bank for the past three months, observing, checking, making pictures and plans of every movement of every member of staff: when they clocked in, when they clocked off, when the alarms went on. And, most importantly, it was him who had managed to sniff out the security numbers to get into the vault. So the success of the whole operation hung completely on him. And these fuckers, who were now about to either bury or cremate him, could never have pulled the heist off without him.

What kind of treacherous bastards did that? There was no honour amongst thieves any more – that was the problem. All lowlifes these days, cardboard gangsters who talked the talk, hawking their heroin and coke, trafficking women, selling kids as slaves. And they were just going to rub him out like he was some old has-been – once they got their hands on the safety deposit boxes that would not just make them millions, but, as it would turn out when they saw the contents, would also make them bombproof. That was why he hadn't told them the truth about where he'd stashed the gear. And he would take that secret to his grave if he had to. Which was looking pretty imminent. He tried to control his breathing. If this was it, then he was fucking sure he wasn't going to go out screaming and thrashing, and have his cold-blooded murderers dining out on the story of how William Joseph Wolfe met his end a snivelling wreck. And who knows, maybe there *was* something better on the other side. He could hear piped music. Piped fucking music! 'Nearer My God to Thee'. Jesus fucking wept!

Then suddenly, the crack of gunfire. One shot, two, then

the familiar ratatat of machine-gun fire. His heart stopped. The plinking of glass shattering, groans and angry, urgent shouts. Someone banging hard on the coffin. He kicked with all his might and gagged as he tried to shout. The sound of the lid being hacked and battered and finally prised open, and daylight on the face of big Tommo Gourlay. Wide-eyed and flushed, Tommo leaned in and ripped the masking tape off his face.

'Halle-fucking-lujah! What took you cunts so long?' Wolfie rasped, breathless.

'Sorry, boss. Trouble trying to find the right fucking funeral parlour.'

CHAPTER ONE

Kerry had thrown a party at the house for everyone in the Casey family. They were forty million quid up from the sale of the Colombians' cocaine they had nicked from the truck bringing it over from Spain, after lying in wait for it in an industrial estate in Manchester. Billy Hill's men had been standing by when the shoot-out started, and they had jumped straight in the back of the truck like a team of professionals, moving the massive haul of cocaine and getting out before the cops came. In the weeks that followed, Billy had shifted it to buyers he'd lined up, just as he'd promised he would. The money was a windfall, over and above the healthy earnings the Casey organisation already amassed on a weekly basis from their various businesses. The coke money had been squirrelled away by the Casey accountants who would then drip it into the hotel complex on the Costa del Sol under the name of the company set up to build the hotel and acquire more property in Spain and the UK. They were already looking at high-end restaurants along the Marbella coast which they could plough money into as a legitimate, expanding business empire. That side of their business was all squeaky clean.

For a few moments Kerry stood alone at the far side of the room, focused on the faces that had become so important to her – the people who were now her family. Most of them career criminals – killers, hitmen, robbers, whose life stories were mapped out in the scars on their faces. All of them loyal to the Casey family, and several among them who had murdered on their behalf. The body count after Manchester had been five dead, including Frankie Martin – Kerry's brother's trusted friend and right-hand man, who had ended up betraying him to his killers. Kerry tried to pretend she hadn't relished settling that score. But the biggest scalp of all had been down to Jake Cahill. The story of how he took out Pepe Rodriguez would go down in history among these people and their friends. But few people would ever dare talk to Cahill about it, and as he stood by the window in conversation with Jack and Danny, Kerry could see that people were in awe of him. No doubt Jake would slip out of the room later without a fuss, and Kerry probably wouldn't hear from him again until she needed his help. That was his way.

From across the room, Kerry saw Sharon Potter, the woman who'd fled to the Casey family after her husband, Manchester hood Knuckles Boyle, tried to have her executed. It was Sharon who'd delivered Boyle to the Caseys, in revenge for the murder of Kerry's brother Mickey, and then her mother, who died in the bloodbath at Mickey's funeral. When she looked back on that now, so much had happened in such a short space of time that Kerry sometimes struggled to remember her life before she'd come back to Glasgow; her life before she'd taken over as head of the Casey family. Sharon, who had moved among gangsters and hoods most of her life in Manchester, had proved to be a solid friend and confidante, and had become a crucial part of the Casey empire. Sharon looked at Kerry then came towards her.

'You look miles away, girl. You all right?'

'Yes.' Kerry held up her glass of mineral water. 'On my third glass of this. I could fairly sink a large gin and tonic though!'

'Yeah.' Sharon sipped from her gin and tonic, and Kerry could see she was quite tipsy. 'Well you'll be the only one without a hangover tomorrow.' She looked around the room. 'Everyone's having a good time, I think. I'm just so bloody glad to be alive.' She glanced over at Jake Cahill then back at Kerry. 'I owe Jake my life, Kerry. Totally. I'll never be able to repay him for what he did. If he hadn't dropped Rodriguez at the moment he did, you'd probably have got sent my head in a box, same as O'Driscoll.' She shuddered.

'Best not to even think that way,' Kerry said. 'Good times are ahead. No news from Vic yet?'

Kerry knew that Sharon hadn't heard from her lover Vic, who had been driving the truck full of cocaine for Rodriguez, after the carnage at the industrial estate in

Manchester. The last she'd heard was when he called from the boat the night before they docked to give her all the information so that the Caseys could hijack the truck. Kerry had seen him during the bedlam of the shoot-out, and assumed he'd got away. But so far they'd heard nothing. That had been six weeks ago. Kerry felt for Sharon because she knew she had strong feelings for Vic after they'd rekindled an old love that went back a long way, to Sharon's days in Manchester.

Sharon shook her head sadly.

'Nope. I'm worried about him. I'm sure he'll know by now that Rodriguez is dead, so maybe he's worried that he'll get linked to double-crossing the Colombians. In that case he'd have to lie low for a bit. But I'm surprised he hasn't even sent a message or made a call. Danny said he knows for sure he got away after the shooting and before the cops arrived, so he must be out there somewhere.' She shrugged. 'Tell you what, though. I'm just going to have to leave it at that. Not much I can do. And we'll have a lot on our plates in the next few months.'

'We sure will.' Kerry nodded.

'What about Vinny? You heard anything?'

'No. I suppose he's gone back undercover.' She paused, half smiling. 'Probably trying to track down the cocaine.'

'Well. Good luck to him on that.' Sharon raised her glass. 'I'm off to mingle. That old rascal Billy Hill is trying to chat me up. What is it with these old guys? He's quite funny though.'

Kerry watched as she walked off, then Marty Kane came across to talk to her. Marty had been the Casey family lawyer as long as she'd known him, and he'd been a close friend of her father Tim, who he'd kept out of jail as he built up his empire. He was the most respected criminal lawyer in Glasgow, but he sailed close to the wind, defending known hoods and hard men who had murdered and robbed their way through life. He was more than the Casey lawyer now – he was a trusted family member, as embedded with them as any of the other hoods in this room. That association with the Caseys had brought him to his knees just a few weeks ago, when the Colombian cartel kidnapped his little grandson, and for a terrifying week there was a real fear they would never see him again. It had almost broken Marty and his family. It was Kerry and her men who had rescued the boy and brought him back, leaving behind a trail of bodies and a seething Pepe Rodriguez determined to wipe out the Caseys.

Marty looked more relaxed tonight than she'd seen him in weeks. He clinked his glass to hers.

'You all right, Kerry?'

'Yeah. I'm good, Marty. Parties are not really a fun spectator sport for non-drinkers, but I'm happy enough. How's the family? I feel we haven't had a chance to speak since all of that happened. Seems like we've been under siege for months, even though it's only been weeks.'

'I know,' Marty replied. 'It's been a tough few weeks for

my family. I know they see Fin's kidnapping as my fault, and I know they'll never forgive me for it. Joe's wife has been traumatised and is bursting his head about moving far enough away to be safe, but so far Joe has resisted. I hope he doesn't move. Apart from us not seeing the boys so much and being in their lives, Joe has really been doing well since he's taken over the main thrust of the practice from me. He's getting quite a name for himself as a top defence brief. He's very able and gaining respect.'

'A chip off the old block. You must be very proud.'

'I am.' Marty grimaced. 'But he's a different generation, Kerry, and I'm not so sure his wife will be as easy-going as my Elizabeth was when I was on the frontline, working flat-out. It's different these days. Elizabeth did all the hard work, running the home for us and making it a great place for Joe to grow up, but Joe's wife is very different. And I think they've both had a real awakening when they almost lost Fin.'

Kerry gave Marty a supportive smile, but she could see how he would have no real influence in Joe's family. She felt the weight of responsibility for his trouble.

'I'm so sorry, Marty. I wish there was something I could do.' She touched his arm. 'Try not to worry about it. I'm sure it will all work itself out. Give them time.' She said it more in hope than anything else.

From over Marty's shoulder Kerry saw Jack and her uncle Danny come towards her, drinks in hand.

'One of the good days, eh, Kerry?' Danny raised his glass and took a sip. He was looking happy and relaxed.

Kerry smiled.

'Yep. Not been too many of them in recent times, but let's hope we've turned a corner.'

For a moment all four of them stood surveying the room full of people, the laughter and the chatter. Then Danny took a step closer to Kerry.

'Kerry, sweetheart, seeing as the four of us are here right now, I wanted to run something past you. Because there might be a bit of urgency in it.'

Kerry arched her eyebrows, glancing at all three.

'Don't give me any bad news, Danny. Not today.'

Danny put a hand up.

'No. No. Not bad news. Actually, something that has been put to me by a very old friend and associate, and I wanted to see what you thought.' He paused for a beat as all eyes were on him. 'It's a proposition.'

Kerry felt herself sigh inside, but her face showed nothing.

'Let's hear it then,' she said, looking at Danny.

'Right.' Danny sipped his drink. 'Very old friend of mine, well, of mine and your father's actually. William Wolfe. You ever hear his name? William Joseph Wolfe? Wolfie?'

Kerry gave him a puzzled look. Her father never confided in her who he worked with or even really what he did, and because she had been away in Spain from her teens, she had had no idea who he was involved with – though she guessed none of it was legal.

'Can't say I have,' she replied.

'Wolfie,' Marty said, a smile spreading on his face. 'Is that old bugger still around?'

'And how,' Danny quipped. 'Haven't seen him in years, and seldom hear from him apart from the odd phone call and chat maybe once a year. But we go back a long way – me, your dad and Wolfie. Could write a book on it, the things we got up to.' He leaned in a little. 'His speciality is cracking codes, safes, et cetera. Like your father, only more sophisticated, dare I say better.'

'Where's he from? Is he Glasgow?'

'No,' Danny said. 'Cockney as they come, Wolfie. Part of the London mob back in the day, but he went freelance, and we did a lot of work together – here and down south, the three of us. Some big jobs.'

Kerry had heard a few stories from Danny over dinners and nights at his house over the years, but they had never really stayed in her mind. It was only in recent months, since she'd been back home, that she could really see how far the Caseys had come and who they had been. How they had got there had come home to her in the first few sharp days, when suddenly she had found herself ordering hits on killers, and had been astonished that there were plenty of people out there who were available to do it.

'Anyway,' Danny said. 'Wolfie calls me up yesterday

morning and asks if he could have a meeting in Glasgow. I was driving back from Manchester at the time and wanted to tell you about it in person rather than talk to you on the phone. Wolfie wants to meet you, Kerry, as you're the daughter of his old mucker. He says he has a major proposition for you and for the Caseys that could make us very rich.'

Kerry puffed out a sigh.

'We're already rich, Danny. And we're trying to move on.'

'I know, I know. But this would make us even richer, and for not much effort. But not only that, Wolfie said he has information, stuff that could make us all bombproof with the cops.'

Marty looked puzzled.

'Bombproof? What's he talking about?'

'He hasn't said. Just said that he has evidence. Tapes and stuff. Photographs. Incriminating pictures of people in high places.'

'Oh aye,' Kerry said, a little sarcastic. 'Like we're in the mood to go blackmailing cops? I don't think so, Danny. But what else is he saying?'

Danny glanced over his shoulder as though afraid someone could hear, then lowered his voice as they all leaned in.

'You know that Hatton Garden heist a few weeks ago? The diamonds? We were in the middle of all our own shit, so we probably didn't pay attention to it.'

'Yeah,' Kerry said as everyone nodded. 'The strongboxes

and diamonds. Course. It's been all over the news. Must have taken some pluck to carry that off the way they did.'

Danny nodded. 'Yep. Sure did. Wolfie was only at the centre of the whole shebang, the sly old fucker! Sixty bloody two, he is, and he's in there on the biggest robbery the UK has seen since the Great Train job.'

'Really? He was part of the heist? So why is he telling you?'

'Because the bastards he worked with have all turned on him. He says he got the gypsy warning that they were going to cut him out of it, like he was some old bastard past his sell-by date. But he says the heist was not only his idea, but that he masterminded the whole robbery.'

Kerry still looked puzzled.

'So why tell us? What can we do?'

'He stashed the stuff away when he heard they were planning to shaft him. Hidden it in some very secret locations, and he's going on the run before they come after him again. They've already tried to murder him. And if he doesn't get off his mark, they'll try again. Once they get the gear and all the stuff they nicked, they'll get rid of Wolfie. He sounded well stressed out.'

'I'll say he is,' Kerry said, not quite believing what she was hearing. The last thing she needed right now was to become embroiled in a feud with even more gangsters who had pulled off the robbery the whole country was talking about. She glanced from Marty to Danny to Jack. 'Guys.

We're supposed to be leaving all this shit behind us and going legit.'

'I know,' Danny said, looking a little deflated. 'It's just that Wolfie's such a good mate, Kerry, and I think he's in trouble. He wouldn't have called me if he wasn't in real bother. If he's calling me, it's because he's shit scared to talk to anyone else, because everyone is looking for him.'

'Has he family?'

'A daughter. Hannah. About your age.' He paused. 'She's in jail. Or just out.'

'Jail for what?' Marty asked.

'Manslaughter.'

'Jesus!' Kerry said, rolling her eyes. 'Charming!'

'She killed one of the guys who put a bomb in Wolfie's wife's car and blew her to bits,' Danny added quickly, his face serious. 'That was about seven or eight years ago. Hannah went after him, and Wolfie said she vowed to get all of them responsible.' Danny looked a bit perplexed. 'I suppose that sounds a bit complicated, but all I'm doing is running it past you as I said I would.'

They all stood for a moment, nobody saying anything, Kerry trying to get her head around it. All she could really see was a woman in jail for a revenge killing, and that was the part she could identify with. That could have been her. If the Casey family hadn't all been there to pick her up after her mother died at Mickey's funeral, she could have been that girl who went out to hunt down the killers in the midst of her grief. This guy, Wolfie, was important to Danny, and he'd been important to her father all those years ago. That made him matter to her. Before she could stop herself, she spoke.

'Okay. Let's meet him then. Can't do any harm, can it. He's an old family friend. He deserves that much.'

Danny looked relieved and Jack smiled as he put his glass to his lips.

'Well said, Kerry.'

Kerry glanced over their shoulders and around the room, and hoped to Christ she wasn't getting herself into something even deeper than she'd just got out of.

CHAPTER TWO

Hannah Wolfe checked her watch for the umpteenth time since she'd woken up. Fifteen minutes to go. In fifteen minutes her cell door would open and she'd walk out without so much as a backward glance. She would walk down the corridor behind the prison officer, the rhythmic clicking of her heels on the stone floor tapping out her steps to freedom. She'd go through the two locked doors, past the other cells, then down the hall, where other prisoners would look on, burning with envy that it wasn't them. They'd be about to start a new day like any other day, like tomorrow and all their tomorrows until their day came and they could walk this walk just like Hannah. Of course, some of them would never see that. Like old Nellie McDade who had taken an axe to her husband's head the day after she discovered his affair with the bitch down the road he'd been teaching to drive. Or teenager Joanne Carr, who had stabbed the playground bully to death, and was detained at Her Majesty's Pleasure, meaning she would probably never see the light of day. But others, the drug dealers and fraudsters, the whorehouse madam, the hapless drug mules, the violent women who shot and robbed and strangled, would one day be walking out just like her. Truth was, she would miss them.

Hannah had done her time, but her quest for revenge was far from over. The five years she'd spent inside were a small price to pay for the satisfaction of seeing one of the men who'd murdered her mother take a swan dive from the twelfth-storey window of his London flat. One down, one to go, she'd told herself, as she'd waited in his flat long enough to watch him splatter onto the pavement below. The jury had believed her convincing performance of self-defence, and the charges had been reduced to manslaughter. As she was led stone-faced from the dock, she'd bitten back tears when she saw her father standing in the front row, trying not to cry, his heart now crushed not once but twice.

She was glad when the click of her cell door opening shook her from the gloom. She stood up from her bed, pulled on her leather bomber jacket, and slung her rucksack over her shoulder.

'You ready for this, Hannah?' the prison officer said from the doorway.

'I was born ready,' Hannah quipped back, defiant.

The prison officer shook her head and half smiled but didn't speak as she turned and walked down the hall with Hannah at her heels.

When the prison doors were opened, Hannah took a breath and stepped outside into the soft drizzle. She stood on the steps for a moment, enjoying the rain on her face, her eyes scanning the car park, watching for her father to appear as planned. But he didn't. A twinge of anxiety lashed across her gut. This wasn't right. Her father was meticulous about time, to the point of obsessive. He was never late. And he would never have been late today. He would have been here at least an hour ago. She felt immediately exposed as her eyes again flicked across the car park, suddenly feeling a threat from every shadowy figure she could see sitting behind a steering wheel. She watched for any movement, but there was none. She was on her own. The aching deflation after weeks of anticipation took the wind right out of her sails. But Hannah stiffened her shoulders and zipped up her jacket as she walked down the stairs and headed towards the bus stop outside the prison gates.

It was an hour and a half to London on the bus, and Hannah sat gazing out of the window, making sure she didn't make eye contact with anyone who came on and would want to exchange small talk. She pushed her hand in to the zipped pocket of her jacket and counted the notes without taking them out. She had thirty quid, enough to get her to her flat to dig out her old phone SIM card and the bank cards her father had left for her. Then she would go to the phone shop and buy a new mobile. Without a phone, she had no way of contacting anyone. First-world problems. Again, the niggle in her stomach. What if something had happened to her father? William J Wolfe had made plenty of enemies in his long and chequered criminal career. He was over sixty now and hadn't been involved in any capers for the past few years, until six months ago, when he'd come up with the plot to rob the strongboxes at the bank at Hatton Garden where some of the richest people in the country and beyond stored their money, jewellery and anything else they wanted to hide. She'd thought he was off his head for being crazy enough to even consider it, but by the time he'd hinted to Hannah that it was a goer, he was already embedded with some of the biggest gangsters in London in order to pull it off. When she'd seen the news about the robbery on television a couple of weeks ago, she couldn't help but smile to herself. On his last visit, he was more buoyed up than she'd ever seen him. As soon as she got out, they would be off to a new life in a far-off land – the Cayman Islands were his happy place, he'd told her. This shit would all be behind them. But Hannah knew that not everything could ever be behind them, because her grief and thirst for revenge had walked beside her like a ghostly figure, urging her on since her mother had been blown up in the car bomb. Some no-mark, lowlife thugs who'd wanted to get back at her father for some ancient wrongdoing a lifetime ago had ripped the heart from her family. She knew her father would never recover, and part of her in the beginning had wanted to hate him, because it was his life that had brought them to this. But he was all she had, and she could see he was utterly broken. So she took over from her mother, looked after him, listened in almost disbelief to his stories of the old days, and, despite everything, they laughed a lot. He'd always told her there would be one last big payday in him, and it was going to happen, but she never believed him, and let him ramble on. In any case, Hannah didn't care for the trappings of wealth. She'd made money from the property she'd bought and sold on – not all of it legal. But she considered it victimless crime when the only people you robbed were the bankers and the building societies who robbed everyone anyway. She worked and made a small fortune. She could have done anything she'd wanted: settled down, found herself a husband. But ever since her mother had been murdered, she lived only for revenge. And it wasn't over yet. For weeks now, she'd been counting down the minutes until she would walk out of the prison doors and her father would be waiting. She could almost see his smile, the twinkle he had in his eye. He'd have their passports, he'd told her, and they were headed off to a new life far away. And she'd promised herself she would go with him, because she didn't want to see the look of disappointment on his face if she told him she had other plans. A wave of sadness washed over her as she rested her head back and closed her eyes, because she'd be damned if she was going to fucking cry.

*

Hannah emerged from the Tube station at Canary Wharf and walked briskly towards her flat. She'd bought the swish two-bedroom gaff overlooking the River Thames after a sweet property deal she'd been working on for months had come through. She loved the place, but had only spent six months in it before she had been sent to jail. As she got closer to the building, she found she was automatically looking over her shoulder and then glancing around the vicinity, suddenly suspicious that she was being followed. On the bus journey from the jail, she'd considered giving the flat a body swerve for the moment, in case something really *had* happened to her father. Her gut told her something was wrong. Nothing would have kept him from coming to prison to pick her up this morning. And even if he couldn't make it, he would have sent someone else to meet her. It wasn't right. But she needed to get into the flat to get her SIM card and bank cards and then get out and get a mobile phone. She didn't even have enough cash on her to get to her old man's place, but even if she did, she wouldn't go near it anyway. Something wasn't right.

She keyed in her security password and slipped through the main entrance into the empty hallway. She stood in front of the two lifts, watching each floor number light up as they were both descending. She held her breath as one of them stopped and the doors parted. A middle-aged lady came out and smiled at her as she walked past and out of the main door. Hannah stepped into the lift and pushed the button for the ninth floor, watching every floor, hoping it didn't stop, feeling more jittery by the minute. *Calm down*, she told herself. The hallway was as deserted as she would have expected on a weekday morning, as a lot of the building's occupants worked in the city. It had never been a place where you even knew who your neighbours were, but Hannah had been quite happy with the anonymity when she bought the flat. Right now, though, she would have given anything for a friendly face coming out of one of the flats next to hers. She walked to her door at the far end of the hallway, consciously listening for the lift in case it pinged a new arrival. She shoved the key into the lock and opened the door, going quickly inside.

She closed the door and stood for a moment with her back to it, letting out a sigh of relief, but at the same time berating herself for allowing the paranoia to almost overwhelm her the way it had in the past few minutes. Maybe it was because she'd been institutionalised for so long that being out in the open had just hit her? It had verged on being a panic attack and she took a deep breath and let it out slowly. She put down her bag and walked softly down the hall, taking in the pleasant tones of the walls and the warmth of the décor. The living room was bright and welcoming with a view that took her back to pleasant nights she'd spent here, sometimes by herself, sometimes with the occasional lover she'd met along the way. Her last longish relationship had been a couple of years before she went inside, with an English teacher who wanted to be a writer. It had lasted nine months but fell apart because he couldn't cope with her moods and the darkness that often enveloped her. She'd brooded about it for six whole days, but then decided that was long enough. Short term was the best and most convenient way, she'd decided.

She went into her bedroom, opened one of the bedside drawers and took out the bank card hidden at the back below some papers. She felt along the back of the drawer and found her SIM card taped to the wood. She stuffed both of them into her jeans pocket and glanced around the room, a fleeting image of a past life flashing into her mind. For a moment, she wondered if she would ever come back here. Then she went out into the kitchen, glanced around, briefly considered making herself a cup of tea, but then decided against it. She went into the spare bedroom she used as a dressing room and threw some tops, trousers, blouses and underwear into a small bag. Then, as she was going back into the hall, she heard a noise. Like the sound a mobile phone makes when a message drops. She stopped in her tracks, then took two steps along the hall to where the bathroom door was slightly ajar, and to her horror she glimpsed a man's reflection in the mirror. She walked backwards to the kitchen, slid out a carving knife from the stand and held it tight by her side as she stole back down the hall. Whoever the Christ this was, it wasn't a surprise welcome home party. She had to pretend she hadn't seen him, because he hadn't seen her. She went into her bedroom, opening and closing doors as though she was busy, hoping to lure him out of his hiding place. Her back was to the bedroom door, but her senses told her he was behind her. She could almost smell him. In a flash, she turned around, lashing out with the knife, but she missed the squat, sweating figure standing before her, pointing a gun. He drew his lips back in a sarcastic smile and made as though to shoot. But before he had the chance she'd dropped down, then struck out with the knife, stabbing his leg. He gasped.

'Bitch!' he spat, a look of shock on his face. 'I'll fucking kill you.'

He lunged at her and knocked her off her feet, the knife falling out of her hands. Then he was on top of her, punching her face. She felt dizzy, blurred, tried to push him off. She grabbed his wrist and smashed his hand on the wooden frame of the bed, and he winced as the gun dropped.

'Bitch,' he said again.

'Who the fuck are you?' she muttered as the weight on her chest almost suffocated her. 'Why are you doing this?'

'Ask your fucking daddy!' he said.

He put his other hand around her neck and squeezed, choking her. She couldn't breathe. If she didn't get this fat bastard off her, she would be dead in about five seconds. She couldn't move, but she sure as fuck hadn't spent five years in the nick to come out and be strangled by some fat fucker in her own home. Adrenalin, survival and rage kicked in all at once and gave her a renewed strength. In a flash, she jabbed her index finger right into his eye. It was enough to stop him, and she felt sick to see the blood immediately oozing out of the lid. His grip weakened, and he tried to recover, steadying himself, trying to squeeze again, but she managed to push him off, and then crawled quickly across and picked up the gun. She was on her feet, her legs like jelly.

'Fuck you!' she said. 'You've got three seconds to tell me what the fuck you are doing here, and I might let you live.'

'Fuck off,' he said. 'Shoot me then!'

Hannah immediately fired a shot which bounced off the carpet a couple of inches from his body and ricocheted across the room. He looked at her in disbelief.

'Fucking hell!'

'Two seconds. One . . .' she cocked the gun again, 'two . . .'

'Stop! Stop for fuck's sake!' He put his hands up. 'I was only sent here to bring you out.'

'Out where?'

'To them. To Nick and the boys. They've got your old man.'

'What?' she said, images of her father being tortured or beaten coming into her head. 'Who the fuck is Nick? Why have they got my father?'

'Listen.' He tried to sit up.

'Don't get up,' she said. 'Sit where you are. Keep talking.'

He put his hand to his eye and winced. It was bloody and swollen and red.

'You fucking blinded me, you bitch.'

'Shut up or I'll shoot your other eye out,' Hannah snapped. 'Why have they got my father?'

'Look, I don't know the full story, but he wasn't being honest with them. He's got the gear and he won't give it to them.'

'What gear?' She suspected she knew what it was but wondered if he would be stupid enough to tell her and confirm her suspicions.

'I don't know. From the heist. The Hatton Garden heist. Your old man double-crossed the gang. They're going to kill him. Probably have by now.'

Hannah's stomach dropped to the floor. She knew it. He couldn't come to get her this morning because these bastards had kidnapped him. She prayed she wasn't too late. But she had no idea what she was going to do next. It wasn't as if she could go to the bloody cops.

He must have seen the blood drain from her face and as she pointed the gun at him, he looked up at her with his one eye.

'Please. Please don't shoot me. I . . . I've got family. Got a girl. Your age. Please. I didn't want to do this.'

'Fucking hell!' Hannah said.

She stood over him, this middle-aged oaf, his beer belly hanging over the waistband of his jeans, and the smell of fear and fags and stale drink telling its own story. If she didn't shoot him now, then someone else would, as soon as they discovered he had failed to do the job he was sent on. But she couldn't shoot him. Not here, not like this, with the blood on his face, and the fear in the one eye that he could see out of, that was now watering with tears.

'Get up!' she said, shaking her head. 'Let's go.'

He manoeuvred onto all fours and got unsteadily to his feet, his hands shaking.

'Go where?'

'Well you've got nowhere to go, mate, that's for sure. Once they know you fucked up spectacularly here, what do you think they're going to do with you?'

He said nothing, his mouth trembling.

'Move, hard man!' she said, standing aside to let him pass her. 'Go towards the front door. And don't try to run. You're locked in.'

He staggered a little, his hand covering his eye as he limped down the hall. She walked behind him, picked up her rucksack, then went back down the hall and into the kitchen. She grabbed some stuff from the cupboard to put on his eye. *How stupid is this?* she rebuked herself. He was trying to choke the life out of her five minutes ago, now she was stuffing gauze and antiseptic and bandages into her pockets to help him. But whoever he was, she couldn't afford to let him go. He might have pointed a gun at her, but this fat boy would never have used it. And the fact that they'd sent a guy of this calibre to monster the daughter of William J Wolfe and bring her in, said a lot about the kind of stupid pricks they were.

'Let's go.' She opened the door and pushed him out into the hallway.

'What about my eye? It's fucking agony.'

'I'll fix your eye. But listen to me. You try to run when we get out of here, and I'll shoot you in the fucking back. You hear that?'

He nodded, didn't answer. She prodded him into the lift and kept the gun on him until they hit the ground floor. When they got outside the building, they stood for a moment, Hannah glancing along the row of blocks to see if the old café was open. It was.

'This way,' she said.

Even if he wanted to run, Hannah could knock him off his feet in five yards. But he didn't. He walked meekly to the nearby café, where she knew the owner and his wife, a Polish couple, wouldn't ask any awkward questions. When they got to the place and walked inside, the owners glanced from one to the other, then, as though it was all perfectly normal, the husband came out from behind the counter and embraced Hannah.

'Hannah!' he hugged her. 'Long time no see.'

'Sure is, Aleksy,' she said, glad to feel the warmth of an old friend. 'Too long.'

CHAPTER THREE

It had taken Wolfie the best part of an hour and two large brandies to bring him back to anything near normality. By the time they'd pulled into the car park of the hotel outside Watford, he'd been so shaky when he stood up that big Tommo had had to support him until he got himself steady. The very action of having to be helped for the first few steps made him angry and sad at the same time. Twenty years ago he might have shrugged off this morning's trauma, but Wolfie was sixty-two now, and this was the first time he had really felt his age. He consoled himself with the fact that what had just happened to him a couple of hours ago was no minor fracas, that the bastards had actually been about to cremate him or bury him alive in that coffin. Anyone would be left distraught by that, and he'd probably have nightmares for the rest of his life. But at least he'd be having his nightmares far away from this shithole, where Alfi Ricci and his band of robbing, double-crossing fuckers would be turning over every house in London trying to find him. Once Alfi discovered that the hit squad he sent to torture and kill Wolfie were lying in a bloodbath in the funeral parlour, the fat little Tally bastard would be apoplectic. The thought of his rubber lips spraying saliva as he barked out orders to his henchmen brought a smile to Wolfie's face. Even now. Even though he was still in the shit; still sitting on millions of stolen diamonds that everyone wanted, but of which only Wolfie knew the whereabouts.

'What you feeling so happy about, boss?' Tommo said, planking himself down on an armchair next to him.

'Happy isn't exactly the word, Tommo,' Wolfie said. 'I'm just allowing myself a little moment to imagine how the shit hit the fan when they broke the news to Alfi that Lazarus had escaped his own funeral.' He grinned, downed the last of his brandy. 'Little cunt.'

'I'll drink to that,' Tommo said, as he raised his glass. The other two men in the room, who were Wolfie's closest associates, did the same. A bunch of them had all grown up together in a Whitechapel council ghetto in the sixties, where the law of the jungle ruled and to survive you had to outsmart and outfight anyone who got in your way. By the time they were sixteen most of them had seen the inside of Borstal more than once to prepare them for the big wide world.

Wolfie's expression suddenly darkened. He still hadn't

spoken to Hannah since he escaped. And he knew she would be beside herself with worry after walking out of the prison doors earlier that morning and finding he wasn't there to meet her. She would know that could only mean one thing: that her father was in big trouble. For five years, he'd been longing for the moment when she would walk into his arms and they would both be free for ever. And he'd missed it.

'All kidding aside, boys, I need to hear from my Hannah.' He shook his head. 'We need to get to her.' He looked at his watch. 'She should have been to her flat by now, and she'll have been calling my mobile. But those fuckers smashed it to a bleedin' pulp.'

Wolfie had dropped one of the boys off in Watford to pick up a new mobile for him, but he hadn't come back yet. Tommo had been calling Hannah's mobile since they'd made their escape earlier, but there was no answer. Wolfie was beginning to think that maybe Alfi's men had got to her, with some shit story that they were taking her to meet him. There was a gentle knock at the door and everyone recognised the voice of Stan as he said, 'It's me!'

Wolfie breathed a sigh of relief as the door opened and in walked Stan, brandishing a new phone.

'It's all ready to go, Wolfie, mate. You've got half a dozen missed calls there.'

He handed Wolfie the mobile. He scanned the numbers and his heart leapt when he saw all but one of them was from Hannah. The only other one was from Danny, his old mucker in Glasgow who he'd asked for help yesterday, just before he'd been clobbered and kidnapped. But first, he had to talk to Hannah. He stood up, walked towards the bathroom and pressed her number. He closed the bathroom door behind him, surprised at how choked he was that her number was ringing. After several rings he heard Hannah's voice in a soft whisper.

'Dad!'

Wolfie struggled to compose himself, his throat tight with emotion.

'Hannah! Sweetheart! You all right? I'm so sorry I wasn't there, darlin'.'

'Dad! I . . . I . . . He told me you were probably dead by now.'

'What?' Wolfie stiffened. 'Who? Who told you that? Where are you? Are you all right?'

'I'm all right, Dad. Honest. Some guy. In my flat. He was there when I got in.'

'Jesus fucking wept, Hannah! Did he hurt you?'

'Nah! He was just a stupid guy they'd sent to bring me to them. To get back at you. He had a bloody gun pointed at me, but I could see he was shitting himself.' She paused. 'But what happened to you? Are you all right? Where are you?'

'I'm okay. That Alfi Ricci bastard tried to have me done in, but Tommo and the boys saved me. Close shave, though, that's for sure. I'll tell you when I see you. Where are you? I'll send someone. I want you with me.'

'No. Don't send anyone. I'll come to you.'

Wolfie told her the name of the hotel.

'Okay. Got it. I'll be there in the next couple of hours. Don't worry, Dad.' The line went dead.

Wolfie swallowed his emotion. His little girl, the kid he'd made the world safe for, was telling him not to worry. He squared his shoulders, shook himself out of it, then stepped across to the bathroom mirror and looked himself in the eye. Alfi Ricci would rue the day he sent one of his thugs to threaten his girl.

Wolfie's mobile rang and shuddered in his hand, and he could see Danny's name on the screen. He answered after two rings.

'Danny! Hey, mate! How you doing?'

'I've called you a couple of times, Wolfie. No answer. Thought you'd changed your mind.'

'Sorry, mate. I was at a funeral.'

'Oh, right. Sorry to hear that. Anyone I know?'

'Yeah. It was mine.'

Wolfie listened to the silence for a few seconds, then Danny chuckled, 'Aye right, Wolfie! Same old pish from you. Listen. I talked to Kerry Casey. She said she'll see you. So, get your rigor mortised arse up here.'

'I'll be there tonight, Danny. I'm just waiting for Hannah to come over.'

'Tonight?' Danny said. 'It's two o clock just now. You going to fly?'

'No. I'll drive up. I'll get a hotel in Glasgow and it would be great if I could see you and Kerry tomorrow. Would that work?'

Wolfie wanted to get out of London as soon as possible, and as safely as he could.

'Sure. I'll talk to Kerry. I'll book you a couple of rooms at a hotel and send you the details.'

'Good man, Danny. Looking forward to seeing you, mate. Seems like a lifetime ago.'

'Aye. It does that.'

Hannah had seen that Aleksy had slid into the seat opposite the fat man, while she'd talked to her father on the phone from the other end of the café. Not that the café owner would have been able to do much if the fat man had decided to do a runner. But as he'd sat there with his hand on the bandage she'd wrapped around his head, covering his damaged eye, she didn't think he was in the mood to make a run for it. But what the hell was she going to do with him? Hannah wondered as she crossed the room and sat down. Aleksy got up and blinked a nod to her that he was watching out for her. Hannah put the coffee cup to her lips and downed the dregs. Then she turned to the fat man.

'So,' she said. 'Who are you? What's your name?'

'Joseph.' He kept his eyes on the table. 'Joey, to my mates. Joey Mitchell.'

'So, Joey Mitchell. What now? Do you have a plan?'

He looked at her with his one good eye and she felt a bit sorry for him. Of course he didn't have a plan. How could he go back to the people who'd sent him here and tell them what happened?

Joey touched his bloodstained jeans where Hannah had stabbed him. The wound on the outside of his thigh was still oozing blood and probably should have had a couple of stitches in it, she guessed, though she hadn't seen how bad the damage was.

He put his head in his hands.

'Christ knows! I'm going to have to lie low somewhere.'

'They'll be looking for you – this Nick you said who sent you.' She narrowed her eyes. 'Who's he, by the way? Who does he work for?'

'Ricci,' he replied, looking at her. 'Alfi Ricci. The Italian. He put the bodies up for the heist with your father. You heard of him? I work for him too, well a bit. He's a kind of second cousin of my old mum's.'

Hannah shook her head slowly and let the silence hang for a few beats. Then she clasped her hands together on the table and sighed.

'You're going to have to call them and tell them what happened. Then disappear.'

He said nothing, only stared forlornly at the table. Hannah checked her watch. She'd have to get a move on if she was going to be in Watford soon. She was desperate to see her father, even though he said he was fine, and she was keen to see what plans he had. She let Joey sit there for a moment, festering in his own failure. It crossed her mind that even though he'd had a gun in her face an hour ago, he could be useful to her. From where she was sitting, he didn't look like a guy with a lot of choices.

'Tell you what,' Hannah said. 'Why don't you help me out, and maybe there's something I can do for you.' She paused. 'I think you're running out of time. If you don't call your boss shortly, then they'll get suspicious and come looking for you.'

He nodded and swallowed.

'I know.' Then he looked at her. 'But what do you mean, help you out?'

Hannah studied his face, the two-day greying stubble on his jowls, his cream chequered shirt looking a little grubby around the collar.

'Make the call to your boss – to Nick or Alfi or whoever pulls your strings.'

'And tell them what? I got my eye poked out by Wolfie's daughter?' He shook his head and puffed.

'You don't have to put it like that. You could just say I got away, that I was fast and I managed to get out of the flat ahead of you and you couldn't catch me.' She paused, watching it sink in. 'You could tell them that you roughed me up a bit, and got some information out of me, that my father was on his way to Heathrow Airport and headed for Málaga, and that I was meeting him there. You could tell them that. And that you almost choked me to death and got me to admit that my father has a buyer for the diamonds and they are going to Málaga to meet him.'

He looked at her, incredulous.

'You making this up?'

She rolled her eyes. 'Course! You think I'd be telling *you* that if it was true?'

He seemed to shrink a little at the putdown.

'No.'

'If you tell them that story, then it buys me time to get the hell out of here, go and meet my father and get as far away as possible.' She paused. 'But it's nowhere near Heathrow Airport, or in fact any airport. All you have to do is tell them that's where we're headed, and they might be stupid enough to come after us there.'

'I see,' he said. 'And what if I just get up and walk out of here?'

'Up to you. But you might find that before you get very far, a car will pull up, and you'll be bundled into the back of it by Nick or some of his cronies, and the next time anyone hears of you will be when your bloated corpse pops up on the Thames.' She raised her eyebrows for emphasis. 'Get the picture?'

He said nothing for a few moments, and Hannah was working out in her head how much cash she could give him as a sweetener. She had the feeling that he could be useful to her father as a spy in the camp, if he was able to sell his bosses a story that would let him escape with his life. They still might bump him off, but they might not, and keep him alive just to use him as fodder from time to time. He might be able to get some inside information that he could punt her way so that they would know when the next move was being made against them. It was a long shot. But she had to do something, and fast. Because she was going to have to get moving and out of this area pronto in case they came looking for her.

'Okay,' he said. 'I'll make the call. I'll take what's coming from them.' He sniffed. 'But what's in it for me?'

She ignored the question. 'How you going to explain your eye?'

His hand went up to the bandage. 'I'll say I fell, opened a door or something onto it at my house and it got quickly infected, and that I've had to go to hospital. If I can lie low for a few days, I might get away with it.' He stopped, looked embarrassed. 'But I've got no money.'

Hannah looked at him, his head down. Then he glanced up at her, his face flushed.

'I'm a gambler. I've lost everything. Family, my home. The lot. What I told you about having a daughter your age is true – but the real truth is she hasn't spoken to me in two years. My wife chucked me out when she saw I had remortgaged the house and spent the money.' He wiped his nose with the back of his hand, and Hannah thought for a moment he was going to cry. 'I'm living in a hostel.'

'A hostel?' she said. 'And does Nick and his mob know that's where you live?'

'No. They don't ask questions. They just assume I'm at home. They only use me now and again. Sometimes if they need a bit of strong-arming.'

Hannah almost laughed.

'Well I'm not too sure that strong-arming is your bag. Maybe time to look for a different career?'

'Yeah. I'm going to get help for the gambling.'

Hannah still couldn't believe that any half-arsed gangster worth his salt would send such a shambolic wreck on what might have been an important mission. Perhaps this shabby figure before her really had been an enforcer in his day. But he didn't look anything like that now.

'Okay. Let's get out of here. There's a cash point a few yards away. I'll get some dosh out for you, and you can disappear, buy yourself dinner, or blow it at the dog track. Up to you. But I want to hear you making the call first. You got that?'

He nodded. She stood up, and he got to his feet, a little unsteady, wincing in pain.

'Let's go,' she said, striding past the counter, where she turned to Aleksy and his wife. 'I have to move, guys, but I'll see you soon. I promise.'

The Polish couple nodded in that economical way that Eastern European people sometimes did, with very little movement, just a slight incline of the head and a blink of the eye.

At the cash point, she took out three hundred quid – two for him, and one to keep her going for her journey in case she took a taxi at some stage. She glanced around to make sure there were no suspicious cars lurking or cruising. There weren't.

'Make the call,' she urged him. 'Put it on speaker so I can hear.'

He took out his mobile and punched in a number. She heard it ringing, then after three rings someone answered.

'Fuck have you been, Joey? Boss has been looking for you. Where's the bird?' The voice was angry, rasping.

'She got away,' he said sheepishly.

'Fuck me, man! How the fuck?'

'She was a fit, strong bird, and ran like fuck. But I had her on the ground for a bit in her flat, and I got her to tell me some stuff.'

'Christ! What stuff?'

'She says she was going to Heathrow to meet Wolfie. That they were on a plane to Málaga this afternoon. She said they were meeting a diamond dealer. She didn't know any more than that.'

'Why didn't you bring her to us?'

'Like I told you, man. She got away. I couldn't catch her.'

'You think she's lying?'

'I honestly don't know. But I don't think so.'

'Right. I'm going to have to talk to Alfi on this. Don't go far from a phone.'

'I've got a hospital appointment.'

'Yeah, fucking right. More likely to be a fucking bookie's appointment. You really are a useless tosser. I don't know why we even use you any more.'

Hannah watched as he took the shit and didn't answer. He looked up at her, humiliated. The phone went dead.

'Nice guy,' Hannah said. 'You want to look for another job, mate. Seriously.'

She handed him the two hundred quid.

'Listen. I'm trusting you on this, though Christ knows why, given you tried to choke me an hour ago. But you look to me like you need a break. So I'm going to give you one. But watch my lips. You double-cross me, I'll hunt you down. And this time I'll knock your other eye out. You got that?'

He nodded, stuffing the money in the zipped pocket of his bomber jacket. She took his phone and punched in her number.

'Here's my mobile. You call me if you get anything you think me and my father might want to know about Alfi and his bunch of arseholes. They'll have eyes everywhere looking for Wolfie, so whenever they move, I want to know about it. If you don't fuck up, you might make some serious money out of this. But if you double-cross us, you'll be dead. You got that?'

'Yeah,' he said. 'I got that.'

'Okay. Now go to a hospital and get that leg seen to, and your eye.'

He nodded.

'Thanks,' he said as he turned away.

Hannah watched for a few seconds as he limped up the road then flagged down a taxi. She couldn't make up her mind if he was going to the hospital or the nearest bookies. But that was no longer her problem. She walked briskly to the Canary Wharf Underground station. If she was lucky she could be in Watford in an hour.

CHAPTER FOUR

The very last thing Kerry Casey needed to be involved in right now was anything to do with the notorious diamond heist in Hatton Garden. When it had happened several weeks ago, Kerry had only been vaguely aware of it as she had been so wrapped up in her own organisation's battle with the Colombian, Pepe Rodriguez. But the heist had caught the imagination of the nation, and even now, it was still high up on every news bulletin and every newspaper.

The story was always the same – cops were still hunting the audacious robbers who seemed to have waltzed into the bank and removed millions of pounds' worth of diamonds, as well as strongboxes containing whatever it was that rich and privileged, and often crooked, clients wished to stash in their strongboxes. They were never going to admit the contents to police, so the investigation was stymied on so many levels, much to the delight of half the country. Villains from Glasgow to London to the Costa del Sol were dining out on the story, and it would go down in history as one of the most daring raids on a bank ever. And not a single shot was fired nor a life lost. When Kerry had got a chance to finally read back on a few of the stories, she too almost felt like applauding the gang for their sheer genius. But had Danny not told her that his old mate William Wolfe was behind the robbery, and that he had worked with her father many years ago, all Kerry would have been doing was marvelling at the story. Now, she was upstairs in her sitting room waiting for this Wolfie character to arrive along with his daughter Hannah, who was just out of the nick for manslaughter. *You couldn't make this up*, she thought, as she crossed the room to stand at the window of the upstairs living room along with Sharon, where they could see the big steel gates below being slowly opened to let the two cars in. Kerry watched, a little surprised at how fascinated she was to meet this man whose exploits with her father and Danny a lifetime ago had made them the men they were. And it wasn't lost on her that she was living in a swanky villa in the north of Glasgow that no doubt had been bought by the proceeds of their crimes.

Danny got out of the front passenger seat and opened the rear door. Kerry watched as a man in a pair of blue jeans and a tan suede bomber jacket stepped out. He looked younger than his sixty-two years. He had a shock of lush silver hair, which he ran his fingers through and pushed back as he straightened up, his eyes behind dark glasses quickly scanning the house and the grounds.

'So that's Wolfie, the man who masterminded the Hatton Garden Heist,' Sharon said, arms folded, then chuckled. 'I kind of feel like getting his autograph.'

Kerry half smiled. 'I wonder what trouble he's going to bring us.'

Sharon was meant to have flown back to Spain yesterday to oversee the construction of the hotel and look after the other Casey businesses on the Costa del Sol, but Kerry had asked her to stay for a couple of days as she wanted her input on whatever this Wolfie guy was bringing to the table.

'If any of the hoods looking for him knew he was in our neck of the woods they'd be coming after all of us.' Kerry sighed. 'That's what I'm a bit afraid of.'

'Yep. But you never know what he's got to offer.'

They both watched as Wolfie turned to the open car door, where Kerry could see the long legs of a woman step out and stand up. She was a good head taller than her father, dressed in tight black jeans and a black leather biker jacket, topped with aviator shades, and had thick, dark, wavy shoulder-length hair. She kept her glasses on as she too glanced around. Her face was pale and lean, and she stood there looking very calm and collected for someone who had just completed a jail sentence for manslaughter.

Jack and a couple of their men got out of the other car, then Jack led the way as they crossed the courtyard and came into the house.

'Well,' Kerry said. 'We're about to find out.'

Kerry and Sharon greeted their guests in the hallway and they all shook hands warmly. As Wolfie looked Kerry in the eye, he shook his head a little as though her face evoked some old memory.

'Kerry!' he said. 'The last time I saw you, you were this high.' He gestured with his hand to show a height of about three feet. 'I think you were about five, and your mum and Tim were down in London for me and my Molly's wedding anniversary. Christ! I remember that as though it was yesterday – your dad, your beautiful mum . . .' Then his voice tailed off a little as he swallowed. 'I'm so sorry for what happened to your mum at your brother's funeral, Kerry. From what Danny tells me, you made sure the bastards got their due.'

Kerry nodded. 'Thanks,' she answered. 'It was tough when I lost my mother. Still is.'

She glanced at Hannah whose lips tightened a little, as they both recognised the pain of losing a mother in tragic, unfair circumstances.

Then Kerry ushered them down the hall and into the study.

The small talk was over in a few minutes, and Kerry sat

at the head of the table with the others around, as they drank tea and ate sandwiches.

'So,' Kerry said, glancing at Danny, then turning to Wolfie, 'my uncle Danny told me a little about what happened to you, Wolfie. It must have been horrific.'

'Oh yeah! I thought that was it this time, I really did. I mean, Danny will tell you – I know we don't keep in touch much these days – but he will tell you that I've not been involved in much in recent years. Only my own bits, earning a few bob, if you know what I mean.'

Kerry nodded. Danny had told her that Wolfie moved stolen jewellery through his connections, and that had been how he'd come up with the Hatton Garden plan.

'Yeah. Danny spoke a bit about it. But robbing Hatton Garden? I mean, what possessed you, if you don't mind me saying, at your age, to get involved in something on that scale?'

Wolfie put down the sandwich he was eating and sipped from a mug of tea, then placed it down on the table.

'What can I say? It was that one last big job.' He turned to Hannah. 'I used to tell her I had one last big job in me, and then I'd retire somewhere sunny, and be ridiculously wealthy.'

Hannah shook her head, and Kerry could see from the way she looked at her father that she adored him.

'I thought he was joking,' she said, and everyone smiled.

'No. No joke. I knew if there was a way to do this, then it had to be looked at, and I did.'

'So how did the rest of the gang come on board?'

'Well, I'm an old associate of Alfi Ricci.' He looked at Danny. 'You'll remember his old dad, Danny. Passed away about ten years ago, and Alfi runs the show down there now. Mostly Italian boys, people brought over to work in restaurants and the like, and Italian second and third generation. They tend to stick together, these boys. Alfi is a robber, not like his dad, but bigger jobs and sometimes bad news too. He and his mob tied an old Jewish couple up one time in a house robbery in Pinner and the pair died. He got away with that, but I thought he should be ashamed of himself, and I told him so.'

'So why get him involved in this?'

'Well, because I do know him well enough, and I know he's got the bodies around him who will do what you tell them to. And I know they know how to keep their mouths shut. That old Mafia omerta shit. Know what I mean?'

There was a general nod of acknowledgement around the table, and they listened as Wolfie went on to describe the months before the heist, what he did, how he got a job inside and found out all the details and plans. Everything that happened was planned to the letter and was down to him. They hadn't exactly been sure what they were going to target in terms of strongboxes once they were inside, but they'd agreed they would just take everything they could get their hands on. Some of it turned out to be not worth too much, and others had hold millions of pounds' worth of diamonds, some uncut, and other jewels.

'Then there was the DVDs,' Wolfie said, glancing around at everyone. 'They just looked like DVDs, but I figured they had to be more than just old wedding videos if they're in a strongbox in Hatton Garden. So once I got them back to my place, I set about getting the DVD player on to have a look.' He paused for effect. 'And what I saw was fucking priceless. Priceless!'

Kerry glanced from Sharon to Danny to Jack. She raised her eyebrows to Wolfie. He rubbed his chin and leaned forward.

'On one of these videos, there is a very senior detective in the Met . . .' He turned to Hannah and Kerry and Sharon. 'Pardon my language in front of the ladies. But said copper is getting a blow job from some Russian hooker while he's tied up to a bed. And it doesn't look like he's been held prisoner either.' He paused, enjoying the little chuckle that went around the table.

'And in another DVD, there's a prominent politician – one of these anti-gay rights geezers – and he's with male prostitutes, not exactly talking politics. And he's not being held captive either.' He smiled. 'And another part, where money is changing hands to a top QC.'

'How old is the recording?' Kerry asked.

'Maybe a couple of years ago, three perhaps. But that's not the point. It's who that QC is now that is the point.

Everyone waited for him to go on, and Kerry could see that he was relishing stringing out the story.

'He's only the fucking Attorney General now! I give you . . . Quentin Fairhurst, QC! Appointed ten months ago. The top lawman in the country.'

There was a collective shock and Danny let out a low whistle. But for Kerry, this was music to her ears. Quentin Fairhurst, QC. Of all the bastards she'd love to see hanging from the rafters it was him. She'd known him as a lawyer in her very early days in London, and he was a complete privileged bastard, who'd walked all over a case she'd fought for – a young disabled girl's family taking on a multinational pharmaceutical company. It was a long time ago, but Kerry had never forgotten it, or the dad's tears that day as his wife held him when they lost their case. And she had never forgotten Quentin Fairhurst as he swanned his way through the ranks, moving into criminal law and up the scale in the Crown Prosecution Service. If Wolfie was right, here he was caught on camera with evidence of his corruption. She didn't want to impart all of these thoughts right now to the people around the table, but the very idea of having Fairhurst's head on a stick was too tantalising to turn down.

'I like the sound of this,' was all she said, trying her best not to smile.

Wolfie raised a hand. 'But that is only half the story.

There's more. More on the discs. We've got an MP – now a Cabinet minister – who is also in the clips with Fairhurst at some meeting. And later the MP is seen being given money by a Russian oligarch. It's all right there. A Cabinet minister and the Attorney General. and more. And by the way, the meeting with the oligarch where the money changes hands has all been recorded on both film and stills.'

'Who's the Russian oligarch?'

'I don't know who he is, but he's on the disc. You can clearly see money changing hands.'

'Christ!' Danny said. 'That's hot shit. The Russian will be ripping up the country trying to get that DVD back. The recordings are his passport to whatever skulduggery he and his mates wants to get away with. That's dangerous property to be holding.'

'I realise that.' Wolfie nodded. 'Obviously, when we were stuffing all this shit into bags we didn't know what was what. It was all jewels and diamonds the lads were putting in the bags, but I just grabbed this other stuff in these two boxes. Suppose I was curious.'

Danny smiled. 'Yeah,' he said. 'Curiosity killed the fucking wolf.'

'Well, let's hope it won't come to that,' he said.

Kerry pushed the teapot across to the others, then helped herself.

'It never ceases to amaze me how completely stupid people seem to get the higher up they go in the establishment,' she said, her head turning over all the possibilities in front of her.

'That's always been the case,' Danny said. 'They think they're untouchable.'

'Well, they're not,' Kerry said. 'What about the diamonds and all the other jewels, Wolfie? Where you going to shift them in the market when the story is still up there in the papers every day? Bit hot, are they not?'

Wolfie looked around the table.

'Well, Kerry. That's why I came to Danny.' He spread his hands. 'Look. I'll be honest. I'm in over my head here. If the troops who I took on and worked with in this had been honest, then it would have been up to them how they dealt with the loot. But they tried to freeze me out. Bump me off, as you know. So I had no option but to run as fast as I could. And now every bastard from London to Moscow will be after me.'

'That's for sure.' Sharon shot Kerry a glance then rolled her eyes to the ceiling.

'So,' Kerry said, 'where are these discs and all this stuff, Wolfie? I presume you've got them well stashed?'

'Mostly,' Wolfie said. 'I've got one or two things with me to show you. But the rest is hidden down the road. Safely.'

'You hope,' Sharon said.

'Yeah. I hope!' Wolfie said. 'I'm pretty sure it's good though.'

There was a long moment where nobody spoke. Kerry looked around at each and every one at the table and she could see by the look on their faces that they were all hooked, if a little sceptical. Her eyes fell on Hannah, who looked back, her face set in defiance, but she could see the hint of vulnerability behind the dark eyes.

'Okay, Wolfie,' Kerry said finally. 'We're going to have to take a few minutes by ourselves to talk about this. Are you all right with that?'

'Sure.' He pushed his cup away from him and nodded to Hannah. 'We'll go out for a smoke and you can have a chat and let us know what you want to do.'

Everyone stayed silent as Wolfie and Hannah got up and left the room, then there was a collective sigh of disbelief around the table.

CHAPTER FIVE

Alfi Ricci was seething to the point that his temples throbbed. How in the name of fuck could he be the guy who pulled off the biggest heist since the Great Train Robbery, and still be sitting here empty fucking handed? If anyone got wind of this, his reputation would be shot to fuck. Instead of going down in history for leading the gang in the notorious Hatton Garden diamond heist, Alfi would be a laughing stock from London to Spain. Christ! If it got out, they might even get to know about it back in Sicily where his great-grandfather had grown up shooting, robbing and murdering his way to the top of the Mafia before he crossed to England to build up his own empire in London. The old bastard would be spinning in his grave. And right now, Alfi was glad his father had passed away a year ago so he wouldn't have to witness this debacle. If he had, he'd have horsewhipped his son up and down Soho, such would be the shame.

Truth was, as well as rage and disbelief, Alfi did feel ashamed that it had come to this. He had been handed the power base that his father and the wider family had built up in London, and it was his job to make it bigger, better, more successful than ever. And in many ways he had. But these were not the best of times for old-fashioned Italian Mafia families in London, because there were so many rival gangs flooding the place now, with fights and trouble on every corner. The Albanians, the Russians, the Yardies, all of them muscling in, so you had to be up for the fight. And Alfi was. Always had been, and he had shown his father the guts he had over the years with his bold steps and takeovers. The Hatton Heist, when it was proposed to him by that old bastard Wolfie, had definitely been too tasty to turn down. And the way Wolfie had described it and sold it to him, it was there for the taking. It would cover them in money and glory for ever more. It was the glory as much as the money that attracted him. All along he knew he was going to fuck Wolfie right out of it and take everything for himself. Wolfie's deal was a fifty-fifty cut, and although Alfi shook on it, he was thinking, Yeah, in your dreams, old man. You'll get a few trinkets and then off you fuck to play carpet bowls somewhere. If Wolfie resisted, he would just take him right out of the picture.

So much for that. The operation couldn't have gone any more tits up. The bank job had been a bigger breeze than he could have dreamed of, but bumping Wolfie off had been a monumental failure. It was his own fault. He should have done it himself, but he'd left it to four of his trusted hitmen to make sure they got the information out of him before they killed him. Not a fucking word would that *stronzo* Wolfie say. Not a sausage. Then bury the cunt, Alfi had directed them when they'd phoned him from the funeral parlour. He didn't mean to actually cremate him, but he thought if it came to the crunch and Wolfie could smell the fucking fumes of the fire then he'd open up. But no. He was going to literally take the secret of where he'd stashed every fucking thing to his grave. Then the bastard's cavalry had come rattling in from Christ knew where. Alfi didn't even think Wolfie had those kinds of connections any more. He'd known he was an associate of his father's a long time ago, but Wolfie was an old man now and only involved in a few frauds and stuff these days. He was never a standout man with a gun in his pocket and a team of hard men at his back. So Alfi had no idea where his rescuers had come from. But even trying to work that out was pointless now. The bottom line was that the Hatton Garden heist was all over the papers, and he was sitting here with nothing, and four of his men shot dead in the mortuary. Wolfie was on the run, Christ knew where. And that daughter he had hoped to catch him with had also disappeared within hours of getting out of jail. That pissbag Joey Mitchell had managed to let her go, according to his boy Nick who had sheepishly broken the news to him last night.

It was only half eleven in the morning, and already Alfi Ricci's day couldn't have got much worse. Or so he thought.

He was sitting in his office at the back of Benito's, the flagship Italian restaurant he owned in Soho, trying to work out his next step, when his desk phone jingled loudly, making him wince and rub his pulsating temples. He could see it was his secretary. 'Fucking hell,' he muttered under his breath as he picked up the phone.

'Shirley,' he said flatly.

'Alfi, er, two men are here to see you.'

'What? Who?' Alfi was immediately on his guard. The only upside of the farce had been that the cops hadn't paid him a visit. So far, they hadn't even a sniff that he was behind it.

'They . . . Erm. They are Russian gentlemen,' Shirley said, her voice hesitant.

Alfi's stomach lurched. Russian *gentlemen*? That'll be fucking right. The only good Russian in London was a dead one as far as he was concerned. And if they were coming to his place to see him, he was sure as fuck they weren't in to ask for the recipe for his cannelloni. Alfi felt sweat sting under his arms and his face flush. Calm the fuck down, he told himself. You are Alfonso Ricci the Third, a powerful Sicilian, from a powerful family. You are a businessman with contacts from Scotland Yard to Parliament. A couple of Russian pricks are not going to make you wet your pants. He took a breath.

'Alfi?' Shirley was still hanging on the phone.

'Tell them I'll be right out, Shirley.'

Alfi put the phone down and pushed his chair back. He stood up, squared his shoulders, took a breath and walked out of his office.

The restaurant was empty as the waiters prepared tables for the lunchtime onslaught of customers. Benito's was one of the top restaurants in London to be seen in, but it was also the best food in town, according to one of the broadsheet newspaper's food critics. Football stars and celebrities often dined there and the paparazzi were always on hand outside to snap them as they came out of the place in the evenings. This and their other restaurants were the perfect front for Alfi's crime empire which mostly involved trafficking women from the Balkans and Eastern Europe. If the cops had any inkling of what went on, they had no evidence because everything Alfi did in his legitimate business was up-front and squeaky clean.

He ran a hand over his oiled, slicked-back, thinning hair then strode from the back of the restaurant, his handmade leather Oxford shoes clicking on the polished mahogany floor. He could see the two men at the maître d' station, eyeing him up as he approached, their faces like granite. Alfi decided that he wouldn't afford these fuckers a cheery, welcoming smile, since they hadn't shown him the courtesy of a phone call to ask for an appointment.

'Gentlemen.' The word stuck in his throat. 'What a surprise. What can I do for you?' He raised his eyebrows.

Alfi was tall for a Sicilian, but the Russians towered over him, and he resented having to look up at them. The bigger of the two, who looked like he could pull off arms like they were chicken wings, stared at him with black eyes.

'We like surprising people,' he said.

Alfi sighed. He wasn't going to let these bastards monster him on his own turf.

'Well. Do you have names, chaps?' He stretched out a hand.

'Yuri.'

The big one gripped Alfi's hand and almost crushed his fingers. Alfi didn't flinch. He looked at the other one, shaven head, built like a brick shithouse, tight, bloodshot eyes and a ruddy face who looked like he supped straight vodka for breakfast.

'Dima,' he said, his lips barely moving as he shook Alfi's hand in a surprisingly civilised manner.

Alfi gestured to them to sit down at a table.

'You like some coffee? Something stronger?'

'Coffee please. Black,' Yuri said.

Dima nodded for the same. Alfi looked up and he caught the eye of the head waiter who was waiting behind the bar, focused on the trio.

'Three coffees, Marco. Black.'

So far, Alfi thought, no monstering capers. But his mind raced with the raft of possibilities behind the reason for this impromptu visit. Often his restaurant was used by

Russians who were clearly gangsters, made obvious by the rich careless way they threw their money around. But they had all been well behaved and ate and drink a lot, spending big-time. And always they had been courteous. Alfi wondered if this was them making their move on him, showing that they wanted a piece of his business. He had plenty of protection around all of his restaurants and the Italian families were very organised in that way – if need be they could provide plenty of heavies. So far, the Russians and the Albanians, who were muscling in everywhere, had not come to his doorstep. Perhaps this was their moment.

'Is very good place, Benito's,' Yuri said, glancing around. 'I've been here with friends.'

'You have?' Alfi said, glad the ice was broken on the awkward silence.

The waiter came across with a tray and placed the coffees on the table. He looked squarely at Alfi and asked, 'Anything else, sir?'

Alfi knew it was a pointed question, and what the waiter really meant was did he need to call anyone for help.

He shook his head. 'No thanks, Marco. Everything is fine.' At least he hoped so.

Yuri took a sip of his coffee and put the cup down, and Alfi watched as he took a long breath through his wide nostrils.

'So,' Yuri said. 'To the matter we came here to discuss.'

Alfi nodded, sitting back, his hands clasped over his stomach, displaying his pinstriped waistcoat with the gold pocket watch that had been handed down from his great-grandfather. He was a good-looking man for forty-three, his olive skin always with a Mediterranean tan from frequent visits back to the old country. He knew he looked the part, and he could sense them seeing that.

Yuri tore open a strip of sugar and sprinkled it into his cup, stirring it slowly. Then he leaned across the table a little.

'The Hatton Garden robbery,' he whispered, locking eyes with Alfi.

Alfi felt a surge of nerves lash across his gut, but he managed to keep his face straight. He said nothing.

Yuri took the spoon from the cup and set it down. He took another breath and let it out through his nose.

'We know, Alfi. We know it was you. Very good job. Very good.'

Alfi said nothing, remained stony-faced, though he felt his bowels churn.

What passed for a smile spread across the big Russian's face, but his eyes were still dead as he sat back.

'Alfi,' he said. 'Please understand. We are not here to mean you any harm. We congratulate you. It was a very brave thing – to take on a job like that. And from what I see in the television and newspapers, the police are scratching their heads.' He nodded slowly. 'Very good job.'

I'm fucked if I'm going to admit anything around this table, Alfi thought, as he tried to work out what he was going to say next. He stayed silent and glanced at the shaven-headed Russian who was sitting, staring at the table as though he'd zoned out. Perhaps he didn't speak English. It crossed Alfi's mind that, given a nod from the big man, the bastard might lurch forward and grab him by the throat. He picked up a glass of water and took a long drink, grateful that his hands were not shaking as much as his insides.

Yuri leaned across the table and clasped his hands.

'Okay. I do not expect you to say anything. Of course. It is your business. I wish you well and good fortune in moving the diamonds. I really do.' He paused and Alfi watched. 'But we are here because we are interested in something that was in one of those boxes.' He lowered his voice to a whisper. 'Not diamonds. Not jewellery. But for us, it is more precious. It is gone now, as we discovered when we go to our box. Is nowhere. And you will understand we cannot tell the police because the point of the strongbox is that nobody knows. But for us, the contents of this box are very precious.'

Alfi's mind turned over. So much had happened since the heist. He knew from the initial reports from his boys that among the haul were a few boxes that contained other stuff. Photographs. DVDs. Shit like that. But he'd shown no interest in them, and neither had anyone else, to his knowledge.

Alfi sighed.

'Look, I don't know what you mean. But since you are here asking me questions, then you must tell me, for the sake of talking. What are you looking for?'

There was a long silence and Alfi could hear the shuffling of feet under the table. There was a flash of impatience in Yuri's eyes. He wondered how long he could get away with this without this Dima character trying to pull his lungs out. He kept silent. *Omerta*, he told himself. But he hoped to fuck it didn't cost him his life.

'We are looking, my friend, for DVDs and some photographs actually. They were in an envelope. A white envelope. I placed them there myself. And now, they are not there. But the DVDs, they are very priceless to my organisation. I need to find it. And I need it quickly.' His mouth tightened. 'Am I making myself clear?'

Alfi waited two beats, then he decided that he had to say something because these two fuckers looked like they might be about to make his day a whole lot worse. He spread his hands apologetically.

'Yuri,' he said, leaning forward. 'I imagine that whoever robbed this bank was not remotely interested in pictures, or DVDs. People don't rob banks to get stuff like that. You must understand that.'

Yuri nodded quickly.

'Exactly my point. You are not interested in such things. But if some of your men took everything they can find in the heat of the moment, then they must have these items somewhere. My package. They must have it.'

Alfi wished he could tell him something positive, but he couldn't, because this was the first he'd heard of it. But he had to make something up.

'If I was the man who was behind this robbery, right now I would be moving my jewellery, my diamonds, my cash. Then I would be looking at the rest of the stuff in the boxes – whatever it was – and I would probably want to throw it in the bin. But perhaps the people who did this have not got to the stage where they are looking through everything they took. So maybe you should give them time.'

'Time we are always short of in my line of business. We can give a little time, but only if the result is good.' Yuri looked like he'd heard enough, and he was about to stand up. 'I will leave this with you. But, Alfi. You must find my package. And you must call me and give it back to me. It is so precious to me. Is a matter of life or death.'

Alfi got that message loud and clear, all right. He was intrigued to know what he was looking for. But he didn't want to push his luck by asking. Right now, he hadn't a fucking clue where that fucker Wolfie had hidden any of the loot. All that Alfi's men had was a lot of very expensive jewellery which they were sitting on until the time was right to move it. What the fuck was this guy talking about DVDs and photographs? He hadn't a clue. He had to find out. But he had nowhere to look until he found Wolfie, the cunning old bastard. The meeting was over. Yuri stood up, and Alfi got to his feet.

'I will make some enquiries, Yuri. In my restaurant, we get all sorts of people coming in, and sometimes you hear gossip. I will keep my ear to the ground and see if I can find some information for you.'

Yuri nodded and his sidekick shot Alfi a look that could have cut him dead.

'My package, Alfi. That is all I want. You must get that and give it back.'

Alfi said nothing. The pair were about to turn and leave when Yuri leaned over and whispered in Alfi's ear, 'I will return very soon. You will hear from me.'

Alfi felt a chill run through him. He didn't reply, but watched as they walked out of the restaurant and through the door. He stood for a moment, his hands in his trouser pockets, his fingers drifting over to feel that his bollocks were still intact. He knew that in a very short time he had to come up with whatever the Russians wanted. But the goods were fuck knows where. He had to find this Wolfie bastard, and this time he wouldn't escape.

CHAPTER SIX

Quentin Fairhurst, the Attorney General, sat staring at the front page of the report on his desk. He'd already read it from cover to cover at least three times and had been briefed by his minions on the contents before he'd even done that. The Serious Fraud Office had pulled no punches in their thorough investigation into the billions of pounds of Russian money in London. Christ! The Russian oligarchs owned most of Belgravia and half of bloody Kensington. It was eye-watering the amount of money they'd invested in the city in property and business in recent years. The Russian empire in London was growing every year, and every property deal had been acquired in watertight legal contracts so that nobody could point an accusing finger. Of course, everyone knew that oligarch was just a fancy name for gangster, and every bloody one of the shadowy figures were no different from the UK-organised mobsters who ruled their own grubby empires from London to

Manchester. The Russian mafia was harder to pin down though. They covered their tracks so well, and you never saw TV news footage of police in dawn raids banging down a door in Knightsbridge. The Russians were far more sophisticated than that. But if you scratched the surface of an oligarch, you found a thug. Simple as that. Few people knew that as well as Quentin Fairhurst. But the trouble with the Attorney General was that he'd been in bed with these Russian hoods for years.

Fairhurst sat back and swung his feet onto his desk as he turned to gaze out of the window onto the thin grey Westminster morning. He wasn't the kind of man to have a niggling conscience that areas of his life were dark and corrupt. That had been how the cards had fallen for him as he'd moved through the ranks from being a young ambitious solicitor to the top lawman in the country. He had never been one of those zealous fresh-out-of-law-school graduates who wanted to change the world. Fairhurst was about winning, about getting to the top, no matter how many heads you trampled to get there. It had been a means to an end, and if he took bungs and massaged the numbers along the way, then so be it. He didn't care. He knew that once you reached the rarefied air this high up in the legal establishment, nobody dared to question you. But now, he had a dilemma. The Home Secretary had given in to the clamour for a probe into Russian money in the UK – where did it come from, how much of it was corrupt Mafia money?

All of it, Fairhurst could have told them quietly, because he had first-hand knowledge of it. But, of course, he couldn't do that. So, he'd sat back and waited for the Serious Fraud Office's lengthy investigation. He'd covered all his tracks over the years, so if push came to shove, he might have to throw a few oligarchs under the bus for the sake of appearances. The Russians would just have to live with that.

Fairhurst's phone rang on his desk and he pushed the button to hear his PA's clipped tones.

'I have the Home Secretary's office for you, sir.'

'Fine, Charlotte. Put them through.'

The next voice he heard was the plummy tones of the Right Hon. Henry Callan, a privileged Old Etonian with a penchant for vintage wine and fine food. And, as Fairhurst had discovered several years ago, a desire for teenage girls, preferably from Eastern Europe. All of which Fairhurst had ensured he had in ample supply, in return for favours to the new breed of Russian entrepreneurs investing in London.

'Henry,' Fairhurst said cheerily. 'How are you, old boy?'

'Up to my bloody arse in alligators, Quentin,' came the reply. 'Have you read the SFO's report?'

'Of course I have,' Fairhurst replied. 'In fact, I've read it so many times I could probably recite it verbatim.'

Fairhurst let the silence hang for two beats. As he suspected, the Home Secretary's arse was twitching. He waited until Callan spoke.

'So, what do you think?'

Fairhurst took a breath and let it out slowly.

'It's a serious job they've done here, Henry, no doubt about that. But we'll have to break it down and see exactly where we can take it. The way I see it is the Russians will throw millions into defending any question of wrong-doing, so we need to be absolutely bang on whichever case we take forward. But I do think we have to take some of this to the next level. There are a lot of people watching, especially those fuckers on the opposite benches from you. So we need to be seen to be doing something.'

Callan didn't answer for a long moment, and Fairhurst knew that, unlike him, his conscience was niggling away. It had been six years ago that the pair of them had become embroiled. There was no trace that would lead to their doorstep. The meetings with the Russian oligarch and his associates had been social encounters in safe surroundings. Nobody had been there to witness the women, or the money changing hands. Fairhurst wasn't that stupid. He would never have allowed himself to be in a situation that could come back to haunt him.

'And how do you think that will go down?' Callan paused. 'You know. I mean in certain quarters.'

'Well, we'll just have to wait and see, I suppose. I don't speak to these people very often these days. Things have moved on. We've all moved on.'

'Hmmm. Well, I hope they see it that way,' Callan said. 'We can stall things for a little while, but we'll have to look at ways we can prosecute. Even just one of them. We need to be seen to be taking that sort of action.'

'Yes. I agree,' Fairhurst said. 'Leave that to me, Henry. I'll be in touch in the next few days.' He paused for a second. 'I wouldn't worry though. I'm not.'

Fairhurst hung up. He ran a hand across his chin, trying to think of a way he could keep the Serious Fraud Office happy without ruffling too many Russian feathers.

Joey Mitchell sat by the window in the lounge of the hostel off the King's Road sipping from a mug of black tea. It was getting dark outside, and the streets were busy with commuters heading home to lives that were a world away from where he was now. *How had it come to this?* he'd asked himself too many times. But he knew the answer. The problem was chasing after the next win, trying to claw back the money you had just lost, knowing that the next tenner you backed was your last as you stood staring at the TV screen in the bookies, willing your horse on, praying it would get up at the last furlong so you wouldn't be destitute. Gambling. He hated himself for every penny lost, for his entire family lost, yet he knew that if someone handed him a hundred quid today, he'd be down at the bookies straight away. The old grey man lying back on the sofa at the other side of the lounge was snoring like a pig, and Joey looked at him, wondering who he was and how long he had been living this miserable, shitty existence. Christ! It never got any easier. Joey sniffed at his grubby shirt and contemplated going up for a hot shower before he went to bed. He had a couple of clean shirts that would have to last him the week, because he had very little money left. That girl Hannah had dropped him two hundred quid, and he had been so grateful that he'd almost burst into tears. And he hadn't even gone straight to the bookies, either. After he'd gone to hospital, got stitched up and had his eye sorted, he'd gone to a café for a slap-up feed, then come back to the hostel and paid his rent for the week. The money he'd been promised by Nick for the job on Hannah would not be forthcoming now. He would have to live with that. But at least Nick hadn't completely humiliated him in front of Alfi Ricci. Joey sat back and replayed the meeting at Benito's earlier.

'You fucked up, big time, Joey,' Alfi said to him as he'd sat down at a table in the restaurant.

The aroma of garlic and Italian cooking was tormenting his stomach and he'd had to keep swallowing to stop himself salivating.

'I know, Alfi.' Joey put his hands up. 'It was all so fast. I won't lie to you. I should have done better. But this bird could really take care of herself.'

'She slap you about a bit then?' Alfi shook his head. 'Was it her that did that to your eye?'

'No,' Joey lied, touching his eye. 'I opened the cupboard door on it. Got an infection, that's all.'

Alfi looked at him and shook his head, then at Nick.

'So that bollocks she told you about Wolfie being at Heathrow heading to Málaga?' Alfi said. 'That was a pile of steaming crap, that was.'

'I can only tell you what she said,' Joey replied. 'I did say to Nick she might have made it up.'

'So where do you think she went to after she left you?'

Joey looked at him. How the Christ was he supposed to know that? But he had to be careful what he said here, because he'd been lucky so far that he hadn't got a slapping.

'I've no idea. She went in a taxi. That's all.'

It had crossed Joey's mind earlier that he could try and ingratiate himself with Alfi by telling him that Hannah gave him her phone number. That he could get in touch with her on the promise that he was giving her information, and that way they could ambush her and Wolfie. But it made him feel guilty. Maybe if Hannah hadn't looked at him with compassion, maybe if she hadn't given him money, or helped clean his wound. Whoever she was, Joey wasn't of a mind to double-cross her. She was right. He really was in the wrong job. He wasn't expecting to be in it much longer anyway.

'Right,' Alfi said, sitting back. 'Clearly, Joey, there is no place for you in this organisation as an enforcer. I don't think you've got the bollocks for it any more, and you don't seem to have the strength either.'

Joey nodded, shuffling his feet. He was getting bumped

out of the job. Where to next? he wondered. Then Alfi looked at him.

'So,' he began, 'because your old mum was a cousin of my old man's, and because in Sicily we look after our own, I can't kick you out in the street, can I?' He paused for effect. 'I'm not that kind of bastard, Joey. You might be a bit of a stupid fuck, but you're *our* stupid fuck. So I'm going to give you a second chance.'

Joey sat up straight, relief flooding through him. Alfi looked at Nick.

'Nick,' he said. 'Find him a driving job somewhere. Something simple. Nothing that will get him shot or done over, if you know what I mean. Maybe picking up the girls or something. But nothing dangerous.'

'Sure,' Nick said. 'Not a problem.' He glanced at Joey, who gave him a sheepish look.

'Okay,' Alfi said, standing up. 'Now fuck off, the pair of you. I've had some grief today from some big Russian cunt who seems to know that it was our boys on the fucking Hatton job. I mean, how the fuck does he know that? The cops haven't even felt our collars yet, and this big Russian plonker is in here this morning telling me he needs stuff that was in one of those strongboxes.' He turned to Nick. 'Did you hear anyone talking about stuff like documents, photographs or any shit like that? Did anybody mention taking anything other than fucking jewels?'

Nick blanched a little.

'Wolfie,' he said. 'The old bastard was bundling everything he could get his hands on into one of his holdalls. I told the fucker to leave anything that wasn't shiny and valuable. But he might have got carried away.'

Alfi ran his hand over his hair.

'Well that's just fucking peachy, that is. This Russian bastard is looking for something that seems to be valuable to him, and that Wolfie might have it. Christ almighty! Where is the old cunt? You need to find him, Nick. And fast. I don't want to be wrestling on the floor with the fucking Russians.'

'Sure, boss,' Nick said. 'We're all over it.'

Alfi dismissed them with a wave of his hand and they both headed for the door.

CHAPTER SEVEN

It had been a very long time since Kerry had revisited the crushing sense of outrage she'd felt the last time she'd encountered Quentin Fairhurst, QC. Another life, another world. The Kerry Casey then, the young, idealistic lawyer, fighting for justice, was very different from the Kerry Casey now, the head of a notorious gangland crime family. If Fairhurst remembered who she was, and he was so arrogant that he probably didn't, he would chuckle at the irony of the transformation.

The last time Kerry had locked eyes with Fairhurst was across a courtroom at the High Court in London when she had been fighting for compensation for a young girl paralysed from the waist down by a hospital drug that had been banned shortly afterwards. The girl, who'd had dreams of becoming a vet, was left needing ongoing care. Kerry, fresh out of university and on her first few weeks working for a small law firm in London, was given the case by her boss and told it was a no-hoper but would be good experience to research. But she'd been so moved by the parents when she visited their home and saw the desperate conditions they were trying to cope with, that she'd decided she would try her damnedest to get justice for their daughter. She'd spent the next few months poring over reams of documents on the pharmaceutical giant, looking for holes in their processing, gathering evidence for the lawsuit. Her boss had told her there was no point in busting a gut because there was no way this big drug company would buckle, and they would throw everything at her. She would get humiliated, he told her. She was wasting her time.

She pleaded with him to let her pursue it on a no win, no fee basis. He gave in to her badgering and allowed her to run with it. Kerry filed the lawsuit, then set about raising awareness of the case, getting interviews with the family in the press and on television. She prayed they would settle out of court. But the drug company dismissed the claims and wouldn't budge. They hired a top QC, Quentin Fairhurst, a slick, hotshot brief who never lost and who specialised in making sure the big organisations never shelled out money in compensation. When Kerry had been introduced to him on the first court appearance, Fairhurst had been condescending. Strap yourself in, he'd told her, for the biggest lesson of your short life. Fairhurst must have been in his early thirties then, Kerry recalled. Handsome, rich and successful. For the first couple of days she'd felt clueless up against him. But then the case had taken a turn and suddenly seemed to be going her way. Another witness came forward who had worked in the pharmaceutical lab and said there had been discrepancies of the drug during tests, and that the possibility of it being harmful had been flagged up but ignored. The hearing strung out for three weeks, watched by the media, and by the end of it, Kerry had almost collapsed with exhaustion at the energy and work she'd invested. But she was sure she was going to win. She didn't. The High Court judges ruled in favour of the drug company, claiming insufficient evidence. She couldn't believe it. Could the drug company have paid off the witness? Of course not, she told herself. She'd lost and that was it. Fairhurst had turned to her with a smug smile when the verdict was announced. She had to bite her lip to keep from bursting into tears. Then afterwards he'd come up to her as the court was emptying. Let me take you to dinner, he'd said, looking her up and down. He'd been impressed by her gutsy approach. Perhaps they could discuss a job if she played her cards right. Kerry looked him square in the eye and told him to fuck right off. Fairhurst glared at her in disbelief, shrugged, and walked away. She'd been so sickened by the case and her nagging suspicions of corruption, on top of her own self-doubt, that months later she'd decided to move to corporate law, where she would specialise in contracts and money, not in people.

Now, all those years on, here she was, with the outside chance that she could stick the knife into Quentin Fairhurst. He was at the very top of his game, so he had a long way to fall. She hadn't seen any of the documents or discs or photographs that Wolfie had said he had, but she was looking forward to it. Neither had she seen the diamonds and the loot he was looking to move on. The Caseys didn't really need to deal in stolen diamonds. A couple of million quid for shifting stolen jewels was more trouble than it was worth. But evidence from a stolen strongbox that could bring down the Attorney General was a tantalising prospect. She couldn't wait to see it.

There was a knock at the door of Kerry's study and Danny stuck his head round the door.

'You ready, Kerry?' he said.

'Yep.' Kerry stood up as the door opened wide. 'In you come, guys.' She motioned them to the big table. 'Sit yourselves down. Tea and coffee will be here shortly.'

Kerry saw Wolfie carry in two black holdalls, and Hannah had another one slung over her shoulder. They had been staying in the small detached cottage at the back of the grounds of the house, which her mother had built so that guests who were staying for longer than a couple of days could have their own space. Since yesterday, she hadn't seen Wolfie or Hannah, and presumed they were spending time catching up after being apart for so long while Hannah was in jail. Wolfie's mate Tommo Gourlay had arrived last night with the holdalls of stolen jewellery that had been stashed in a graveyard in Southend. He'd gone back down this morning to make sure the rest of the loot was still in the safe places they'd hidden it after the raid.

'Kerry,' Wolfie said as he placed the holdalls on the floor and pulled out a chair, 'I just want to say again, thanks for giving me and Hannah shelter here. Honestly, love, you've no idea how much it means to us. I'm not sure if I'd still be alive right now, if Danny here hadn't given me a break.'

Kerry raised a hand. 'Not at all, Wolfie. Glad to have been able to help you. Danny has told me that you, my father and him were like family back in the old days. The Caseys are on your side. We will do as much as we can to make sure you stay safe.' She glanced around, half smiling. 'Mind you, once you open these holdalls, I'm not sure how safe we'll all feel knowing that half the gangsters in London are looking for you. But we'll do our best.'

'Thanks,' Wolfie said.

He placed one of the holdalls on the table and unzipped it. He reached in and pulled out what looked like cotton cash bags, the kind businesses might use when taking cash to the banks. Then he put his hand into one of the bags and pulled out a handful of jewels. There was a diamond necklace dripping from his grasp, and a couple of pieces of jewellery dropped onto the table. Kerry glanced across at Sharon who was watching as Wolfie slowly emptied the contents onto the table. Eyes widened in the glare of diamonds dropping out of the bag and onto the polished oak. Large diamonds. Kerry knew nothing about diamonds, other than what she'd seen in photographs of models or in engagement rings in a jeweller's shop. But these were bigger than anything she had ever seen. Danny let out a low whistle, his eyes displaying admiration for the daring robbery Wolfie had pulled off, and dazzled by the gems now strewn across the table.

'Now, I'm no expert, chaps,' Wolfie said proudly, 'but the contents of that there bag I've just emptied must amount to something in the region of maybe ten or more million quid. Look at the size of them fucking jewels.'

Hannah shook her head in disbelief, smiling. 'Jesus, Dad! You are fucking mental, you are. There has to be an easier way to slip into retirement with a few quid in your back pocket, without half the gangsters in the country chasing your tail.'

'I know, sweetheart. I know that. But remember, old villains like me don't exactly have a pension plan up our sleeves. So this is my pension. I told you. One last job. Once I move this lot, you and me, we won't have nothing to worry about for the rest of our lives.' He turned to Kerry and Danny and the others round the table. 'That's not including your cut of the loot, of course. You know, guys, we will divvy this up fairly.'

Kerry nodded, but said nothing. She looked at the jewels and was still not sure how much of a part she wanted to play in shifting them. It could be fraught with all sorts of problems and dangers. It was still up for discussion with Danny, Jack and Sharon. She watched as Wolfie meticulously put the diamonds and jewellery back into the bag. Then he pulled out another bag, smaller and tied at the top. He loosened the ribbon around it, and carefully emptied the contents. Kerry leaned forward, peering at the vivid yellow stones spilling out onto the table. Again, she glanced at Sharon who was also leaning into the table.

'Yellow diamonds?' Sharon piped up. 'Christ! Canary yellow diamonds! And look at the size of them! They're worth a bloody fortune. Nobody owns this amount of yellow diamonds!'

Wolfie nodded sagely. 'They are indeed worth a fortune, my lovely. Diamonds as vivid and bright in colour as these are top drawer. But we have to be very careful how we shift them.'

Kerry was thinking that somebody somewhere who had shelled out for diamonds like this must have a lot of money to play with. She wondered if they had been bought by legitimate means by an investor or collector, or some gangster with an eye for the finer things in life. Maybe they'd even been stolen from someone else before they were put in a Hatton strongbox. Part of her could see how much money there was to be made here, and she could see around the table that everyone else was thinking of the money. But the part of her that hadn't been a criminal all of her life was slightly recoiling from throwing herself fully in with the robbing and looting lark that everyone else seemed to be marvelling at. She loved most of the people who sat before her, and they were her family now. But she was still different from them. She kept her thoughts to herself as Wolfie continued to display the contents of the holdalls. Everything from necklaces to tiaras to gold watches and even small gold bars. So much stuff. She was glad when it came to an end and he produced the last holdall.

'And now,' Wolfie declared like a magician about to reveal his next trick, 'for an inside glimpse at the secret life of our Attorney General. And, if you look closely, you might recognise another face in the movie.' He held up the envelope. 'Do we have a DVD player?'

'We do,' Kerry said. 'But do you also have photographs, Wolfie? I wouldn't mind a quick look at them first.'

'Of course, darlin'.' He stuck his hand in the white A4 envelope and pulled out a couple of blown up colour pictures. Everyone's eyes turned to the first photograph of three men sitting in a booth in a restaurant. There were bottles of wine and glasses and a couple of empty plates and an ashtray. Two of the men had distinctive Eastern European or Slavic looks. It was hard to say. But the man sitting opposite them looked British.

'Can I get a closer look?'

Kerry reached across the table as Wolfie handed the photograph to her. She stood for a long moment staring at the handsome, arrogant face she remembered looking at across the courtroom. She didn't need to read the caption that whoever had taken the secret snap had typed onto the foot of the photo. Kerry smiled and she shook her head.

'This guy you may recognise as the Attorney General for England and Wales, Quentin Fairhurst, QC.' She handed the picture to Danny who passed it around. 'I'll tell you a story about this bastard, and why this part of the loot you brought us, Wolfie, is more valuable to me than anything.'

Just as she sat down, a mobile went off in someone's pocket. It was Hannah's and she fished it out, pushing the phone to her ear.

'Joey,' she said softly. 'How are you?'

Then for what seemed like a long time she didn't say anything, just listened. Kerry remembered Hannah mentioning Joey as the man who'd failed to kidnap her in her flat the other day. Eventually, Hannah spoke into the phone.

'Thanks for this, Joey. Much appreciated. I'll be in touch.'

Hannah turned to her father, then glanced at the others and back to her father.

'That was Joey,' she said. 'He was with Alfi Ricci earlier. And Ricci is banging on about some Russians who came to his office this morning and told him they know he was behind the Hatton robbery.'

'What the fuck?' Wolfie said. 'How the fuck can they know that? Was my name mentioned?'

Hannah shrugged.

'No. Not so far. But the Russians told Alfi they are looking for the contents of what was in two of their strongboxes. And it's not just diamonds.' She paused, pointing to the envelope on the table. 'It's that shit there, Wolfie. Right now, that appears to be hotter than the yellow diamonds.'

'Fuck me!' Wolfie said. 'They must be going to blackmail the bastard.'

Kerry said nothing. But her mind was already wondering how soon it would be before the Russians came calling.

CHAPTER EIGHT

Kerry didn't know the first thing about moving stolen diamonds, but millions of pounds' worth of them were now in her house, and she wanted rid of them as quickly as possible. She'd chatted to Danny and Sharon the previous night over drinks and they'd decided they could do one of two things from here. They could give Wolfie a few more days in the house waiting for the dust to settle, then seriously look at moving the diamonds on. Or they could simply put their hands up and tell Wolfie that much as they were grateful for the offer of a cut, stolen diamonds weren't something the Caseys wanted to be involved in. They'd given him and Hannah refuge when they'd needed it for old times' sake, so perhaps they should quit while they were ahead, and before anyone came looking for them. But Kerry kept coming back to the damning tapes and photographs of Quentin Fairhurst and the Home Secretary. What they were doing, taking bungs from the Russian mafia, was just plain wrong. Not that she was in a position to stand on the high moral ground, having just stolen forty million quid of cocaine in her quest to go legit. When it came down to it, she was as much a villain as the rest of the mobsters out there shooting and robbing. Fair enough, she'd told herself during a restless night. She was the head of a gangland crime family with blood on her hands. But she wasn't a public figure, like Fairhurst and the Home Secretary. That was the point she was making to Danny and Sharon. And that was why she wanted the tapes above all else.

'I think if we're in with Wolfie, then we have to be all-in, Kerry,' Danny said. 'I don't think we can sit here with his bags of swag and pick out the bits that suit us. Remember, we took no risk in getting all this loot – including the recordings. Wolfie is the man who took that risk, and we have to respect that.'

Kerry knew that, from the outset, Danny had relished the tale of robbing and looting that Wolfie had regaled them with. That had been meat and drink to Danny and her father many years ago, and how they all lived now was on the proceeds of that crime. And she could see that.

'I know what you mean, Danny, but it feels like it's going to be fraught with danger. Don't you think that as soon as anyone makes a move to shift these diamonds and jewellery, then alarm bells will go off?'

'I suppose it depends on where you go,' Sharon said. She turned to Kerry. 'I do see your point, Kerry, and it makes me nervous that we might be getting pulled into something that could end badly. But there will be crooked jewellers out there who will fence this – anywhere from Glasgow to Amsterdam – and keep their traps shut.'

'Of course,' Danny said. 'It's a long time since I was in the business of moving stolen gear to the jewellery trade, but there are plenty of people who'll do it. Especially this stuff. Okay, some won't want to touch it for obvious reasons, because it's just too hot, but I do know somebody in Glasgow who could put feelers out. Old associate of your dad and me. Manny Lieberman. He'll be a good age now, but he's still on the go. And he'll know people – that's the main thing.'

'Where is he?' Kerry asked.

'He has a shop in the town centre – but his son runs most of the business now. Manny is in and out of the place – spends much of his time in Israel soaking up the sun. But he'll definitely have connections. We should talk to him.'

'Sure,' Kerry said, glancing at everyone, who seemed to agree. 'Let's do it. Get him in or organise a meeting somewhere very private. If we're going to show him some of the stuff, we need to be ultra careful.' She paused. 'I'll be honest with you, guys, this diamond lark makes me even more nervous than stealing Rodriguez's cocaine.'

'But look how well that turned out,' Danny chuckled.

They all smiled.

Sharon's phone rang and she picked it up, looking

puzzled by the number. She put the phone to her ear, and they watched as her face lit up, then fell. She stood up.

'Vic! Jesus Christ, man!' She turned away from everyone. 'I . . . I thought you were . . .' Her voice tailed off as she walked across the room to the window.

Everyone looked at each other, incredulous. Then Kerry nodded towards the door, so they could give Sharon some privacy. Vic was alive. Kerry didn't know him, but Sharon had trusted him and was clearly smitten by him. And, as good as he'd promised, he'd delivered the cocaine right into their hands. Wherever he was, and why he'd taken so long to get in touch was up to him. As they were walking out of the door, they heard Sharon speak.

'What? You're in jail? Fuck! Where?'

Everyone stopped and looked at each other as Sharon spoke again.

'In Spain! Christ! When?'

Kerry and the others left the room and went down to the kitchen to wait.

A couple of minutes later, Sharon came through the door, her face flushed.

'Well,' she said. 'Vic's in jail in Spain. Got picked up yesterday by the Guardia Civil.' She paused for a moment, swallowed hard and bit her lip. 'Bloody hell. Poor Vic. He couldn't say much as he said they'd be listening. He's been lying low for weeks, didn't even want to phone me, he said. Spanish cops picked him up, apparently, on a joint investigation with the British police probing the truck load of cocaine that came in. The one we stole. They have him on CCTV at the port in Spain in the truck with the driver.'

'Shit,' Kerry said. 'At least he's alive, Sharon. I was beginning to worry the Colombians had got him. But he's alive, and we'll have to get him out of there. What else did he say?'

'Nothing. Only that extradition proceedings will be lodged, as the Brits want to get him in the UK. They also have him on CCTV at the docks in Portsmouth.' She shook her head. 'Jesus. How do we get him out of that?'

'I'll get Marty on the case. He can look at bail prospects. Sometimes these things look clear-cut because they got him on CCTV at the port, but they're never that simple. What about the truck driver?'

'No idea. I thought he was dead – caught in the crossfire at the warehouse.'

Kerry nodded slowly. A sudden image flashed into her mind of the thud of the bullet hitting her stomach as the gunfire raged, and the realisation she'd been hit, and how she had woken up in hospital later crying with relief that her baby was alive. She had much to be grateful for, and she should be quitting while she was so far ahead. But that was not how the Caseys did business. Even though she'd never met Vic: by his actions, he'd become one of their own. And she would not desert him.

'We'll find a way to fix this, Sharon,' she said, and meant it. She turned to Danny. 'Okay, Danny. Let's get a meet with your mate Manny, and meantime I'll talk to Marty about Vic.'

Three hours later, Kerry was having dinner in a private room at the swish Kimpton Blythswood Square Hotel in the centre of Glasgow with Wolfie, Hannah, Sharon and Danny. Opposite them was Manny Lieberman. The old Jew must be in his early seventies, Kerry thought, but he had a twinkle in his pale grey eyes, accentuated by his deep, weathered tan and shock of snow-white hair. He cut a well-dressed figure in a dark blue suit, white shirt and red tie. As he sat, swirling the brandy in his glass, a diamond pinky ring glistened under the lights. Money and class oozed from him, from his impeccable manners to his charm, and he'd already amused the table with stories of the old days and how Kerry's father had been fearless and determined, and how everything he'd done had been for his family. He was glad Kerry was taking the Caseys on to a different level. It's what her father had worked towards. Kerry had explained to him at the start that she was helping Wolfie as a friend, and that was her main concern. The plates had been cleared and now it was time for him to see a sample of the goods. The old man watched as Wolfie took out the small cash bag and spilled a few yellow diamonds onto the table. They shimmered in the light, and Manny watched them silently for a long moment, then picked one up and gently caressed it between his thumb and fingers.

Then he went into his jacket pocket, pulled out a magnifying loupe and wedged it in his eye. He put one of the diamonds on the table and examined it closely. Then lifted it, slowly moving it around, scrutinising its surface. Then he picked up another, and another, saying nothing until he had studied all of them. Eventually he sat back and clasped his hands on the table. He looked at Wolfie and a smile played on his lips.

'Well, well,' he said. 'Quite the haul.' He glanced at Kerry and Danny. 'Somebody, somewhere, will be very upset that they have lost a fortune like this.'

Nobody spoke. Manny picked one of them up again and turned it around expertly in his fingers. 'Yellow diamonds,' he said, 'as you will probably know by now, are rare and very expensive – and because of this they are much sought after. Only the very rich can afford these. And, of course, the crooks.' He smiled, the lines around his eyes crinkling. 'And sometimes being rich and crooked go together.' He took a breath, sipped his brandy. 'These diamonds,' he shrugged. 'Obviously you don't know who they belong to. It could be some rich, private investor. But is probably more likely to be wealthy Russians. They use diamonds as a way to launder their money and move them around because diamonds never lose their value, unlike so many things. And especially yellow diamonds. If you found this many diamonds in one strongbox alone, then I will be surprised if they are not owned by some Russian oligarch. Placed there as collateral if and when they should be required.' He paused. 'If this is the case, then, as I said, someone will be very upset.'

Wolfie nodded. He reached across and touched a couple of the diamonds.

'Yeah. I agree, Manny. I'm pretty sure that whoever put them in the bank is in a right old state about it. But the question is: how difficult will it be to move them on? In the present climate, as it were.'

Manny nodded, glanced from Kerry to Wolfie. He sighed.

'In the present climate,' he said, 'most people who would readily move these and pay top dollar for them will not go near them. They are very hot. Very hot. If it had been a one-off robbery – say a house robbery or something like that, then it would not be so high profile. But right now, every crooked jeweller will be watching closely to see what comes up on the market.' He shrugged. 'And so, my friend, will the police. The robbery is still on the news most days, and the police are looking pretty clueless. Don't get me wrong, many people I know in my trade are applauding the ingenuity of the heist – especially as it was done without bloodshed. They will be watching for the proceeds being moved. But not too much has come out in the news about the exact items that were stolen. Many of the people whose boxes were stolen will not want to put their hands up and admit it, because many of the goods are there illegally. So nobody really knows the level and degree of the contents.' He smiled and shook his head. 'Until now.'

'So what do you think?' Kerry said. 'Too hot to handle or what?'

The old man shrugged. 'Nothing is ever too hot to handle if it is moved and handled by the right people.'

'So what would your advice be?' Wolfie asked.

'It depends on how much time you have. If you had time, you could sit on them for a while, but then you are running the risk of someone doing some detective work and finding out who was behind the robbery and it may lead them to who has the items in their possession now. And I don't mean the police. If the police find them in your possession you will be lucky. You will go to jail for a very long time. But if, for example, these diamonds belong to some Russian gangsters, then you would have to pray that they do not find them in your hands.'

Kerry felt a little shiver run through her, and for a few seconds nobody spoke. Eventually, Manny pushed the diamonds towards Wolfie.

'So,' he said softly, 'what would you like me to do?'

Wolfie glanced at Danny then at the old man.

'Would you be able to move them?'

Everyone sat watching while Manny took a long breath. Then he nodded.

'I know someone who may be interested in them. Not here in the UK though. In Amsterdam.'

Wolfie nodded, looking relieved.

'Would you be prepared to make a connection for me?'

Manny looked at Kerry. She realised he was waiting for the request to come from her. He didn't know this Wolfie character from Adam, but the Casey family were his friends.

'Can you make a move for us, Manny?' Kerry asked.

She knew better than to say anything cheap like he would be well rewarded. Manny would know that his cut would be handsome.

'I'm not going to lie to you, Kerry. It is a big risk,' said Manny. 'But it can be done. If you leave it with me today, I will make a phone call. After that, it is up to you, if there is an interest.' He paused. 'But I know my contact will not come to the UK. So if it works, then you will have to go to Amsterdam – show him the diamonds.'

'I'll take them,' Hannah piped up.

Surprised, Wolfie put his hand up, and frowned at his daughter.

'Hannah, sweetheart. You just heard what the man said. It's a big risk. And I'm not going to let you waltz off to Amsterdam on a bloody mission like this when Christ knows what might happen.'

Hannah flicked a glance around the table then glared at her father.

'Oh, you think I can't take care of myself, Dad?' She sat back, folded her arms across her chest and stretched out her long legs. 'You're forgetting where I've just come from. And what I was in there for. Believe me, I can more than look after myself.'

Kerry kept her face straight but inside she was smiling at Hannah's boldness. She was only a few years younger than herself, but how different their journeys had been to arrive at this point. She'd already served time for manslaughter, and here she was, ready to face down anyone who got in her way. Kerry got the impression that Hannah had some way to go before she was finished. Everyone looked at each other, then at Kerry, who took a long breath before she answered.

'I think if Hannah wants to go, then we should send her. We can have her well protected every step of the way.' She glanced at Jack. 'You should go with her, Jack. What do you think? And take someone else too.'

Jack looked from Kerry to Hannah, then back to Kerry. He shrugged.

'Sure. We just need to look at exactly where we're going, survey the set-up. Make it as safe as possible.'

'You'd have to go on the Eurostar,' Sharon said. 'Don't want to be flying with that kind of gear in your possession.'

Jack nodded. Hannah looked at her dad and half smiled as he shook his head.

'So that's settled then,' Kerry said, looking around the table and finally at Manny.

CHAPTER NINE

Alfi Ricci stepped out of Benito's in the heart of Soho, his gaze sweeping left and right. He'd heard nothing since the visit from the Russians two days ago, but his nervous gut told him it wouldn't be long till they came back. The problem was he had nothing to tell them. Wolfie had vanished into thin fucking air. Nobody had seen him since the day his boys failed to bury him, and only Nick had survived to throw any light on where he might be. Nick had been knocking on doors of all Wolfie's old mates to see if anyone knew anything. He'd even been offering money around, but so far there was nothing. What a right fucking mess this was.

Whether it was paranoia or sixth sense, after walking just a few hundred yards down the road, Alfi had the feeling he was being followed. Beak Street was close to the hub of the city, near Piccadilly Circus and Carnaby Street, and was usually bustling at most times of the day with punters and tourists as well as cars. But right at this moment it was quiet.

There was nobody in front of him for a few lamp-posts away. He could hear footsteps behind him. He quickened his steps. The sound of the footsteps behind him got faster. Alfi felt his heart begin to race. Calm down, he told himself, as he tried to take a breath. He couldn't resist the urge to glance over his shoulder. When he did, he saw a blacked-out Mercedes limousine, cruising along the street just behind him. His stomach dropped and he suddenly froze as he felt what he knew to be a gun poking into his back. Then the car door opened. He came face to face with Yuri, the big Russian.

'Get in,' Yuri said.

It wasn't an invitation. But Alfi stood for a moment, trying to work out his options. Would they really shoot him dead in the street in the middle of Soho? The guy behind him was so close now that Alfi could feel his breath on his neck as he nudged him forward. Alfi bent his head to look in the car, and he could see another man sitting inside, with a hood over his head.

'What the fuck is this?' Alfi said. 'Who's that in there?'

Muffled noises came from behind the hood. Alfi felt sick with fear.

'I won't say it again,' Yuri said. 'Get in.'

Alfi eased himself off shaky legs and into the car. The man with the gun at his back climbed in and pushed him over. Then a bag was pulled over his head too.

'What the fuck, man!' Alfi said. 'What the fuck is this, Yuri? What do you want from me?'

'We need to talk, Alfi. It is serious now.'

'Who the fuck is this next to me with the hood on?'

'This is Nick, Alfi. He works for you.'

Again he heard the muffled tones of Nick and concluded they must have gagged him.

'Fucking hell! What are you guys playing at?'

The limo pulled away, gathering speed. Even with the hood on, Alfi knew every corner and street in this part of London and he could have negotiated it with his eyes shut. He kept his concentration as the car sped along. He sensed by the twists and turns and traffic he was up Grosvenor Street, then past Marble Arch and Park Lane. And he had a feeling even before the car slowed down and pulled into the kerb that he was in Kensington Palace Gardens. The limo turned into what felt like a driveway then down into an underground garage. The man next to him yanked the hood off his head and pulled Nick's off too. Alfi saw the terror in Nick's eyes and the sweat on his face as he yelped when the squat Russian ripped the masking tape off his mouth. Nick's whole body was shaking, and as the light came on Alfi could see a swelling round his eye. These fuckers were not going to mess about.

The car stopped and the engine was switched off. Alfi and Nick sat while Yuri and Dima got out of the car. Dima beckoned them out. At least they didn't drag him out and start beating the shit out of him, Alfi thought. But he wasn't under any illusion that this was going to be a friendly chat.

He wished to fuck he had something to tell them. He glanced at Nick and puffed out a sigh.

'We'll be all right, mate,' Alfi said, because by the look on Nick's face he felt he had to say something.

'No, we fucking won't, Alfi,' Nick rasped. 'These cunts will cut us to pieces.'

Alfi didn't answer and followed the other two as they went through a door into a bright basement room with harsh strip lights on the ceiling. The room was empty apart from a chair, and a drum that looked to be full of water. The man standing beside it was holding a watering can. Alfi's heart sank to his boots and he felt his legs go weak. They were going to fucking waterboard them. Jesus wept!

'Now,' Yuri said. 'You first, Alfi.'

Dima grabbed Alfi roughly and pushed him towards the chair. Then he tied his hands behind his back. He caught a glimpse of Nick who looked like he was about to pass out. Alfi tried to take a deep breath to compose himself but it wouldn't come. He had seen this done before in punishment beatings to get information and he hated even watching it. Dima took the hood out of his pocket and pulled it onto Alfi's head. He felt himself suffocating and it hadn't even started yet.

'So, Alfi. As I said to you when we met. We know it was you who was behind the Hatton robbery. All you have to do is tell us where our property is.'

Alfi heard the water being poured into the watering can and his whole body began tremble.

'Stop! Stop! Please!' he managed to say. 'Please! Don't do this. It *was* me and my people behind the robbery. I can tell you that, Yuri. But my men were murdered in the aftermath.'

Silence. Alfi felt the hood being pulled off and he glanced at Nick, then at Yuri.

'Speak,' Yuri said. 'Go on.'

'My men were murdered. There was a shoot-out, the day after.'

'Why? Your men are fighting among themselves?'

'No. I ordered them to kill a man.'

'What man?'

Alfi looked at Nick who was staring at the floor.

'His name is William Wolfe. Wolfie. He was on the job with us. He helped plan it. The whole thing. And his job was to stash the gear we took.' Alfi paused. 'But, when it came to it, he wouldn't tell us where it was.'

'So you killed him?' The Russian's voice had a hint of incredulity. 'Did he tell you where the gear was before you killed him?'

'No.'

'So you killed him before you know?' He raised his hands in despair. 'You cannot be that stupid.'

'No, no. Listen, please. We were in the process of trying to get information out of him when we got, well, we got ambushed.'

'Ambushed? Who by?'

'I don't fucking know, man. From nowhere. I wasn't there. But Nick was. Weren't you, Nick? Tell him what happened.'

Nick opened his mouth to speak, but nothing came out.

'Come on, Nick. It's all right. Just tell him what happened. All we can do here is tell the truth, mate. We're in trouble if we don't. We want to help these men, don't we.' Alfi looked up at the Russians who stood, faces deadpan.

Eventually, Nick spoke.

'Yeah, guv's right. We were trying to get Wolfie to talk and in comes this fucking firing squad. I don't know who they are. Wolfie's an old man and I had no idea he had that kind of backup. I mean, he's not a big shot or anything like that, even if the robbery was his idea and he kind of masterminded the whole thing.'

'Why would he not tell you where the gear was? You had fallout with him?'

There was an awkward silence and Alfi shifted in his chair.

'Yeah, well, Yuri. We did kind of fall out. You see, the old man was getting really greedy, and he said he wanted a bigger cut. I mean, it was me who provided the men for this job and all the stuff needed, but here was Wolfie now saying he wanted a bigger cut. That's just not on.'

Nobody spoke.

'Go on,' Yuri said, looking at Nick.

'So these guys came in firing every fucking where and four of our men got bumped. I caught a bullet to my leg. It just grazed me, but I lay down anyway, because the way it looked to me was that anyone who was still breathing was getting it. So I stayed still.'

'And what happened then?'

'Well, they got a hold of Wolfie and they all disappeared.'

The silence seemed to go on for a long time, and Alfi was praying the Russian believed him.

'Where did this Wolfie go?'

'I don't know. That's what I've been trying to find out for the past two days. I've turned over every mate who knew him, but nothing. I didn't know Wolfie all that well – he was a mate of my old dad before he passed away, so I don't know who his mates are. He could be anywhere.'

'And he has all of the things stolen from the bank. Everything?'

'We had only one holdall with some jewellery in it the first night it happened. But it was Wolfie's job to get the rest of the stuff well hidden. And the plan was to lie low until the police investigation died down, then we could move it on.'

Yuri pulled a packet of cigarettes from his coat pocket, slipped one into his mouth and sparked a lighter under it.

'Why should I believe anything you say?' He addressed the question to both Nick and Alfi.

'Because it's the fucking truth, mate. I promise on my father's grave. We're both telling you the truth, as it happened. I'm sat here with not a fucking penny from the robbery that the whole country is talking about. You're about to waterboard me and probably kill me. Believe me, I have no reason to make up a story.'

Again, the silence.

'There were documents in a strongbox that we need. They are very important.'

'I know, Yuri. You said. I wish I could help you.'

'And not just the documents. My associates tell me that also some very rare diamonds belonging to them were taken. Yellow diamonds. You know what they are?'

Alfi glanced at Nick and they both shrugged.

'No. I don't. I've never seen a diamond that isn't just a normal clear diamond. I don't know what a yellow diamond is.'

'Well. They are very expensive. And very rare. And in one box alone, my associate had more than seven million pounds' worth of diamonds. Now they are gone.'

'Fuck me!' Alfi said. 'Believe me, Yuri, if I had the faintest clue where that bastard Wolfie had planted your stuff I'd take you right there now and get it back for you, and I'd put a bullet in the cunt myself. I promise you that.'

'You must have some idea where he may be.' Yuri looked at both of them.

Nobody spoke for a few moments then Nick's voice squeaked, 'I ... I might have an idea. This afternoon, I turned over a mate of Wolfie's down in Bethnal Green, who seemed to know a bit more than he admitted in the beginning.' Nick sniffed, shuffling his feet. 'We put a bit of pressure on him, and he said Wolfie was heading north. To Scotland.'

'Scotland?' Alfi asked, surprised. 'Why?'

'Wolfie has some old mate there. Name of Danny ... They used to go on the rob years ago with some other geezer from up there. Some guy Casey. Tim Casey. I was going to phone you earlier, Alfi, to tell you, then these men had other ideas.' Nick was seeming a bit more his old self now that he had something to tell. 'So this plonker that we roughed up a bit said he might be up in Scotland. With the Casey mob.'

'The Casey mob?' Yuri looked surprised. 'What is that?'

'It's a crew up in Glasgow. They run the show up there. I don't know them. Never had any dealings with them. But there was a lot of trouble last year – the son Mickey Casey got murdered, then his old mum got killed at his funeral. Bloodbath apparently. It's the sister who runs the organisation now.'

'The sister?' Yuri asked. 'A woman? Running what?'

'The crew,' Nick said. 'They are criminals. Top drawer. She's called Kerry. Kerry Casey. They're big up there, and also in Spain – got a big hotel business getting built on the Costa del Sol, I hear. I made some more enquiries before I got ... well ... before I got kidnapped.'

'So do you know if this Wolfie is with them? Why would he go to them?' Yuri asked.

Alfi shrugged.

'Desperation, I suppose. He knew he had to get out of London toot sweet or I was going to hang him from the fucking eye in the sky. Robbing cunt.'

Yuri looked down at both of them, a little smile almost playing on his lips at Alfi's righteous indignation.

'So much for honour among thieves, eh?' the Russian sighed. 'Where we come from, honour is everything.'

They sat in silence for a few moments. Then the Russian nodded to Dima to untie Alfi.

'So,' Yuri said. 'Now you have your new information, Alfi. You must go and find Wolfie and bring him to me.'

Alfi nodded. He knew he had to agree but he hadn't the faintest fucking clue how he was going to go about it. He couldn't just march up to Glasgow and knock on the Caseys' door without staring down the barrel of a gun.

'We will try, Yuri. That much we can promise you.'

Yuri nodded.

'Not try, Alfi. You must succeed.' He glanced at Dima, then at Alfi. 'But we will help you. We can provide help. But you must have a plan, and you must tell me every step of it. Have you got that? If you don't, then you will be back here very soon and we won't play games any more.'

Alfi looked at Nick and they both nodded vigorously.

'Come,' Yuri said. 'We will take you back to the restaurant. You both look like you could do with a drink.'

CHAPTER TEN

Sharon had spent most of the journey back to Málaga trying to process the roller coaster her life had turned into. In the space of six months, she'd survived an attempt by her husband Knuckles Boyle to have her executed, then witnessed him being shot dead. With her teenage son, Sharon had walked straight into the arms of the Caseys – one of the biggest gangland families in the UK. It had turned her life around. In the Caseys she'd found more loyalty and sense of family than she'd ever known. But that also came at a price. And by agreeing to work with them as they took on the Colombian drug cartel, she had made herself a target as she handled the task of building up the Caseys' hotel complex and businesses in Spain. She'd survived an attempt by the Colombian thugs to kill her, and they would have succeeded if it weren't for Jake Cahill. As she glimpsed the mountains on their approach to Málaga, her mind drifted.

Years living with Knuckles Boyle, despite the trappings of wealth and the jet-set life, had reduced her to no more than a gangster's moll, to be discarded when he'd no more use for her. Sure, it was her who'd kept him out of jail over the years, shifting his money around, making his drug dealing look legit. But that counted for nothing once Knuckles had moved onto younger flesh. Just thinking of the rejection still stung at her heart, even though he'd tried to have her killed, even though she was glad he got his comeuppance, dying in the dirt like the thug he was. She'd loved him for a very long time and, over the last few months, life had been moving at such a pace she hadn't even taken time to reflect on all that was lost. She wasn't grieving, because how could she feel grief for a bastard who'd ordered her murder? But somewhere in her darker moments, like when she had time to string a thought together, she did feel a level of loss for what she had. The good parts, anyway. Now, she was on her way back to the Costa del Sol, where for so long with Knuckles her life had been a social whirl of dinners and parties with other hoods and their wives, living what some people may have thought was a dream. But the life she lived now was very different. She'd become a crucial part of the Casey empire. Just weeks ago she'd fought off attackers on all fronts from the Colombian mobsters trying to tear the Caseys down, and who'd even kidnapped her son Tony to show how powerful they were. And she'd looked their boss in the eye as she'd put a bullet in him. Everything that had happened had been such a whirlwind. But now, as the plane began its descent into Málaga, Sharon gazed out of the window at the mountains and the coastline stretching as far as the eye could see and she breathed a sigh of relief. She thought of Vic Paterson, and being swept up in an unexpected romance by the man she'd had a fling with more than a dozen years ago. There was enough going on in her head to make it explode. But the fact was, she had never felt more alive in her life. She took hold of her son Tony's hand, and he smiled up at her, his fourteen-year-old face full of trust. He melted her heart. Whatever was going to happen over here, she was ready.

Sharon had spent the evening at their villa in the hills near Marbella, still surrounded by heavy security, after looking into the hotel complex, which was now a fortress, but was moving along after a brief meeting with her people. She and Tony had had dinner together at home, and he'd flopped into bed, while she lay in a long hot bath before crashing out. The next morning she was up and out as soon as he was at school. Her driver took her on the long road out towards Alhaurin de la Torre prison where Vic was being held, pending the extradition hearing to get him brought back to UK to face trial. In conversation with lawyers she'd been told the Spanish police were in the mood to prosecute him too, as they knew he was leaving their country with a cargo of cocaine. But the wrangling continued with the Brits to see who was going to bag him, so they could get the bragging rights to having brought down one of the biggest smugglers of cocaine in history.

The prison was a few miles into the backroads and wild landscape, and set well back from the road. The high walls were an imposing sight on the skyline. They drove into the car park and went through the door where other visitors seemed to be going. Inside the prison there was a waiting room full of Spanish and Moroccan families, some with young children on their laps, waiting for the shout to see their fathers, brothers, sons. There was a twinge of something like regret for the many visits she'd taken Tony on when he was that age and they'd sat in waiting rooms just like this before going to see Knuckles. How could she have lived like that? she asked herself. Because she thought she had to, that she had no choice; and also because she had been ashamed of the fact that she enjoyed the lifestyle that Knuckles' life of crime brought her, and so had thought she didn't deserve better. She felt a wave of shame, and she hoped Tony had little memory of those days – after all it had only been for a few months at a time over the couple of sentences his father had been in jail.

The guard, jangling his keys, came and told the visitors to assemble in Spanish. She hadn't been able to let Vic know she was coming because the prison didn't allow that, so the visit would be a surprise. She wondered what kind of shape he was in, and even if he would want a visitor. She knew he was tough and hoped he wasn't letting it get him down. She was sure Vic was made of stronger stuff and that he'd survive. But the niggle was: how the hell he was going to get out of this, being caught red-handed with a container load of coke? And he'd done it all for her. Whatever state she found him in, Sharon vowed that she would never desert him, no matter what.

The visitors had their passports checked then were taken into a locker room where bags were taken off them, and guards checked inside their mouths for drugs, then ushered them to a long corridor in single file to rooms where there were lines of booths separated by thick glass. There were no prisoners in yet, so Sharon sat down with the others and watched as the place filled up with visitors until they were all sitting waiting to see the prisoners. Then there was the noise of doors buzzing open, and gradually a stream of prisoners in single file walked in, looking along the line of people. Sharon wanted to stand up but she restrained herself as the big prison guards were walking up and down behind them. Young men, old, many with bulked up muscles – tattooed masses – began to file through. Then, eventually, she saw him. Vic hadn't seen her as he walked in, his big square shoulders hunched, hands in pockets. He still looked like the old Vic, but his face was pale and tired. Then he saw her, and at first he looked surprised, then his face lit up. She stood up a little as he approached and then stood before her. For a brief moment he looked really emotional, his lips tightening, but he was tougher than that. Sharon did the same and forced herself to smile. He pushed his hand forward against the glass, and she put her hand up to his. They stayed that way for a moment without saying anything. Eventually, Sharon spoke.

'Vic,' she said, and her voice felt as though it was echoing. 'Christ! How are you?'

For a moment Vic said nothing. Then, 'Champion, darling.' He shrugged. 'As you can see, the hotel here has everything I need – decent grub, a gym, friends, and kinky sex in the morning if I don't have my fucking wits about me.'

His face broke into a smile when he said the last part, and Sharon was glad to see he was still punching, even if it was a front.

'Christ, Vic! I'm so sorry!'

Again the shrug. 'Well, I took my chances and I knew if I got caught I'd get my arse felt. But I just have to buckle down for the moment.'

'I've got the lawyers working,' Sharon said quickly. 'Here in Spain and back in the UK. They're desperate to get you back to Britain so they can prosecute you. But the Spanish are digging in.'

He nodded. 'Yeah. They'll do that a bit, Shaz. But if you've got a good brief on the case, he'll get me back to the UK.

I don't want to be sitting in this shithouse for the next year awaiting trial.' He looked straight at her and for the first time she saw a flicker of something like anxiety in his face. 'You've got to get me back to the UK, darlin'. If I go to court there and get banged up for ten years, I can live with that. I've done it before.'

'We will, Vic. We'll get you back. Marty Kane is working on it with some top counsel, so we're hoping to get things moving soon. We'll get you back, and then see how we can get you out.'

He snorted, but forced a smile.

'Well, I wouldn't go planning any long holidays for me, sweetheart. Because the way they've got me I'm in the slammer for a long time.'

'But you were only a passenger in the truck. There is nothing to tie you into the drugs. And the driver is dead, as far as I know, so he can't say you were working with him.'

'I know. That's the only positive. But I was still found in a truck with a haul of coke. It doesn't look good.'

For a long moment they said nothing and sat looking at each other.

'I got weighed in, by the way, by the Colombian. Remember I was getting paid for riding shotgun? Big bucks. The money was in my bank account by the time I got to the UK, so I moved it smartish somewhere safe.' He grinned. 'Good timing before Rodriguez popped his clogs.'

Sharon shifted a little in her seat. She wanted to ask him

why he hadn't got in touch for these past weeks, even after everything had appeared to have died down.

'Well that's good news. And now that Rodriguez is out of the game, he can't get his money back. But Kerry has got to pay you what we agreed too, to do the job for us. But . . .'

Vic looked at her and seemed to read her mind.

'But I disappeared off the radar, is what you're thinking.'

Sharon looked at the back of his hands and then at him.

'Well. Yes. Look. It's not that anyone was thinking bad of you. We . . . I was really worried. In fact I was bloody frantic and that's the truth. I thought maybe even if you didn't want to use your phone or something you could have found a way to contact me.' Sharon felt a little choked and her voice tailed off. She looked at him.

'I know,' he said. 'But that's not how to do business like this. For me, it was important that I completely disappeared. Like a ghost. For the past few weeks I've been living everywhere – Belgium, France, Amsterdam. Using a different passport, mostly driving everywhere. I've got plenty of money. I was going to get in touch when bang, the bastards picked me up. So I'm guessing the DEA are out there doing a victory dance somewhere.' He paused, put his hand to the glass. 'But, Sharon, believe me, I thought about you every single day. I missed you. Maybe that's not what you want to hear, but I had stuff in my mind about you. I thought we could be together. I wanted to talk to you after it was all over and I wanted to tell you how I feel. But now, well it's all fucked up, isn't it.'

For a few beats Sharon said nothing, just looked at him, at the tired eyes, more lined now than they had been, and the shadows under them. He'd also lost some weight.

'Oh, Vic,' she said. 'I'm so sorry. I just . . . I don't know what to say. Everything has happened so fast. My life has been in absolute turmoil – and honestly, despite everything, you have been the best thing that's happened to me in a very long time. But it seemed impossible when we last were together that we could really work out what to do. I was leaving everything until you got in touch. I didn't dare to make any decisions or plans until I saw you.

She could see him swallow hard.

'And now?' Vic asked softly.

Sharon looked at him.

'Now . . . We have to get you out of here. I missed you every day. I promise you that. I still do.'

'But when I get out . . . I mean, if I don't get out.' He shook his head. 'Ah, Christ! I don't know what I'm trying to say. Look, I know that if I get banged up then the last thing I expect is for you to be sitting and waiting for me. I honestly don't want that. I . . . I . . .'

Sharon put her hand to the glass. She could see the frustration and hurt in his eyes.

'Sssh. Don't say that, Vic. One day at a time. One thing at

a time. But listen. Don't ever think for a moment that I will abandon you. Jesus, man. You saved my life back in San Pedro that day. I'll never abandon you.'

She wanted to say she loved him then, that she wanted to be with him, that she had never felt as good with a man in her life as she had with him in those weeks they had had together. But something was holding her back and what it was she didn't even know herself.

The bell went and one of the guards called that the visit was over. Vic looked at her, despondent suddenly. He stood up.

'Look after yourself, Sharon. And that boy of yours.' He hesitated for a second and glanced around him. 'And . . . please get me out of this shithole.'

'I will,' she said. 'We'll get you back to the UK and take it from there. I'll come and see you next week and we can talk again.'

He was about to turn away, then he looked at her.

'Do you want to see me, Sharon? If you don't, please, sweetheart, do me a favour, leave it to the lawyers. You don't have to feel obliged to come and visit.'

He looked defiant and vulnerable at the same time, and it brought an ache to Sharon's chest.

'Vic,' she met his eyes. 'I want to be here. I want to see you. I promise you that.' She swallowed. 'But try to understand: everything has moved so fast for me in the past few months. But one thing in my life I don't want to let go of is you. Please. Please believe me.'

He nodded, his face brightened a little, then he turned and left. She watched him in the line of prisoners snaking along the narrow corridor towards the big steel door. He didn't look back.

CHAPTER ELEVEN

So far so good, Hannah thought. She'd been surprised when Jack had introduced her to Cal and Tahir, the two hands who'd be accompanying them to Amsterdam. They were lucky if they were sixteen years old, and she didn't fancy her chances if things went tits up on the trip and they had to fight their way out. Jack must have noticed the look on her face, and he'd quietly told her it was all about appearances as they travelled, but not to worry – these guys had earned their stripes in the Casey family. He'd filled her in on their story. They might look innocent, he'd said, but they were far from it. Jack, she'd decided, knew his stuff, so she didn't question it. On the way over on the Eurostar, the boys hadn't said much. The Kurdish boy Tahir seemed sullen, with black, liquid eyes that looked as though they'd seen too much in his short life. Cal was more open, but watchful, always glancing at Jack as though seeking approval for anything he said. To anyone on the train, they looked like a couple with two teenagers going on a trip, in the heart of Amsterdam with its colourful landscape and canals. Hannah was glad, though, when they were met in Amsterdam by one of the Caseys' handpicked associates who operated out of the city. He'd be watching their backs wherever they went, and in the backroom of a bar in downtown, he'd handed them each a revolver in case of trouble. Hannah had watched as the boys glanced at each other and shoved the weapons in the waistbands of their jeans.

Moshe Dolgin gently kissed his wife on the forehead as she slept in the armchair in the lounge of their apartment overlooking the Amstel river in the heart of Amsterdam. They'd been together so long, he couldn't imagine his life without her. Had it not been for Freida who knew how he could have lived with the horrors of the concentration camps in Auschwitz seared into his mind. They'd met as starving waifs in a children's hospital in Krakow, part of the first wave of Jewish prisoners to be rescued from the hellhole where both their families had perished. If it hadn't been for Freida, his life would have been driven by hate rather than the love that she brought to it. He was seventy-five now, and Freida one year older. Soon they would up sticks from Amsterdam and live out the rest of their lives in Israel, where they spent most of their summers at the home they had built years ago. Moshe was richer than he could ever have imagined as a young boy learning the diamond trade. Yet he still worked; still he liked the wheeling and dealing, the thrill of turning a diamond into something beautiful that glistened and shone with promise. And still, despite the dangers that lurked, he fenced diamonds for an occasional, trusted hood who he knew would look after him. So when the call had come from his old friend Manny Lieberman, Moshe couldn't resist it. Yellow diamonds. You didn't see them every day, and he knew he could shift them without any great problem if he played it carefully. He pulled on his camel overcoat and scarf and closed the door softly behind him, on his way to meet this Hannah lady who had been sent by Manny, who'd told him he was helping out a long-trusted connection he had in Glasgow.

The man on the counter of the jewellery shop disappeared behind a velvet curtain once Hannah had told him her name. He emerged a few seconds later with Moshe Dolgin, who greeted them with a smile. His silver hair was thinning on top, but he kept it slicked back, making him look immaculate and groomed. His fleshy hand felt warm in hers as he introduced himself, then motioned them forward behind the curtain. As she sat opposite the old man at his desk, Hannah waited for him to speak, feeling just a little out of her depth, though she would never have admitted that to Jack. Her father had told her all she had to do was show Dolgin the diamonds and watch and listen to his response. Then she had to phone him. This was testing the water, he'd said.

'So, Hannah,' Moshe said, smiling to her. 'My good friend Manny tells me you have some beautiful yellow diamonds.'

He spread his hands, and Hannah took it as an invitation to produce the goods. She slipped off her shoulder bag, unzipped it and reached in to pull out the velvet pouch. She'd been touching and caressing it obsessively since they'd left Glasgow, to keep reassuring herself that it was still there. She opened the pouch, leaned forward on the desk and gently shook the contents onto the mahogany table. The yellow diamonds twinkled in the lights as they tumbled out, and Moshe watched them closely, seriously at first, then with a smile beginning to play on his lips. When the last gem dropped onto his desk, his eyes scanned them for a long moment, then he looked up from Hannah to Jack.

'Well, well,' he said. 'They are very beautiful. Quite a collection.' He reached into his waistcoat pocket and brought out the eyeglass. 'But let me look closer.'

Hannah and Jack looked at each other and said nothing, as Moshe picked up the biggest of the diamonds and turned it over several times, slowly examining it. He was nodding and making little nasal noises as though he was tasting a beautifully prepared meal. They watched as he put one down, then lifted another, and another, until he had looked at all of them. It seemed to take for ever, and he still hadn't spoken. Finally, he put the eyeglass down, sat back and clasped his fingers across his stomach. He continued to gaze at the diamonds for a few moments, then up at Hannah. Eventually he spoke.

'Beautiful,' he said. 'All of them. But a couple of them may be the best I have ever seen.' He took a breath, let it out slowly, then picked up the largest diamond. 'This one, for example, is worth a lot of money. It's very large, maybe as much as ten carats, I believe. I would say this could fetch at least two million euros by itself.' He waited for a response. Hannah simply nodded. Jack showed nothing. Moshe fingered the other diamonds, turning them over a little. 'The others, some individually, a hundred thousand, others more, and some less. But within that there is another three million at least.'

Hannah didn't know what to say. She looked at Jack for guidance.

'Good,' Jack said. 'And, Moshe, do you think you would be in a position to move these? To find a buyer?'

After a long sigh, Moshe said, 'For all of them together, it is not a good idea. But I could find a buyer for the biggest couple of diamonds. Yes. I could find one buyer who would take these, I think.' He shrugged. 'I think you, well, I mean whoever these diamonds belong to, could expect to earn for the big ones alone, around four million euros. In pounds, that is a bit more. Maybe four and a half. Because, as I'm sure you know, once you start moving diamonds then the cost can drop.'

Out of curiosity, Hannah wanted to ask who he had in mind. What nationality. It couldn't be a Russian, she thought, in case it filtered back to the Russians who were no doubt already looking for them. But she kept quiet.

'And how quickly do you think you could move them?' Jack asked.

After a sniff and a clearing of his throat, Moshe said, 'In two or three days, I could have them sold. And the money in your hands through Manny. The money would go to him. That is how I would do it, and he would give it to you.'

They all sat in silence. It was a lot to take in, and she knew she could make no agreement here. She glanced at Jack but felt that as she had been sent by her father with the diamonds, she should say something.

'Okay, Moshe,' she said. 'As far as I can see, that all sounds very good. I will have to speak to my father, if you give me a moment, as I need to know what he wants me to do.'

He nodded a couple of times. 'Yes, yes, and it goes without saying that Manny knows you can trust me.'

'Yes,' Hannah said. She stood up. 'Give me a moment please.'

She stepped out of the room and called her father. She relayed what Moshe had told her.

'Let me speak to him,' Wolfie said. 'I need to know a bit more. What's he like? What's your gut feeling, sweetheart?'

'Dunno. He seems okay – like a kind old man. I think

I like him. But I've never done this kind of thing before. I don't know anything about diamonds or how to move them.'

'I know. It's not really fair sending you there, but I couldn't take the risk of being seen. Listen. Put him on the phone to me and I'll ask him a couple of questions. That all right?'

'Sure. I'll ask him.'

She went back into the room and held out the phone.

'My father, Moshe. He wants to talk to you. Is that okay?'

He shrugged. 'Of course.'

She handed him the phone and sat down beside Jack. They watched as Moshe listened. Eventually, he spoke.

'One and a half million,' Moshe said.

Hannah looked at Jack and he raised his eyebrows. That must be his cut, Hannah thought, and assumed Jack was thinking the same thing. Not a bad little earner, considering Moshe didn't have to actually go on the rob. But she knew that was how these things worked. If you wanted to move stolen gear at this level, the fence took the risks and he got paid top dollar. You paid for what you got, and if you went cheapskate, you could end up in serious trouble – and a stretch in jail was not the worst thing that could happen. After a bit more conversation, Moshe handed Hannah the phone.

'Okay, darlin',' Wolfie said. 'I'm going a lot here on the trust of Manny back in Glasgow, who is in turn trusted by the Caseys. So let's hope it's all good. But we need to get moving, as you know. So I've agreed a deal with him. You hand over the diamonds that he can move quickly. He'll move them, then we wait for Manny's call to say the money is here. And by the way, I've told him not to even think about moving them to Russians. You know what he said to me? He said some Russians would kill to get their hands on this lot.' Wolfie chuckled. 'Yeah, tell me about it, I felt like saying. But I think Moshe will probably know by now that these diamonds came from the heist.'

'Jesus, Dad. What if the Russians come looking for them here? It sounds well risky.'

'It is, sweetheart. Not as risky as it was that morning when I was in the bank emptying the fucking stuff into bags, though.'

Hannah detected a little bit of bravado in her father's voice and she couldn't help but smile.

'Okay. If that's what you want,' she said. 'But I feel we need to kind of protect Moshe.'

'No. That's not how these guys do business. I've told him we'll give him the two biggest diamonds. I'm sure he'll have someone in mind for those who's only a phone call away, believe me. He'll have them out of there by tomorrow. Just give him the two big ones, bring the rest with you for the moment, then we sit back and wait for our ship to come in. Just get yourself back here asap.' He hung up.

Hannah sighed. Ever the optimist was her dad. He could

see diamonds in the middle of a pile of shit, but in this case, there actually *were* diamonds. She hoped she hadn't seen the last of them.

Hannah put the phone in her pocket.

'Over to you now, Moshe.'

He nodded but said nothing as he separated the big diamonds and put them into a small piece of velvet material he took from a drawer. Then he placed them aside and carefully put the rest of the diamonds into the pouch and handed them back to Hannah.

'If it goes well, then perhaps we can do business again with the other diamonds,' Moshe said.

He stood up and came from behind his desk and shook her hand, then Jake's. Hannah couldn't help glancing at the small black velvet bundle on his desk. But it was too late now to worry if they'd done the right thing.

'Don't worry, my dear. Everything will be good,' Moshe said as he walked towards the door of his office.

Hannah and Jack walked out of the door of the shop and looked across to where Cal, Tahir and the minder Billy sat at a pavement café on the canal drinking coffee.

'Jesus,' Hannah said as they crossed the road. 'Did that really happen in there?'

Jack let out a low whistle.

'It sure did, pet. It sure did.'

CHAPTER TWELVE

Kerry, Danny and Marty listened as Wolfie relayed the story from Amsterdam back to them. It had gone to plan, and this Moshe Dolgin character seemed sound enough, he said, and was now in possession of the two biggest yellow diamonds. She hoped for Wolfie's sake that this wasn't the last they'd see of them. The four-million-euro figure that the old jeweller had put on them was eye-watering, but deep down she worried that it might be more trouble than it was worth – especially now that they were hearing that the diamonds belonged to some Russians. The DVDs and pictures that could ruin Fairhurst were the real reason she was in this, and for that she felt a little streak of selfishness.

When Danny and Wolfie left, Kerry glanced at Marty Kane as the door closed and she let out a long sigh.

'I'll be glad when this is over, Marty,' she said. 'Won't you?'

'Yes. Definitely.' Marty reached across to the table and

picked up a folder. 'Let's hope we can contain any problems, and we don't bring the wrath of the Russians upon us.' He smiled. 'I don't think I could cope with that after the Colombians.'

Kerry found herself smiling too at what they had got themselves into. But Marty wasn't here to discuss the diamonds. He'd been working his way through the red tape to try and get Vic Paterson brought from jail in Spain to the UK. He was wanted in the UK for the same reason that he'd been picked up in Spain – smuggling a truck load of cocaine. The UK had the same evidence of him arriving as a passenger in the truck as the Spanish had of him leaving.

'It's one of these situations that gets a bit political,' Marty said. 'You get the Spanish wanting the kudos of having captured someone involved in the smuggling of Colombian cocaine, and at the same time the Brits want him to go to trial in their courts so they can claim victory. So far, the Spanish are digging in their heels, and to be honest, I'm not getting a huge deal of luck on this side either. The legal paperwork has been done from my side, but even here they're dragging their feet. In Spain, well, to be honest, if we go by the way they work, Vic will still be sitting there awaiting trial this time next year.'

'That's awful, Marty. I've not met Vic, but everything he's done, he did it for us, and we've got to be able to help him.'

'Yes, I totally agree with that. But it's not going to be easy.

I've got a very good QC in London working on the case, so I'm hoping he can make a breakthrough, but we're very much in the hands of the legal system.'

Marty closed his file and put it back in his case. He stood up.

'So how are you feeling these days, Kerry? I mean with the baby – are you getting time to enjoy your pregnancy?'

Kerry felt herself smiling at the question. She'd never really even considered that she was supposed to 'enjoy' her pregnancy. The last few weeks had gone by like lightning, as the Caseys regrouped and organised themselves after the battle with the Colombian cartel. And she hadn't heard from Vinny since the day she'd got home from hospital after she'd been shot. He'd come to the house to tell her that he was going back undercover, and that he would only be able to make contact with her now and again. She had no way of calling or texting him, as he told her he wouldn't be using his mobile for the foreseeable future. She didn't even know what country he was in. There was nothing she could do about it. She had no control over whatever their relationship was, and she accepted that and got on with things the way she'd always done. But days like today, she wished she could talk to him. She was going for her twelve-week scan at the maternity clinic in the afternoon, and she would have to do it without Vinny.

'I'm fine,' she said. 'Actually, I'm a bit nervous as I'm going for my scan today, and even though they told me the baby was fine after I got shot, I'm just worried that something might have changed.'

'Don't worry,' Marty said. 'That's normal. You'll be fine. You're a Casey.' He winked, then turned and headed for the door.

It was mid-afternoon by the time Kerry arrived at the private maternity clinic in Glasgow's West End. She'd taken Maria – Cal's mother – with her for support, and they sat in the empty waiting room, Kerry fidgeting with her phone.

'Don't be nervous, Kerry,' Maria said. 'It'll be totally fine.'

'I wish I could talk to Vinny,' Kerry said, turning to her. 'He hasn't been in touch since the day he left.'

'Well, if he's undercover, then maybe he can't even do that.'

'I know.'

'But you're not alone, Kerry. You'll never be alone. You have Danny and Pat and all the guys.' She squeezed her arm. 'And you have me.' She grinned. 'Changed days, eh? You and me sitting in the maternity unit? Seems like yesterday we were hanging around Jaconelli's café in Maryhill waiting for the boys to come in, then pretending we weren't interested in them.'

The memory made Kerry smile and took the heat out of her for a moment. Then the receptionist came over and told her it was time. They looked at each other, and Maria gave her a supporting nudge.

Inside the examination room they were greeted by the sonographer and Kerry was ushered up on to the bed. When she'd stripped down the sonographer had noticed the scar on her stomach. It would have been in her notes, but she didn't mention it. Kerry glanced at Maria and she wondered how many people she got in here who'd been shot in the stomach while pregnant. The sonographer spread the gel across her stomach, then Kerry felt the coldness of the ultrasound transducer. She looked again at Maria as the hand-held probe went across slowly, stopping briefly at a couple of areas as though she was searching for the foetus. Kerry could feel her gut churning, watching the sonographer's expression closely. Was there not supposed to be a heartbeat by now? Nothing. The woman's face was set in concentration and the screen above was just a blurred image, dark and mysterious. Then, suddenly, a tiny figure came into view, and there was a rapid pounding. The sonographer's face broke into a smile as she turned up the volume.

'Here we are.'

Kerry looked up at the screen. At first, she couldn't see anything that she could figure out was a baby. Then the sonographer enlarged the image. And there it was. A little mass of flesh – she could clearly make out a head and a tiny body – and the constant beating of the heart at a hundred miles an hour.

'Is . . . is that my baby?'

'It certainly is. Heart pounding away there like a wee champ.'

Kerry bit her lip and glanced at Maria who was giving her the same look. Then the tears came. She wished her mother could be here to see this and hold her hand. After all this time, the nausea, the panic, the past weeks of frenzied activity, the fear that she'd nearly lost it in the shoot-out. And now this little figure on the screen would change her world for ever. She sniffed.

'Sorry,' she apologised. 'I'm just so . . . It's just been . . . It's been a tough few weeks. I'm a bit overwhelmed.'

The sonographer squeezed her arm.

'Everyone is overwhelmed when they see that little life for the first time. I've got the best job in the world on a day like this.'

'Thanks,' Kerry said, wiping her tears.

The sonographer clicked a button and across the room a little picture came out of a printer. She went over and took it out, then handed it to her.

'For your album,' she smiled.

Kerry sat up, gazing at the photo and fighting back more tears. Maria put her arms around her and hugged her.

'Congratulations, Kerry. This is just the best moment ever.'

Kerry nodded. She had never considered that seeing that picture on the screen would take her feet from under her the way it did. Nothing could have prepared her for the flood of emotion coursing through her. The love she felt for this little dot in the blurred image was overpowering, and she knew that her life would never be the same again, no matter what the future held for her.

CHAPTER THIRTEEN

Vic's mind was made up. He had to get out of here pronto. There was no way he was going to sit in this shithole waiting for the Spanish and the Brits to finish arguing over who was going to put him on trial. He knew how these things worked: despite the promises of Sharon the other day, deep down he knew he would still be sitting here a year from now if he left it up to other people. He knew she would try her best and he trusted her. More than that, he had real feelings for her. If he was honest with himself, seeing her through the thick glass partition that separated them was what finally made his mind up. It was down to him to make it happen now.

All his life, Vic had relied on nobody but himself. He'd learned that lesson very early on in the harshest way, when his mum had died and his dad fucked off, leaving him and his two little sisters to fend for themselves. His mum had died of breast cancer, and for almost eighteen months he had watched her fade away to a frail figure. She'd held his hand

and made him promise that no matter what, he would take care of his sisters, because she knew what a feckless bastard their father was. Vic had watched as she took her last breath, her hand slipping from its grasp on his. He was only fifteen. He'd dried his eyes, stuck out his chin at the world and, almost overnight, Vic had gone from teenager to man. The very last thing he would allow to happen was that they would all end up in care. He cooked and cleaned, and made sure there was food on the table every day, so that his sisters went to school clean and fresh and well fed. To make that happen, he had his first venture into the criminal world. In the council estate where they lived, you either left through education or you made your way through crime. Vic had been taken under the wing of the top crime lord in Salford, who knew his set-up, and that he'd been abandoned by his dad. The big man used him to do small jobs at first. Vic was tall and well-built for his age and able to handle himself, so he used to collect protection money, and now and again pick up stolen goods and move them on. He kept himself very much in the background at first and for four years, he did the job, kept his mouth shut, and made sure his sisters got through school the same as all their friends did. When the girls left home and got jobs – one going to college – they very quickly met boyfriends, and Vic let them go. He'd done what he could. That was probably as close as he was ever going to get to being a father. And it hadn't mattered to him. At eighteen, the world had been at his feet. He could take on anyone, and he did. But that was all a very long time ago. Now, in the prison cell, Vic went over the conversation he'd had with his Spanish *amigo* last week.

At first Vic had thought it was a joke. He'd sat and listened to the Spanish lag he'd become close to over the past few weeks. Vic had stepped in when Juan was getting the shit beaten out of him by some new gorilla who'd just arrived in the jail, and who was trying to show the other hard men in the wing that this was his show from now on. In about five seconds, Vic had decked the big man and three of his sidekicks, and he'd picked up Juan, bleeding and battered, from the exercise yard. Of course, when the prison officers finally came around, nobody said a word. And Vic and Juan had become instant mates.

Juan was teaching Vic Spanish and he was trying to teach him the basics of English, although it didn't seem that Juan would need English, because he was in for fifteen years for the murder of a bar owner who had taken over his business by force. But Juan had assured Vic that he had no intention of staying in prison, and that for the past year he had been working on his escape plan. At first, Vic had only paid lip service to his idea, nodding in all the right places, trying to humour his friend who he'd become fond of. He'd felt Juan got a raw deal in life, a bit like himself. But the little Spaniard had endeared himself to the prison staff and was now a trusty – a trusted prisoner given a key to certain places. So Juan had a real knowledge of every area of the prison, of the comings and goings, and had been examining every possibility of escaping. His problem, he'd told Vic, was money. To get out, he would have to be able to bribe one or two people, and he had no money. The more Vic listened, and the more desperate he became, the more his plan had begun to seem quite credible. Vic told Juan he could come up with the money for his escape, if he included him in his plans. To his surprise, Juan agreed immediately. Then a couple of days later, in his fractured English, over lunch in the dining hall, Juan outlined his escape plan.

'The prison,' he said, 'they buy their fruit and vegetable from the local farm. I know when he deliver. That is how my plan will work.'

Vic wiped his plate with a piece of bread and took a bite from it. Keeping his eyes down on the table, he mumbled, 'So how you going to get the farm truck to take you out?'

Juan picked up his plastic mug and took a sip of water.

'I see him every time he come, and we talk a bit. He an okay guy. I make joke with him one day that I hide in his truck, and he laugh and tell me, sure, if money is good.' Juan paused. 'He was smiling. But in his eyes, I can see that it is no joke.'

'How can you trust someone like that though? I mean, it's a bit crazy. You must know that yourself.'

Juan shrugged and leaned forward.

'Yesterday, I ask him again. Only this time I was serious. I said how much to take me over. And he said two grand.'

Vic couldn't help but smile.

'Just like that? You give a guy two grand and he'll take you out of this shithole in his truck? And what are the screws doing while this is happening?'

'When he comes with deliveries, is always lunchtime for the guards. Lockdown for most of the prisoners except for ones like me who have certain jobs. So when he is here, there is not much supervision. Only maybe one guard, two, and they don't sit and guard. It's not like that.'

'But you have no money to give to him. And I have no money here. But if he takes us both out, I can get him the money immediately.'

'You can? Two grand?'

'Sure.'

'Then we do it. You and me. On the day he comes with his vegetables I make some excuse that you are helping me for a while. Then, we are out of here, *amigo*.'

That was last week, nearly two weeks after Sharon had visited. Now he was ready. If this all went tits up, Sharon would never forgive him for not telling her, not giving her the opportunity to talk him out of it. But Vic wasn't leaving his fate to anyone but himself – and, of course, Juan, who had told him yesterday to be ready and poised for freedom. Vic had even allowed himself a little laugh about it when he had been lying in his cell the previous night, convincing himself he was doing the right thing.

After lunch the prisoners hung around for fifteen minutes in the yard smoking and enjoying some sunshine, before the bell rang signalling time for lockdown. The wardens shepherded them back to their cells as they began drifting away from the halls. Vic was delivering a box of garbage to the back-kitchen utility area on the ground floor where the delivery man was. Juan was working, taking rotting food out to be used for the farmer's pigs. By the time Vic had joined him the truck was already reversing in and the driver, a thickset little man in his fifties, had got out of the cabin and come to the back. He worked on the latches and bolts, sliding them over and opening the huge doors. He began unloading one or two boxes, and Juan took them out and into the walk-in cool storage room. Vic helped him, lifting a couple of boxes, and so they went on until they'd removed the lot, and the driver stood having a cigarette, chatting to one of the guards. The guard looked at his watch, indicated he was going for lunch and disappeared.

Vic looked up, at and around at any watchtowers. Just as Juan said, there was only one guard up in the high lookout tower, and he was on his mobile. The driver didn't make eye contact with Vic, but when Juan talked to him, he glanced briefly in Vic's direction and gave a slight nod. He took one last drag of his cigarette and stubbed it out. Then as Juan carried out some empty crates and shoved them into the truck, he climbed into the back with them. He told Vic to go and bring out some more. It was as quick as that. Vic took out one, two, three crates, returning twice, glancing around all the time, amazed that the guard hadn't come back. Then from the inside of the truck, behind the crates, Juan grinned and beckoned him in. It was now or never. Vic jumped in, and in seconds they heard the doors being closed and latches and bolts being slapped on. Then came the drone of the big truck's engine and they felt it move off. It was dark and chilly inside, but their eyes got used to the darkness, and Vic looked across at Juan, his eyes shining. They sensed the truck going through the main doors and heard the electronic gates shut, then the truck moving a little faster as it came out of the prison yard and down the drive onto the country road. They could hear the roar of the engine as the truck picked up speed, and Vic felt his palms start to sweat and his stomach churn with an excitement he'd not experienced in a very long time.

'We are free, *amigo*,' Juan said, a smile breaking out in his dark stubbly face.

Vic listened to the sound of the engine as it got faster, sensing the twists and turns of the country road. He wondered how long it would be before they started chasing them. Probably once the two hours of prisoner lockdown was over and the screws started emerging from lunch, they'd discover there were two missing. But Juan was right. For the moment they were free. And Vic resolved to make sure it stayed that way.

CHAPTER FOURTEEN

Hannah stepped out of the riverside hotel in Amsterdam and stood for a moment taking in the stillness of the morning. The colourfully painted buildings made a picture-perfect scene, with the river gently meandering under the ancient bridges. Jack had been advised by his people on the ground here that they should stay in the canal district of the city, so they would look like any of the other tourists who flock to the area to take in the atmosphere. When she'd woken up, Hannah had considered sitting tight in the hotel for the duration of the trip. She'd stayed in her room or around the lounge all day yesterday, reading and watching movies. But she'd never been to Amsterdam before, and after five years banged up in jail and the stresses of the past few days, she'd decided it was too good an opportunity to miss. It was only eleven in the morning, and the city was beginning to get busy with tourists out for a morning stroll. As she crossed the street, she nodded to the guy in the car parked at the edge of the corner. She'd met him yesterday and he had been introduced as Stevie. He'd been with another two blokes, John and Bruno, the men on the ground Jack had organised to keep an eye on things in case there were any unwanted visitors looking for diamonds.

Hannah went across to the bridge and stood for a moment watching a canal boat negotiate its way along a narrow stretch of the water. No wonder the Dutch were so laid back, she thought, living in a place as calm and easy on the eye as this. She crossed the bridge and wandered along the canal path until she came to a pavement café tucked off into a side street. In her leather jacket and scarf it was warm enough to be outside, so she sat down at a table where she could still glimpse the water and stretched out her legs. When the waitress came she ordered a white coffee and a croissant. This was as close as she'd been to a holiday in the past five years. She smiled to herself at the thought, and wondered how some of her old friends were coping behind bars. When the coffee arrived, she raised the cup in a private toast to them, just as she said she would as soon as she enjoyed her first real taste of freedom.

Hannah watched as a party of four tourists came and sat by a table close to the café window, and she listened to their chatter about afternoon plans to visit the café district to sample some of the cannabis freely available in shops and bars. It was a rite of passage in Amsterdam, but

Hannah would be giving it a miss. She picked up a magazine and flicked through the photographs of city life and celebrities, nibbling on her croissant, wondering where life would take her in a few months from now. Her father was determined to get out of the UK and go to the Cayman Islands as soon as he could get paid off from the heist. As far as he was concerned, she was going with him. And she would. But not long term. She had an old score to settle in London first and when the time was right she would get it done and tick the final box of payback. Hannah thought about Kerry Casey and the empire she had going in the UK, and by all accounts in Spain with Sharon. From what she'd heard about Kerry and her background, being sent away as a teenager by her father for her own protection, she felt a bit of a kindred spirit with her. Kerry didn't at all come across like any of the hard-case women she'd met over the years in jail and on the outside. She looked and sounded a cut above all that, without being a snob, and with a big heart, according to Jack and Cal. Last night during dinner, Jack had told her how Kerry had stepped in to help Maria – and how the Casey lawyer had got Cal out of deep water in Manchester when he got arrested. She wondered if she could maybe work with these people in the future. Though it would probably be impossible for someone to come up from London and move into any kind of job with the Caseys. She liked the cut of Sharon too. She was more like the tough nuts she'd met – looked and sounded as though she feared no one and would fight to the death for her son and for herself. She'd listened to some stories over the past few nights back in Glasgow. The one about how Sharon had looked the Colombian in the eye and put a bullet in him after Jake Cahill had downed him was straight out of Hannah's book of how you deal with the people who hurt you. *Who knows what the future holds?* she thought. But it was far too early to start even speculating on what she might do. There was a job to be done here, and it wasn't over yet. She finished her coffee and walked back to the hotel.

It was early evening and Hannah was showered and ready to go downstairs for dinner in the hotel with Jack. She stood by the window and looked down to see Cal and Tahir leaving the hotel and crossing the road to the bar they'd gone to last night. She looked at her watch. It was nearly an hour before dinner, so she decided to join them in the bar to pass the time. Downstairs, the hotel foyer was quiet and she went outside, zipping up her jacket as she went down the steps. She was about to cross the street when she stopped and turned towards the corner where, earlier, Stevie had been keeping a watch in his car. Whether out of instinct or paranoia, Hannah found herself walking to the corner just to make sure he was still there. He was. She saw his car and bent her head a little hoping he would see her. From where she stood he seemed to be leaning over the steering wheel, so he hadn't seen her. But she had to be sure. She walked towards the car, her stomach tightening with every step. Then she froze. Stevie wasn't leaning over the steering wheel. He was slumped. Hannah reached into her bag for her gun as she nervously glanced around her, braced for someone to jump out of the shadows. But the road was deserted. She took a step towards the car, her gun in her hand, and carefully opened the door. Stevie was dead. Blood dripped off the steering wheel and oozed out of the back of his neck. Hannah pulled out her phone and called Jack. It rang and rang, but there was no answer.

Cal was delighted to be told they'd be staying in Amsterdam for a couple of days longer than they first thought. It had been Kerry's suggestion that instead of going straight back to Glasgow, they should wait in the country until they knew the diamonds had been moved on and the money was showing up in Wolfie's account. It made sense. From what he could make out of the conversation between Jack and Hannah, Wolfie had been reluctant at first because he wanted Hannah home. But Kerry and Danny had told him it was the best way. And what if the money didn't arrive in the account? Nobody even wanted to go there right now. So for the past two nights, everyone had been kicking their heels in Amsterdam playing a waiting game.

Cal and Tahir had been dying to have a look at downtown Amsterdam to see if all the hype was true. But Cal knew they daren't even mention that to Jack. They were here to work as backup. They had to be vigilant at all times, Jack had told them when they'd arrived. That was enough for Cal and Tahir. They were happy to be sitting at the table with these people, listening to stories, enjoying being part of a top team. They ate in the hotel, and Cal and Tahir only went out to a nearby bar for an hour in the evening.

The bar across the street from the hotel was a modern-looking effort with bright lights and thumping disco music. It was always busy, mostly with young people in groups chatting and drinking, some standing around the bar, others at tables. Cal had clocked the two men who had come in just after them, who stood at the end of the bar. Whoever they were, they looked a bit out of place in a bar like this, as the music blaring from speakers and the general look of the place would not attract older people. He wondered if the guys were perhaps staying in the hotel and were on their way downtown but stopping for a quick drink first. Maybe he was paranoid and overzealous, he told himself, but the big guy in the leather bomber jacket was definitely stealing little glances at him.

'Don't look now,' Cal said quietly to Tahir as he sipped his glass of Coke, 'But those two guys at the bar. They look kind of old for this place.' He put down his glass. 'And one of them keeps looking over here.'

Tahir nodded slowly.

'I saw them when they came in and thought the same.'

He shrugged. 'Maybe we're getting a bit paranoid. Maybe one of them fancies you.'

Cal gave an exaggerated laugh, but it was more to look natural, because now the guy in the leather jacket was definitely talking to his mate, and he had turned his head around to look in their direction. Cal felt uneasy. These guys looked Eastern European, not Dutch or Afro-Caribbean or Spanish or any of the mix of people in the bar.

'I think we should get out of here,' Cal said.

As he said it, the main door opened and another two walked in and ambled across to the men at the bar. There was no obvious show of friendship or camaraderie between them. All were stony-faced. One of them was huge and bald, with a tattoo on the back of his thick neck, dressed in a bulky knee-length leather coat. Almost as soon as they joined their friends who were ordering drinks, one of them glanced in their direction.

'I don't like this,' Cal said.

Then, as Tahir put his drink down, Cal slipped his phone out of jacket pocket. 'I'm going to phone Jack first. This doesn't feel right.'

Jack answered his phone after two rings.

'What's up?' he asked.

As calmly as he could, Cal told Jack about the men at the bar, how they looked and that he was feeling uneasy.

'Right,' Jack said. 'Hang up and sit tight for a couple of minutes until me and Bruno get outside the bar so we can see you as we leave. You'll not see us, so don't look for us. Just walk straight across to the hotel. Don't look at these fuckers or even nod in their direction. Just get yourselves out of there.'

The tone of Jack's voice told Cal everything he needed to know. He was right to be worried. How the hell anyone could know that the Caseys had a crew in Amsterdam right now was anybody's guess. He slipped his phone back into his pocket and whispered to Tahir.

'In a couple of minutes,' Cal said, 'we get up and just walk straight out. We don't even look at them, but just go right to the hotel. Jack and Bruno are going to be somewhere looking out for us. Tahir blinked an agreement and they sat quietly. Cal's stomach was going like an engine, and he was trying to picture how many steps it was to the hotel, and if they could sprint it in a few seconds. But he was getting ahead of himself with worry. *Calm down.* After what felt like several minutes, but was probably only two or three, Cal looked at Tahir.

'Let's go.'

They both got up and walked towards the door, their eyes straight ahead, but Cal was aware that the men at the bar were eyeing them up as they walked past them. Cal pulled open the swing door and walked through. Outside, the air was crisp and cold, and Cal took a deep breath and glanced around. There was no sign of Jack, but he hoped he was there somewhere in the shadows. They only got a few steps away from the bar when it happened. At the same time as a black SUV screeched to a halt in front of them, they heard the swing door of the bar open and shut and the sound of heavy footsteps running towards them. For a second both Cal and Tahir were like rabbits caught in the headlights, both frozen to the spot, not sure whether to watch the car where a huge gorilla of a guy had got out of the passenger seat and was thundering towards them, or turn around to face what they instinctively knew were the guys from the bar. Cal found himself automatically slipping his hand up his sweatshirt to feel the metal of his gun. He turned around, and just as he did, the guy with the tattoo struck out and punched him in the face. The force of the blow knocked him off his feet, but he quickly got back up again. As he did, the others from the bar rushed forward and grabbed hold of Tahir and began to drag him away towards the SUV. Cal pulled out his gun and stood back, pointing it at anyone who was coming near him. But as he did, a shot rang out, and one of the two guys who were dragging Tahir dropped to the ground. Then another shot, and another guy dropped. Christ! Tahir quickly rolled over and crouched behind the wheel of the car. It was all happening so fast, Cal didn't even get a shot off before everyone began to scatter apart from the two injured hoods on the ground. Then he saw Jack and Bruno emerge from behind a four-by-four parked in the street.

'Come on. Let's move it.'

*

As he spoke, another car screeched to a halt and Cal braced himself for the next onslaught. But then he could see it was Hannah in the driving seat, and she pushed the passenger door open. In a few strides, Jack was in the passenger seat and Cal, Tahir and Bruno had thrown themselves into the back, closing the door as Hannah roared away, tyres screeching as she raced through the tight streets and on through the city.

'Fuck me!' Jack said, glancing in his visor mirror. 'There's a car chasing us.'

'I see it,' Hannah said as she stepped on the accelerator and roared through a red light, swerving to avoid a lorry then turning right. 'I've no fucking idea where I'm going, Jack, but I'm hoping it's out of the city.'

'Did anyone see Steve?' Bruno asked. 'He was in his car close to the hotel, but I didn't see him as it all kicked off.'

There was a stony silence and Hannah stared straight ahead, then Jack spoke, softly.

'Steve is dead, Bruno. Hannah saw him slumped over the wheel just before it all happened. I'm sorry.'

Nobody spoke. Bruno's face was like flint.

Jack turned to him.

'I know John dropped one of the fuckers. I'm hoping he's in a car somewhere. He knows the city so he'll have seen us leaving and will hopefully follow us.'

'Would be good if he was behind this bastard who's catching up with us. Christ!' Hannah said.

'I know,' Jack said. 'We'll just have to keep driving.'

Cal and Tahir both turned around to see the black car getting closer.

Hannah wasn't sure if they were heading further into the city or out to somewhere at the edge, but there were now fewer people and cars, and the bastards were still behind her. She kept switching streets, taking sharp turns, but still they were catching up. Then as she turned into a street that looked deserted, she dropped a gear and sped up, thinking if she could get to out of the other end quickly she would lose them. But just as she did, a car came flying round the corner towards her, then suddenly screeched to a halt and blocked the road.

'Fuck! They must be with the guys from the bar. We're trapped.' Jack pulled out his gun. 'We're going to have to shoot our way out of this.' He half turned to the back. 'You boys all right? Get ready.'

Cal swallowed the dry ball in his mouth and cocked his gun. He could feel his heart pounding. Tahir stared straight ahead, his face pale and expressionless.

Hannah's stomach dropped. There was no way out. She had no idea how many people were in the car behind her, and now the car in front was an even bigger threat. She stopped the car.

They sat there as the driver's door and the passenger door opened in the car that was blocking the road. One man got out of the driving seat brandishing a rifle. The other, from the passenger seat, had a handgun. They started to walk towards them.

'Jesus!' Hannah muttered. 'What now, Jack?'

'Just wait,' he said. 'Cal. What's going on in the car at the back?'

Cal turned around to see two men come out of the car, armed.

'Two of them,' he said. 'Both armed.'

Jack didn't answer, just stared out of the windscreen. Hannah flicked a look around the street and up at the roofs but could see nothing in the darkness. Then the man with the rifle came up to the car and pointed the gun at the windscreen. Everyone sat, barely breathing, waiting for the gunshot.

'Out of the car!' the man with the handgun barked. 'Now.'

'What do we do?' Hannah asked.

She could see the fear and concentration in Jack's face, his jaw tightening.

'We have to get out,' he said. 'We're not going to sit here and let these cunts shoot us. Put your guns out of sight, boys, or that's the first thing they'll take.'

Cal didn't dare ask if there was a plan. There was none. There were gunmen in front of them, and more behind. Jack opened the door and Hannah did the same. Then Cal and Tahir got out of the car. They all stood, hands in the air. Cal thought of his mother. *We might not get out of this alive*. Everyone stood rigid, waiting. Then the man with the handgun, who seemed to be the group's leader, jerked his head towards the guy with the rifle. He stepped forward, pointed the gun at Cal, then grabbed him by the hair. Cal winced, terrified, as he caught Jack's eyes, cold with fear and rage. The man dragged Cal by the hair across to the head gunman, who then pulled him into a headlock so that he was facing the others. Cal could feel the beefy arm around his neck and then the cold of the gun pushed hard against the side of his head. He felt dizzy but tried hard to hold his nerve. Deep down he wanted to cry, because he knew if he died like this it would break his mother.

'The diamonds!' the man shouted, squeezing Cal's neck a little tighter. 'You have five seconds to hand them over or everyone is dead. Starting with this boy.' He pushed the gun harder into Cal's head.

Cal looked at Hannah and their eyes locked. He could see the panic and fear in her, but her face was set in defiance. Nobody moved.

'Five, four . . .' he barked.

Cal saw Hannah put her hand up. Then with her other hand she slowly unzipped her jacket but stopped halfway.

'You have three seconds,' he said, almost smirking. 'Three, two . . .'

Then the shot came from nowhere, and the man with the rifle was down. And by the time he hit the ground, another shot had rung out. In the blur, Cal thought he had seen Hannah go into her jacket and pull out a gun, but it happened so fast he couldn't be sure – at least the guy who was crushing his neck had now let him go. Cal dived to the ground, pulling out his gun, and as he did, all hell broke loose. There were so many people shooting, he crawled along the ground, not sure where everyone was. Then he saw Tahir fire his gun at one of the men in the car behind him, and he fell to the ground as Tahir went across and put two more bullets into him. Then he turned like a pro and dropped the other guy.

'Cal,' Jack said. 'Get into that car and move it out of the way so we can get the fuck out of here.'

Cal dashed across and into the gunmen's car, shaking as he tried to start it up. Then he heard the engine roar, reversed and pulled it back round the corner at the end of the street, clearing the way. He jumped out and ran across to the others, who were piling back into their own car. Hannah eased it past the gunmen's abandoned car and roared out of the street.

Nobody spoke as they sped back towards what looked like the end of the city. By the time they hit the motorway they could hear the sound of police sirens in the distance. Only when they were on the motorway and Hannah was doing over a hundred miles an hour did Cal risk a deep breath. And only then did he notice the throbbing pain in the side of his eye and feel the blood trickling down his face.

Finally, Jack put his head back and spoke.

'Fuck me, troops! What the fuck just happened?'

'Did you see the shot from the roof of the building?' Hannah turned to him momentarily, grinning. 'Must have been John.'

Jack turned to her, surprised.

'Seriously? Did you see any of them, Hannah? I didn't. I just wondered where the fuck the shot came from to drop that big bastard with the rifle. I mean he was there one second, then he wasn't.' He shook his head and turned to the back. 'You lads all right?' He smiled. 'Now don't tell me you didn't enjoy that!'

Cal and Tahir laughed, but Cal was still in shock. Tahir gave him a playful punch.

'You okay, mate?'

'Yep,' Cal said. He wasn't, but he knew he would be.

Jack looked at Hannah.

'And where the fuck did you learn to shoot like that, Hannah?'

Hannah smiled.

'Jesus, Jack. I didn't know I could. I mean, Wolfie took me to the gun range when I was a teenager and I got quite good at it. But it's been a long time.'

'Yeah,' Jack said. 'But that was fucking precision stuff. You shot that bastard right in the head. If you'd missed, Cal would have got it there and then. Risky as fuck!'

'I know,' Hannah said. 'But I'd caught a glimpse of someone on the roof just as we got out of the car, and there was nothing I could do to alert you to it, so I just kind of knew by instinct that it had to be John. And when the shot came, I knew if I didn't do it then, then that bastard choking Cal might have killed him just for badness.'

'Still some fucking shot, though.' Jack shook his head.

'Well,' Hannah said, opening the driver's window and breathing in the cold night air. 'I suppose nothing concentrates the mind like fear.'

Nobody said anything for a few minutes, everyone processing what they'd just been through, then Jack took out his phone and they listened as he spoke.

'Danny. It's me. We've been rumbled. Some bastards in a bar next to the hotel. Looks like they knew who we were and where we were. How the fuck does that happen?'

Cal couldn't hear Danny's reply, then Jack spoke again.

'We're on the motorway heading for Brussels. It wouldn't be smart to take the Amsterdam route back in case they're watching for us. We'll hole up somewhere near the terminal overnight and get the train in the morning. At least that's the plan. But fucking hell, man! How the fuck did this happen?'

There was a moment's silence, Jack still with the phone at his ear.

'No. Everyone's fine. I'll tell you about it later. Cal got a bit of a slap. But Hannah's okay. We'll let you know where we are in a few hours.' He paused. 'But, Danny. We need to find out how anyone could possibly know where we were.'

Cal and Tahir exchanged glances as they both let out a sigh.

'You're bleeding, mate,' Tahir said.

'It's nothing,' Cal said.

'You lads all right back there?' Jack said. 'Did you get any sense of what nationality those guys were?'

'Didn't hear them speak, but to look at, I'd say they were Eastern European,' Cal said. 'We clocked them as soon as they came in, and we saw them looking at us. That's why I phoned you. I had a bad feeling about it.'

'You did the right thing,' Jack said without turning around. 'But this isn't over yet.'

By the time they got to Brussels, Hannah was beginning to feel exhaustion creeping in. The initial rush of adrenalin from the shoot-out was wearing off. She was glad when they drove across the city and found a hotel close to the Eurostar terminal. She parked the car and everyone climbed out and took their belongings from the boot. Jack turned to Cal and Tahir.

'Bet you're glad you've got a change of drawers in the boot – you must have just about shat yourselves back in Amsterdam.'

His jibe lightened the mood a little, and everyone smiled as they slung their bags over their shoulders and headed to the hotel entrance. Jack went to the reception and sorted the rooms he had organised by phone on the journey, then handed everyone keys.

'Right. Everyone down to the bar in ten minutes. I'm sure we could do with a stiff drink and a bite to eat.'

Hannah let the others go to their rooms, then she walked into the bar to have a quick look around. It was quiet, apart from a couple of men who looked like reps or businessmen on an overnight. Nothing to be suspicious about. She turned and left, climbing the stairs to her room on the first floor. On the way up, her mobile rang, and she could see her dad's name on the screen.

'Sweetheart. You all right?'

'Yeah,' Hannah said. 'I'm good. Bit knackered.'

'Did you get a look at these bastards who came after you guys?'

'No. There was a bit of a shoot-out. So we're lying low in case the cops are after us. We can't be shooting people in a foreign country. But it had to be done.'

'Cops will be the least of your worries, pet. I want you back here where I can look after you.'

Hannah couldn't help but smile.

'I don't need looking after, Dad. You should know that by now.'

'Yeah, sweetheart. But you know what I mean.' He paused. 'Anyway, all that aside, the bad news is coming in thick and fast.'

'Really? What's happened?'

'Well, it might not be that bad, but on the face of it, something stinks. You remember that old Jewish jeweller we met here in Glasgow? Manny Lieberman?'

'Course I do. What's happened?'

'Well, he's fucked off, that's what.'

'How? I mean where? How do you know?'

'Well, Kerry had her boys keeping an eye on his shop for the last few days after we saw him. I mean, you know that any money Moshe gets from shifting the diamonds was to go to him, then to me.'

'Yeah. But we're not expecting the money until tomorrow at least. I only saw Moshe the day before yesterday and he said it would be a couple of days before he could shift them.'

'I know that. But I didn't expect Manny to fucking disappear in the meantime.'

'How do you know? Have you checked him out, at his house? Maybe something's happened to him.'

'We've checked him out just the last couple of hours. Turns out he's only fucking gone to Israel.'

'Israel? When?'

'Don't know. But in the last twenty-four hours. We had someone make a discreet enquiry with one of his neighbours and they said him and his wife had gone to Israel. They have a house there. But she said they left quite suddenly.'

'Oh fuck!'

'Yeah. My sentiments exactly.'

'Surprised all of us. Kerry didn't know him that well, but Danny did, and he's assuring us that Manny wouldn't do the dirty. If he's in Israel, then there must be a reason for it, Danny says.'

'I hope so,' Hannah said, not really knowing what else to say. 'So, what happens now? What about Moshe?'

'That's why I'm calling. Kerry will speak to Jack shortly. She's getting someone on the ground in Amsterdam to go out to Moshe's address to make sure he's all right. Or to find out if he's also fucked off somewhere. Because if he has, then I think we've got problems.'

It certainly sounded that way to Hannah. And she was beginning to ask herself if she had been right to part with the diamonds there and then to a complete stranger. But she had been working on advice from connections in Glasgow. Somehow, she couldn't believe Moshe would do the dirty.

'We have to wait and see, Dad.'

'We will, darlin', but I'll be one fucking angry man if I've just been stung by a couple of old bastards.'

'Don't think that way. It's early days. Let's see what they come up with at Moshe's house.'

By the time they were on their second drink, Cal and Tahir were tucking into extra chips after demolishing huge burgers in the bar. The shock of being ambushed by hoodlums earlier had clearly washed off them. Hannah still thought the boys were too young to be involved at this level, but she'd noticed how quick Cal had been to reach for his gun earlier when the guys were dragging Tahir away outside the bar in Amsterdam. He was plucky enough despite his age. Hannah had eaten very little and was about to say she was off to bed when Jack's mobile rang. He picked it up from the table and pressed it to his ear.

'Danny,' he said. 'Tell me something good, for fuck's sake.'

A couple of whiskies had made Jack feel relaxed after the mayhem of the past few hours, but now his face fell.

'Fuck me! Israel?' He shot Hannah a glance.

Hannah couldn't hear the rest of the conversation as Jack nodded and shook his head as he listened. But she knew what he was going to say by the time he hung up.

'Well fuck me!' Jack said, tossing the phone onto the table. 'Our old mate Moshe has fucked off to Israel. With the diamonds, I presume.'

'Christ,' Hannah said. 'I had a feeling about that when Wolfie called me earlier to say that Manny had gone to Israel. What the fuck?'

'Aye. Exactly. What the fuck!' He sighed. 'I can't believe old Manny would double-cross the Caseys. He's known them for years – was an old pal of Kerry's dad. Moshe Dolgin I don't know, but well, he seemed all right. But you never can tell. He was pretty bowled over by those yellow diamonds. What do you think, Hannah? I mean it's not as if we can report it to the police!'

She shrugged. 'Same as you, Jack. I can't believe we've been stung. But what the Christ has made the two of them disappear to Israel?'

'Time will tell,' Jack said. 'If the money isn't in Wolfie's bank by tomorrow or the next day, then it's a different story.' He paused, his eyes scanning everyone. 'But I'll tell you what the bigger problem is right now. Someone was looking for us in Amsterdam – like they knew we were coming here. That can only mean one thing. Either they were tipped off by Manny, or by Moshe. Or, worst of all, we have a spy in the camp.' He shook his head. 'I find that hard to believe. But only a handful of people knew we were coming here and why, so Danny is looking into it. And he'll find out.'

CHAPTER FIFTEEN

'The signs are not good, Kerry.' Danny sat opposite her with his arms folded, shaking his head. 'The only person who knew exactly where the boys were staying in Amsterdam was Alex. I didn't even know myself what hotel they were in. Jack got Alex to organise it all.'

Kerry didn't like what she was hearing. As soon as the word came last night that the troops had been got at in Amsterdam, she'd known it could only mean one thing. Someone had betrayed them. Someone on the inside. A traitor in her family. She knew Danny would have run his investigation into every corner before he would come up with any solid accusation or acceptance that it was one of their own. She'd hoped he would come back with something pointing to Manny Lieberman or someone who knew the old jeweller. Even though it would have been hurtful and shocking that an old friend of her father's had betrayed them, it was better than discovering that it was one of your own. But not even Manny knew where they were staying in Amsterdam. Danny was almost a hundred per cent certain it was Alex. It was Alex who'd booked the hotel rooms and organised the travel for Jack and the rest of them. Nobody else knew. Not even Kerry or Wolfie or Danny knew where they'd be staying.

'I hear you, Danny,' Kerry said shaking her head. 'I just don't want to believe it.'

She stood up, went across to the window and looked down at the courtyard where the bodyguards and security were. Men she trusted with her life. Most of them she knew by name, but in truth she had no real idea who they were, how they lived their lives, whether they had ever felt slighted by the Caseys over the years and harboured a grudge. She had never known anything but loyalty from everyone who surrounded her, and even though she didn't know each and every person's background, she knew that Danny did and so did Jack, so loyalty was never in question. Until now.

'So what now?' Kerry said as she came back and sat opposite Danny.

Danny's lips tightened.

'A traitor has to be dealt with. No matter who it is.'

'Tell me about Alex,' Kerry said, spreading her hands almost apologetically. 'I've only met him once in Jack's office.'

Danny let out a long sigh.

'Alex. He must be in his forties now, but I've known him most of his life. His father worked for us. Did similar kinds of work. More of an administrator than someone you could send into a scrap. But like his father, Alex can think outside the box. Many's the time he's come up with a solution moving money or setting up new situations here and abroad. He's smart.'

'Married?'

'Yeah. Well. Was. Divorced now. He's a bit of a womaniser. Bit of a drinker too, but nothing he couldn't handle, I'd say. He likes to be a bit of a man about town. When Mickey was alive, he and Frankie quite often used to go to bars and clubs with Alex. He knew a lot of people. But there was never any sign he wasn't to be trusted.'

'Kids?' Kerry's question was out before she could stop herself.

Danny gave her a long look, his face like flint. He shrugged.

'Grown up by now. Don't know what his set-up is there. Right now, Kerry, that doesn't matter.'

His comment felt like a rebuke to Kerry. The message was clear. Alex's private life was of no concern. The only concern was that he was a traitor.

For a few moments they were silent, and only the sounds of the house – Elsa from the kitchen, and activity outside with cars and security men talking – could be heard. Life going on as normal downstairs while up here they talked of the fate of one of their own. Eventually, Danny spoke.

'Do you want to speak to him yourself, Kerry?' he asked.

She hid her surprise at the question. Speak to him? Could she really look someone in the eye before handing out a death sentence? Because that's why Danny was here. For her approval.

'No,' she said. She felt the colour rise in her neck. 'I'll leave it to you, Danny.'

Danny nodded slowly.

'I'll deal with it. Boys are trying to find him right now. He didn't turn up for work this morning. That says it all.'

Kerry nodded and looked away.

'So what does it mean, Danny? Who has got to him? Obviously one of Wolfie's enemies who knows he's up here with us.'

'Yeah. I talked to Wolfie this morning. He says it'll be Alfi Ricci's men who've got to him. But it wouldn't be them who were in Amsterdam. So Ricci must be under some pressure from the Russian mob who want their stuff back.'

Kerry nodded. 'We need to see what we can get out of Alex.' She stopped herself from saying 'first', because by saying it, she would really be saying 'before you kill him'.

Danny looked at her as though he could sense her inner turmoil. He had known her all her life, and if anyone knew that Kerry struggled with what she had become it was him. He stood up, and looked straight at her.

'I'll deal with it, Kerry. We'll see what happens. I'll keep you posted.' He turned to leave, then stopped. 'The troops will be back from Brussels this evening.'

Kerry nodded but said nothing, because right now she was lost for words. She shouldn't be, but she was.

Alex Mackie couldn't stop himself shivering, even though the car he was being driven in had the heating on full blast. He sat in the back, flanked between big Tonzo and Reilly who stared straight ahead, their faces blank. They'd been his mates for as long as he could remember. But not any more. They'd found him in the little one-bedroom flat he rented just as he was packed up and ready to blow town. He'd bought the flat on the Broomielaw down by the River Clyde as an investment a couple of years ago, because he was always thinking ahead, working out ways to make a fast few quid. Not that Alex was struggling for money. He was on a good wage for doing the job he did for Jack, organising all the admin, preparing books for the accountant, and keeping tabs on all the business interests Jack handled for the Caseys. Plenty of times, he supposed, he could have siphoned off some dosh and squirrelled it away, but he was always too scared in case Jack found out. That was before the blackmail had started. Never in a million years could Alex have imagined betraying the Caseys. He was family. His father had been family and he grew up alongside Mickey, Jack and Frankie. Alex had never been a strongarm like them, and old Tim Casey and Danny could see that early on. But he was smart, good with numbers and organisation, so he was perfect for the job he did. He made good money, but somewhere along the line it went wrong for him. He was always a womaniser but nobody knew of his penchant for young girls, some as young as early teens, and he used a secret escort contact who would provide him with them. Paid plenty of money, too, and had enough to keep going, if it hadn't been for the blackmail. The escort contact turned out to be a bitch who blackmailed him with pictures of cocaine-fuelled romps in country houses with young girls under the age of consent. Eight months ago his contact and her associates had threatened that if he didn't pay up they would spill the beans to the cops and the Caseys. He'd be dead meat. He paid them off, thousands, but they kept coming back for more. And every demand brought a new, fresh picture. He was desperate by the time this London guy connected to Alfi Ricci had got in touch with him through connections and asked to speak with him. He met them in a bar in Charing Cross and they told him they were looking for some people. Big money in this. More than he'd ever dreamed of – maybe even some diamonds. The guy hadn't said too much about it, but said his clients were looking for stolen diamonds. They'd said he could help, because they knew some guy called Wolfie they were trying to track down was being sheltered by the Caseys. They'd offered him a hundred thousand quid if he just kept his ears open. So he did, and he heard that a guy called Wolfie was staying with Kerry, and then Jack had told him to book travel and rooms in Amsterdam. When he had done that, Alex had asked for a meet. And the London boys gave him a hundred thousand hard cash in a brown envelope. Right now, that cash was sitting on the front passenger seat in a holdall to take to wherever they were going.

The driver took the car down through Shettleston Road in the East End, and then turned into a derelict car garage and up the side street, rattling over the potholes to a builders' yard at the end. The car pulled up and Tonzo turned to Alex and jerked his head. Alex opened the door and got out. He stood on shaky legs and walked behind Tonzo towards the Portakabin. Inside he could see a small strip light on the ceiling throwing shadows on the ground as Tonzo and Reilly marched him on, feet in puddles, Alex's whole body shaking. Then they pushed him up the wooden steps and through the door. When he saw Danny leaning on the desk and facing him, Alex felt his legs buckle. Danny nodded to Tonzo to put him on the chair and tie his hands and his ankles.

'Danny . . . I . . .' Alex struggled to speak, his chest tight with panic.

'Shut the fuck up!' Danny snapped. 'I don't want to hear your fucking voice unless I tell you.'

Alex nodded his mouth dry.

Danny stood, arms folded.

'So talk. Everything.'

'Danny . . . I . . . I'm sorry.'

The force of Danny's slap almost knocked the chair over, and blood seeped from Alex's nose.

'I don't want to hear your fucking sorry pish,' Danny said. 'Okay? Just fucking talk. Tell me everything.' He raised his hands. 'How the fuck did it come to this?'

Alex knew there was no point in denying anything. If he'd been brought here, it was because they knew he was the traitor. He opened his mouth to start talking, but his voice croaked. He cleared his throat and began.

'I was getting blackmailed, Danny. I was desperate for money.'

'Blackmailed by who?'

'An escort bitch.'

'Why?'

Alex took a moment to answer, shame washing over him.

'Young birds. I got myself involved with young birds. Illegals. They took pictures when I was coked up. A few times. Different birds. They said they were going to the cops. So I started paying them off, then it got out of hand. I was running out of money, going to lose my flat. My son is at uni studying to be an accountant. I couldn't let him know what his father was.' He started to cry. 'Danny. I'm so ashamed. It's all my fault.'

'I'm not your fucking parish priest. You're not getting any fucking absolution in this room. Who got in touch with you over Amsterdam?'

'Some guy up from London. His name was Nick. He

seemed to know that I worked for the Caseys. How the fuck did he know that?'

Danny didn't answer, just jerked his head for Alex to go on.

'They gave me some money a few days ago. Promised me that there was a big reward going if I kept them posted. Said it was something to do with diamonds and they wanted them back. Just said it was Russians. Said it was nothing personal against the Caseys. It was Wolfie they wanted. I didn't know who Wolfie was apart from hearing he was staying at the big house. So I told them.'

'Told them what.?'

Alex hesitated, blood trickling onto his upper lip.

'I told them about the trip to Amsterdam. That's all. I told them where they'd be staying. I didn't know anything else. I booked the tickets so that's the only information I had. They didn't say what they would do.'

'What the fuck did you think they would do? Organise a surprise fucking party? An open top fucking bus tour?' Danny snapped, his voice full of disgust.

Alex didn't answer. The silence filled the room. Alex let his head sink to his chest, then looked up pleadingly from Danny to Tonzo, whose faces were like flint.

Finally, Danny shook his head, and looked at him.

'Your father will be spinning in his fucking grave. Make your peace with that, you worthless shitbag.'

Then Danny nodded to Tonzo and Reilly. Tonzo reached

into his jacket and brought out his gun. Alex's face crumpled.

'Please,' Alex pleaded. 'My boy. Don't tell him what I did.'

Danny didn't answer as Tonzo stepped behind Alex, pushed the pistol into the back of his neck and fired.

Danny watched as Alex slumped over, blood pumping out of the back of his head onto the grubby vinyl floor.

'Phone Jamie. Tell him to get rid of this cunt.'

CHAPTER SIXTEEN

Vic Paterson rolled down the passenger-side window of the old pick-up truck. He took a deep breath and filled his lungs with the air of freedom. He closed his eyes, relishing the sun on his face. He even felt himself smiling.

'You are happy, *amigo*.' Jorge the driver grinned a tobacco-stained smile as he reached for a pack of cigarettes from the dashboard. 'You are free now.'

Vic opened one eye and turned his head in Jorge's direction.

'I sure am, *amigo*. And that's how I'm going to stay.'

From the back seat where Juan was lying with his feet up, he said, 'Vic. We must go as far away from this area as we can, as soon as we can.'

'Yep,' Vic said. 'Soon as I get the money and some stuff.'

It had taken a bit of convincing, but Vic and Juan had managed to persuade the farmer to ask a friend to drive them the hour-long journey to Estepona. Vic owned a small studio apartment there which he kept for emergencies. Little did he know when he bought the place a few months ago that it would become so crucial to him. In it, he kept various bank cards and a false passport, as well as several thousand euros. The deal Juan had agreed with the farmer was that it would be two grand cash as soon as they escaped. The farmer didn't want to run the risk of driving them all the way to Estepona, so he'd called on his friend Jorge and promised he would be well paid for the trip. Juan had done the negotiations with the farmer who was growing more nervous by the minute. He knew he might be the first port of call for the cops chasing the missing prisoners, so he wanted them as far away as possible – and quickly.

Estepona had grown bigger over the years with spreading apartment builds and a bustling port. The town centre was busy enough with tourists and locals that Vic could be anonymous. But as they drove in, they saw a lot of police around, and they were stopping some cars on the way in and out. He felt his gut tighten. He knew he could hold his nerve, but he hoped Jorge and Juan could if they were stopped. Vic was wearing borrowed sunglasses and a baseball cap pulled down to cover most of his face, and was pretending to be asleep as they approached the line of traffic.

'You okay with this, Jorge?' he said. 'If we get stopped?'

Jorge shrugged. 'No problem. Just keep quiet. I do the talking.'

It was sheer luck that the cops stopped the two cars in front of them but waved the pick-up truck on, and Vic breathed a huge sigh of relief. He directed Jorge to his apartment, slipped inside the building in a backstreet and took the five grand cash he kept there from a small wall safe in the room. He also took bank cards and a mobile phone. Then he threw some clothes into a small holdall. So far, so good.

'We're done, Jorge. Let's go,' he said as he climbed back into the truck.

As they drove to the next town, Vic lent Juan his mobile to make arrangements with a friend. When he handed him back the phone, he told Jorge to go to the small town of San Pedro where his friend would meet up with them. It didn't take long to get there, and when they did, they sat in a side street waiting for Juan's friend. When he turned up, Vic climbed out of the truck and made his farewells to Juan, dropping him a thousand euros to keep him going. The little Spaniard was almost tearful when he handed him the money.

'You save my life,' Juan said, giving him a bear hug.

'No,' Vic said, 'you saved mine, my friend.' They exchanged phone numbers and said they would keep in touch. They had to keep on running, Vic told him. That's what they would be doing from now on, to make sure they didn't go back inside. Vic watched as Juan got into his friend's car, then looked back and waved to him. It had only been a few weeks, but he'd grown close to the plucky little guy who'd got him this far. and he promised himself that if there was anything he could do to give him work in the future he would. He nodded to Jorge to go, and they headed to Cadiz for the train to Seville.

Now, relaxing with the sun on his face in the backstreet pavement café in the old part of Seville, Vic reflected on the last few hours as he sipped a cup of black coffee. No doubt, before nightfall, the daring escape from one of Spain's toughest jails would be all over the news, and his and Juan's faces would be appearing on TV screens here and in the UK. He had to get moving fast. He rubbed his chin, scrolled down his phone until he found Sharon's mobile, and pushed the call key. She answered after a few rings.

'Sharon. It's me.'

There was a moment's silence, then she spoke softly.

'Vic?'

'Yeah. Listen, sweetheart. I'm out.'

'What?'

'I'm out. Of jail. Escaped.'

'Fuck me!'

'Oh, sweetheart, you have no idea—'

'Cut the shit. Are you seriously out?'

'Yeah. I escaped this morning with another con. Long story. But I need your help.'

'Jesus, Vic. They'll be all over the place looking for you. How the Christ did you manage to pull this off?'

'I'll keep that story for dinner sometime soon, darlin'.'

'Where are you?'

'Seville. But listen, Sharon. I need your help.'

'Of course. Whatever you want. Jesus. I can't believe this.'

'I'm going to the UK. That's my plan. Once I'm there, I'll see about turning myself in. I'd rather take my chances with the Brit justice system than the crap over here.'

There was a long silence.

'You're really going to do that? Give yourself up in the UK?'

'Yep. Can't stay on the run for ever. You know that. They'll find me sometime. I'd just rather it wasn't here.'

'What do you need?'

'A car. Can you come and meet me? Give me a car so I can drive north and get a ferry somewhere? Maybe from Santander or maybe I'll have to drive to France. But I need to get out of this area, and I don't want to keep taking trains. I came here on the train from Cadiz. It's too risky. I need to be on the road as quick as possible before the escape really hits the news.'

'Christ. I hardly know what to say. But, no problem. I'll drive up and meet you. I'll get someone to follow me and take me back down the road. I'll leave in the next half hour. I'll call you on this number when I'm closer.'

Vic was so relieved and touched at her response that he felt his throat tighten a little.

'Sharon,' he said. 'Thank you. So much. I . . . I . . .' He

wanted to say, I love you, but it wasn't the time. But just hearing her voice and how quickly she was rushing to help him, he knew with every fibre of his being that he did love this woman, no matter how much that complicated his already complicated life. But that was for another day. And anyway, Sharon had already hung up. It was that kind of feisty shit that made him love her even more. He sat staring at the screen and allowed himself a smile.

By the time Sharon was on the motorway heading for Seville, she had already spoken to Kerry to tell her about Vic's phone call. She was glad Kerry was pleased to hear of his escape, even if she was as shocked as Sharon had been when Vic had told her what he'd done. Within fifteen minutes, Kerry had phoned her back to say she had already briefed Marty Kane on the situation and he was looking into how it would pan out if Vic handed himself into a police station in the UK. Marty had told her the Spanish would try to extradite him without a doubt, but the Brits would fight it, now they had a big collar in their grasp. However it worked out was not important right now for Sharon. She was almost in Seville, followed by Paddy, one of her security men from the house, who would drive her back. She pushed the ringback key on her mobile. Vic answered straight away.

'You nearly here, Sharon?'

'Yeah. At the edge of town. Tell me where you are, you big lunatic.'

She heard Vic chuckle.

'I'm at the Hotel Alminar. It's in the centre of the city, near the big cathedral. You can't miss it. Meet me there.'

'Okay. Soon as I can.'

Sharon couldn't believe how ridiculously excited she was to be seeing Vic. She had been like a dizzy teenager on a first date, the way she had raced around the house after his phone call, making arrangements for Tony when he came in from school and getting into her car to hotfoot it to Seville. It was all sorts of crazy, and she was old enough to know better, but this feeling of being alive every time she was with Vic was exhilarating. She told herself to calm down. This was a serious business. She had to be careful for several reasons, not least because cops might suddenly pop out of nowhere and arrest both of them. But she worried the feelings she had for a man like Vic were too strong. You never knew where you were with him because of how he led his life, and the last thing she needed was to be hurt again. That was why she had never told him how she truly felt, and why she always made a joke every time she thought he was going to put her on a spot by declaring his feelings for her. She wasn't ready for that. Especially right now. But then, as she drove into the hotel car park, she spotted him outside at a table in the empty patio bar. Her heart skipped a beat, and she pulled the car around and parked. Paddy nodded to her as she got out – he would wait here for her. As she walked towards Vic, he stood up, his face pale in the sunshine, but his blue eyes twinkling as he smiled. He held out his hands to greet her.

'Sharon. Darling. What can I say? Are you a sight for sore eyes or what!'

She walked straight into his arms, and the feel of him holding her tight made her realise how much she had longed for this. They stayed that way for a long time, then Vic released her and they looked at each other. He cupped her face in his hands then kissed her softly on the lips, then harder, pulling her close to him again, before Sharon finally prised herself away.

'Steady on, Vic, or they'll be shouting at us to get a room,' she joked.

'Christ, Shaz. I wish. You have no idea how much I wish. I've thought about nothing else these past few weeks.'

She smiled. 'Yeah, well, apart from how to tunnel your way out of bloody jail, El Chapo! How the hell did this happen?'

Now they both smiled. He motioned her to sit down and pulled his chair closer to her while he held her hands.

'You've no idea how crazy it felt at the time. It was one of the other lags – Juan – in for murder. It was his plan, and I thought it was completely bonkers. But here I am. It worked.'

'Tell me about it,' Sharon said.

'I'll give you the brief version.'

Sharon listened as he told her the story of his escape,

stunned by the gutsiness of it all. He looked well, though his eyes had dark smudges under them as though he needed a few early nights and a rest. Part of her still couldn't believe she was sitting here with him, having visited him in jail so recently.

'I need you to talk to Kerry,' Vic said. 'I have to get a lawyer on my case when I get to the UK.'

Sharon put a hand up.

'Already done, pet. I talked to her as soon as you phoned.'

'You are such a fucking star!' Vic leaned over and kissed her again. 'What does she think?'

'Like me, she was bloody shocked. But she was glad to hear it. She likes you, even though you've never met. It didn't sit well with her, you being banged up over here for something you didn't have to get involved in.'

Vic shrugged.

'Well, I knew the risks. And I was well paid.' He squinted his eyes in the sunlight as he looked at her. 'Let's hope I get to spend it someday.' He held her hand. 'With you.'

Sharon smiled. How could she resist him when he looked at her like this, when she knew he meant everything he said, and when she knew that he was in this mess because he put himself on the line for her? But she said nothing. Just reached across and gently touched his face.

'You are a one-off, Vic Paterson. You really are.'

'So is Kerry going to get me a lawyer?'

'Of course,' Sharon said. 'The very best. Don't worry about

that. She already has the Casey lawyer looking into what will happen once you give yourself up. The Spanish will try to get you back here, but the Brits will resist that. They're not going to let a big-time smuggler like you out of their mitts.' She paused. 'But you might get banged up for a very long time if you get found guilty.'

Vic shrugged again. 'They have to prove it first, don't they?'

'Yeah. They do. And they'll throw the kitchen sink at this.'

Vic kept his eyes on her, studying her face, then touching her hair as though he had to make sure she was really here. He ran his hands down her arms and she felt her whole body tingle. He leaned across and kissed her again, his tongue probing her lips and inside her mouth and she was bursting with desire. She pulled back.

'Enough already, Vic. We'll get arrested.'

He stayed close to her, his lips brushing her face and neck and the feel of his breath on her made her want him more than ever.

'I want you so much, Sharon.' He glanced at the hotel. 'Shall we get a room?'

Sharon pulled back. This was beyond reckless.

'Yeah,' she said. 'Like we've got nothing better to do.' She stretched out her hands. 'No. Jesus, man! Stop this or we'll drive each other crazy. We can't. You literally don't have time for this. You need to move as quick as you can and head north. You know that.'

He sat back and pushed out a frustrated breath.

'I know. I know. But I don't want to go back without being with you one more time. Once I get to the UK, everything might happen really fast, then I'll be locked up.'

'I know,' Sharon said, feeling the frustration as much as him.

'What if I can find some place once I get out of Spain. Maybe in France. Could you fly up and meet me before I get away?'

'Christ, Vic. I don't know. Honestly. I just don't know if I can – if it's safe,' she said. 'We really have to be sensible about this.'

He sat back, looked crestfallen. She held his hands.

'There'll be other times, Vic. I promise.'

'You promise?'

'Yes. But right now, you have to be smart. You're on the run, so get on the run and get the hell out of Spain before somebody spots you.' She stood up, looked over her shoulder where Paddy was parked. She handed Vic the keys of the car. 'Just take it to wherever – to the UK if that's how you want to do it – and let me know. Kerry will deal with it. Just get yourself out of here and into the UK.'

As she said it, she knew that once in the UK, Vic would be in even bigger trouble, because then he would not only be a suspected cocaine smuggler, but he'd be an escaped prisoner on the run. Whatever happened in the next few months, she promised herself that she would be with him.

She stepped forward and into his arms again and he held her tight. Then he kissed her on the lips and they parted. As she walked back to the car, she felt suddenly deflated, because no matter what her heart was telling her, or how much she wanted to be with him, the reality was that she might not even see him again. And worse than that was the sudden realisation that she was in love with him.

CHAPTER SEVENTEEN

Kerry's sleepless nights were filled with guilt and worry. Her thoughts were all of Vinny, wondering where he was. Weeks had passed now and she hadn't heard anything from him. Not a phone call or a single text to say he was safe and still working. It had been such a special moment at the scan when she'd seen a real live image of their baby for the first time, and she knew that Vinny would have loved to have been a part of that, given how tearful he'd been when he found out she was carrying his baby. The selfish part of her felt he could at least have found a minute to get in touch since he'd gone, especially when he knew she was pregnant. But nothing. She had to keep reminding herself that her life was not about *her* any more, it was about the little heart beating inside her. She would never let this baby down.

Last night, her guilt had been over Alex who had betrayed the Caseys, and how she'd given the nod for Danny to deal with him. She hadn't even asked Danny if the deed was done. There would be no messing around on a job like that. Alex's body was probably weighed down somewhere along the coast, or buried in a shallow grave in some remote forest. She'd rather not think about it, but she even chastised herself for that, for not being able to face up to who she was these days. What an ugly paradox of inner turmoil she had become. But Kerry had to be bigger than this. There were things she couldn't change, but there were some things she could. And in time she would. She stood at the window looking down at Danny and Jack, with Wolfie and Hannah, arriving for their meeting. She took a deep breath and headed downstairs to the study.

As everyone sat around the table, Wolfie was first to speak.

'Well,' he puffed, 'you might not be surprised to hear that there is still no fucking money in my bank account. Not a fucking sausage from the old guys.' He sat back. 'What do you think is going on? Apart from the possibility that this couple of old geezers have legged it with the diamonds.' He shook his head and his face broke into a smile of incredulity. 'Fucking couldn't make this up, could you?'

In the silence, everyone looked at each other. Then Danny spoke.

'I can't believe old Manny would do that kind of shit. Seriously. That's not his game. He just wouldn't.' He looked at Wolfie. 'I do think there's something suspicious, though, about both of them getting out of the country and going to

Israel, but I don't think it's because they've stolen your gear, Wolfie.' He paused. 'I think the pair of them have decided if they're going to move hot shit like stolen yellow diamonds, then it's wiser to get as far away from here as possible. I mean, these guys will probably have contacts in Tel Aviv or wherever they live who will know how to move stuff like this.'

'But why no news yet?' Wolfie asked. 'That's my problem. Why no phone call? Even to you Danny, or Kerry or somebody. Why the fucking radio silence?'

'Maybe there's a reason for that,' Kerry chipped in. 'Maybe they've picked up some info or intelligence that suggests the best thing to do right now is sit tight and keep silent.'

'Hmmm.' Wolfie folded his arms, looking a bit petulant. 'Still. Might have fucking phoned.'

There was a quiet moment while coffees were poured and pushed across the table to each other, and then Kerry spoke, glancing at Jack, Hannah and Danny.

'Anyway, guys, good to see you got back in one piece. That was some shit to have to deal with. We definitely didn't expect that.' She looked at Danny. 'But you'll know by now we had a traitor. It's been dealt with.'

Danny nodded slowly.

'Aye. Wasn't pleasant. Old family connections. Never is, shit like that. But it had to be done.'

'So Alfi Ricci is out there paying people to find me,' Wolfie said. 'Cunt!' He glanced at Kerry and Hannah. 'Pardon my

French, ladies, but if I could just get two minutes in a room with that fucker . . .'

Another silence.

'I'm a bit disappointed that I didn't get any tip-off from that Joey guy I told you all about,' Hannah said. 'It was him who contacted me and told us about the Russians having got at Alfi, as you remember.' She shrugged. 'I know we're not bosom buddies or anything, but I had a connection with the bloke, and I'm just a bit surprised I didn't get the wire that they'd got to someone up here and found out about Amsterdam. Especially when your man had told them it was something to do with diamonds.'

'Maybe they've bumped the geezer off, Hannah,' Wolfie said. 'Wouldn't be surprised. Maybe they got wind that he told you about the Russians and stuff and they just got rid of him.'

'I hope not. He was a bit of a sad bugger in a lot of ways. I quite liked him. I've tried phoning him, but no answer,' Hannah said. 'I think if he gets in touch again I should go down to London and meet up with him. Maybe get some more information.'

'Nah,' Wolfie said. 'Too risky, darlin'. And what could he tell you down there that he couldn't let you know about on the phone? Nah. I think that Joey has had his ticket punched.'

Hannah didn't answer. Kerry looked at her and thought she looked genuinely disappointed that she hadn't been able to help the Caseys further.

CHAPTER EIGHTEEN

Alfi Ricci was watching his chef at Benito's put the finishing touches to the cake for his son's tenth birthday party later that day, when his head waiter came bursting through the kitchen doors.

'He's here again, Alfi,' the waiter said. 'That big Russian guy.'

Alfi's face fell.

'Aw, for fuck's sake! Who's with the prick?'

'That same knuckle-trailer from the last time.'

'Jesus fucking wept!'

Alfi could feel his insides churning. He'd pulled out all the stops for this bastard to try and flush Wolfie out. He'd even sent Nick and the boys to Glasgow to get information out of one of the Casey crew. And to his surprise it had been successful, with this Alex bloke telling him that the Caseys were off to Amsterdam, and as far as he knew they were moving diamonds to a dealer there. Nick didn't even have to strong-arm anyone to get the information. He just threw money at the bastard and he spilled it out. Whatever the Russians did with the information was up to them. Alfi had kept his side of the deal so they could fuck right off. But he knew they wouldn't. He shook his head, puffed out a sigh and strode through the kitchen, throwing open the swing doors to the restaurant.

'Yuri!' He spread his hands as he walked towards the Russians. 'What a surprise! You are here for lunch? To celebrate?'

The big Russian was stony-faced and dead-eyed. He shook his head.

'No. Not to celebrate.'

Alfi made sure his face showed nothing, and he shrugged a little. He motioned them to a booth and the Russian and his sidekick moved across and slid in. Alfi sat opposite them, feeling a little warm under his collar. He hated this bastard – something about the raw power he exuded made Alfi feel small.

'So,' Alfi looked Yuri in the eye. 'You have a problem? My information was good, that much I'm sure of.'

Yuri nodded. 'Your information was good. We went to Amsterdam, found where the Caseys were, and ambushed them.' He looked down at the table and Alfi saw the muscle in his jaw tighten. 'Well. We tried to.'

Alfi sat back. Epic fail. He managed to conceal his delight.

'Oh. Did the Casey crew get away from your boys? That's

a pity.' He glanced from Yuri to his sidekick. 'Because sometimes you only get one shot at it.'

Alfi waved to the waiter and when he came across to the table, he gestured to the pair. 'Coffee? Something stronger?' He was still in the shit with this bastard, but he was enjoying Yuri having to admit failure. Everyone ordered coffee.

'They got away,' Yuri muttered. 'We have to work out a new way to get to them.'

'So do you think the Caseys were over there moving the diamonds to some dealer?'

Yuri shrugged. 'For sure. But we don't know who. Amsterdam is full of dealers.'

Alfi was enjoying this. The only thing that dulled the pain of him losing the millions of pounds' worth of diamonds his boys stole in the heist was the fact it didn't look like this bastard was getting them back. But if Wolfie had managed to move them on with the help of the Caseys, then the sly old fucker would be in for a massive payday. He had to find a way to get to him and at least get a share of it. All in good time.

Alfi sipped his coffee, took a breath and cleared his throat.

'Yuri, look. I don't see what I can do to help you now. I did as you asked. I got good information for you. It was up to your boys to make it happen.'

In a flash, Yuri reached across the table and grabbed Alfi by the throat so hard he almost lifted him up. Alfi choked for breath as he saw the Russian's face turn crimson.

'Listen you bastard!' he said, twisting his grasp so that Alfi could barely breathe. 'You are acting like you are not to blame here. This is all down to you. You are the fucking thief who sent your men to break into the bank and steal everything. You robbed the diamonds and stole the important papers from the strongboxes. This is all on you. Not me.'

Alfi felt the room sway as he was about to pass out. He managed to reach a hand across pleadingly, and the Russian released his grasp. He sat back, coughing and trembling.

'Fuck's sake, Yuri.' Alfi wiped the sweat from his face. 'I know this. I've done my best to help you. Believe me, I wish I had never listened to that bastard Wolfie in his plans for the heist. I was stupid.'

Yuri breathed heavily through flared nostrils.

'Stupid! And greedy!'

Alfi managed to glance across to the waiter who stood helplessly at the bar. In any other situation Enrico would be on this. But these were Russian mobsters and he could hardly come up and throw them into the street.

'Look,' Alfi said, 'I did what I could, and if I can help any more then I will. But if the diamonds were taken to a dealer in Amsterdam then my guess is that they will already have been moved.' He sniffed. 'I . . . I don't know what else to say to you.'

They sat in silence as Alfi got his breathing back to normal. Then Yuri looked at him.

'Here is what you do.'

Alfi shifted in his seat, manoeuvred his chin out to stretch his neck a little. It felt tender next to his shirt collar, but he didn't want to touch it in front of this vicious fucker. He nodded, listening.

'If my diamonds have disappeared then I want to find out who has them. There must be a trail. But at the moment, the people I represent are also very concerned about the important papers and DVDs that were stolen. They are, well, they are priceless. You have to find them.'

'Priceless? DVDs?' Alfi asked, confused.

'Think about it.' Yuri gave him a look as though he was thick.

The penny dropped. Whatever paperwork and stuff that was in these boxes was for blackmail. What else could it be? But where the fuck was it? And why in the name of Christ did Wolfie take it? There was no way the old bastard knew what he was looking for. Sure, he knew the strongboxes would be full of jewellery and cash, but documents would mean nothing to him, and everything had been done so fast he wouldn't have paid attention to them. Probably just stuffed them in the bag. Christ. He might even have dumped them by now. Not that he would be suggesting that to this prick at the moment. Just get the fucker out of here. Tell him what he needs to hear and get him out. Alfi nodded.

'Yeah. I think I see it now, Yuri. Documents and papers

and DVDs can be used for all sorts of purposes, can't they? Am I right?'

'Yes.'

'So I'm pretty sure Wolfie would not even pay any attention to them. Probably just shoved them in on top of everything else. It was all done so fast. He might not even have opened them yet, if he still has them.'

'You have to find out.'

Alfi wanted to say, why don't *you* find out you Commie fuckwit? Why don't you send one of your gorillas up to Glasgow and monster the Caseys on their own turf and see how you get on? But he said nothing. The problem was, this was all down to him. No robbery, no problem. And in the end it was all down to Wolfie, who'd fucked off with nearly everything. That bastard had some grief coming to him, Alfi vowed to himself. He would have to get the boys together and decide what to do next. There had to be a way to get to Wolfie, even behind the wall of protection the Caseys were giving him. And when he got his hands on him this time, he'd personally make sure the cunt would stay dead.

Joey Mitchell was sipping a mug of tea in the greasy spoon café next door to his hostel. The racing section of this morning's *Sun* was spread across the table, and he was draped over it, meticulously studying the form of every horse in the race meetings at Chepstow and Haydock. There were a few he fancied, and one or two were sure things, if only he had decent money to bet on them. He studied jockeys too, had favourites on good days who'd made him big wins at the last minute just when he thought he'd lost it all. The same jockeys he'd cursed when he'd trusted their abilities with his last few quid. He couldn't help himself. Even though right now he knew he couldn't afford to go to the bookies and bet the last of the money he had in his pocket, Joey couldn't start his day without studying the form. As he picked out the horses he fancied, he fantasised about accumulators and doubles, and all the permutations that, if they all came up, could bring in nearly twenty grand for a fiver. Ridiculous as it was, and he knew it, Joey still kept up the dream. If only he could get one big win, he would set himself up and put all this shit behind him. He would stop gambling for ever. Definitely. He had twenty quid on him. He could afford an accumulator bet that might net him a right few quid later in the afternoon.

Joey sat back, gazing out of the window at the dismal street in the driving rain. He wondered how his daughter was doing but didn't have the heart to phone her or arrange to meet her. He was scared in case she asked too many questions – where he was living, working. She would see by the way he was dressed that he was on the bones of his arse, and he was too ashamed to let her see that. He'd been working doing driving jobs for Alfi in the past couple of weeks so at least there was regular money coming in, as long as he was able to hold onto the job. Mostly it was driving Nick around, picking him up late at night if he'd been out drinking or carousing, or sometimes picking up girls who were being moved around by the various escort agencies Alfi owned. He hated that more than anything. Most of the girls were the same age as his daughter, and some even younger. They all had that same waiflike, miserable look, and sat silently as he took them from place to place implied. That had been the extent of his work, and he noticed he'd been kept in the dark about this business with the hunt for Wolfie up in Scotland. It was only because he had been in the car a few days ago driving Nick that he picked up a bit of conversation that they had got to some guy in Glasgow who was close to the Caseys and had passed the information onto the Russians. If he had got wind of that before, for sure he would have phoned Hannah. She was the only person who had shown him any kindness in a very long time, and he had slipped her information before. His mobile rang and he fished it out of his pocket. It was Nick.

'Where are you, Joey?'

Nick seldom exchanged the time of day other than business.

'Just out and about, Nick. Nothing much. You need me?'

'Yeah. Got something in mind. It will involve you going up to Scotland for a bit. Driving a couple of the lads.'

'Sure,' Joey said, pleased that he was going somewhere that wasn't sitting in that shitty hostel. 'When? How long for?'

'Dunno yet, mate. Might be a couple of days, could be longer. Get some changes of kecks and get yourself organised.'

'That won't take long. I can be ready when you are. You going?'

'Dunno yet. Might be. Will call you later. Just giving you a heads-up. You and the lads will be in a hotel somewhere in Glasgow.'

Joey knew he might get slapped down if he asked any details of the job, but he couldn't resist it.

'Chasing someone, are we?'

'Well. You'll probably not be chasing, given your recent fucking track record. But yeah. Still trying to flush out that Wolfie cunt.'

'Oh, right,' Joey said. 'Well, whenever you want, I'm ready.'

'Good stuff.'

Nick hung up without saying goodbye. Ignorant fuckwit. Joey folded over the newspaper and pushed it away. No time for that shit at the moment. He had to go back to the hostel and pick up some clothes and get down to the launderette. Knowing Nick, he would only get about an hour's notice on the next phone call, so he had to look sharp. But he liked the idea of a hotel. Proper food, a clean bed, and a shower that had nobody else's fucking pubes in it. Christ. All the shit people take for granted, Joey had flushed down the toilet chasing a big win. He sat scrolling down his mobile phone until he came to Hannah's name. Then he pushed the call key. She answered after one ring.

'Hannah?'

'Joey. How you? Haven't heard from you lately.'

'No. Been doing some driving work for Alfi and Nick.'

'Right.'

Hannah sounded almost hesitant.

'Yeah. Been a bit out of the loop.'

'Yeah? So, you're calling me, Joey. I'm intrigued here.'

He was silent for a moment, recalling her swift put-downs during their encounter. He still felt a bit humiliated at the complete arse he'd made of the job.

'Well. I . . . I got some information for you.'

'Really? I'd be glad to hear that.'

'Yeah. I'm going to be driving a crew to Glasgow in the next few days. I guess you probably know why.'

'Wolfie?'

'Yeah. That's all I know. But I don't think they're coming up to deliver any Valentines to him or anything like that.'

'No. So when?'

'Don't know yet. But I might know later in the day. I'll let you know as soon as I do.'

'I appreciate that, Joey. I really do. That's a big help.'

'Sure. Whatever I can.'

Silence.

'By the way, Joey, I thought I might have had a nod from

you that Alfi's boys were up here recently, tapping up one of the Casey's men for information.'

'Yeah. I only heard about it after it happened. I didn't know anything about it, Hannah. If I'd known I'd have tipped you.'

'Well. It's done now. But there was a big leak in the Casey organisation, and it caused some problems for them.' She paused. 'It didn't go well for the traitor either, if you get my drift.'

'Yeah.' Joey didn't have to ask. Whoever had passed on the information would be history by now. He had a little punch in his gut that reminded him that what he was doing right now was betrayal, and if Alfi or Nick got wind of it, he would end up at the bottom of the Thames with a bag of bricks tied to his ankles.

'Okay. Well thanks for calling. Good to hear from you. And I'll be glad to hear from you as soon as you know you're moving.' She paused. 'Oh, and if there's a chance in Glasgow I'll buy you a drink.'

'Sure,' Joey said, knowing there wasn't a snowball in hell's chance of him going for a drink with Hannah, much as he would love to.

She hung up, and Joey got to his feet, dropped two pound coins onto the table, then headed out into the rain.

CHAPTER NINETEEN

Quentin Fairhurst didn't relish delivering bad news unless it was to someone he liked to see squirm. He didn't much care for the Russian oligarchs whose day he was about to ruin. But he didn't want to rile them too much. After all, they had paid him a handsome sum on several occasions over the years to make sure they were able to bypass the financial regulations that would have hamstrung others who used London as a huge laundry to wash their dirty money. There was loads of it floating around, and plenty had floated his way. So in many ways he felt obligated to the Russians who swanned around the city flashing their wealth. But his tacit support wasn't without limits, and he had made that clear to them in the beginning. If their reckless activities ever encroached on his jurisdiction, then he would have to make a move. And so it was that over the last few weeks he had been poring over the financial reports from the Serious Fraud Office, trying to work out how he could come up with some show prosecution that would satisfy the clamour, but keep the oligarchs out of jail. They knew too much about him for a start. But if it came down to threats from them, who would believe them anyway? That was always his get-out card that helped him sleep at night. Under their Savile Row suits and Cartier watches, they were still thugs, gangsters who'd plundered their way forward after the fall of the former Soviet Union. No amount of tarting up was going to change that. He wasn't planning to put it as clearly as that, though, when he met his old friend Anatoly and his hard man Yuri in the Greek coffee house off Euston Road.

By the time Fairhurst arrived, he could see through the café window that the pair were already there, sitting far enough away from the lunchtime crowd that they wouldn't be overheard. He smoothed back his hair and pushed open the door.

From the back of the café, the Russians glanced up from their conversation, but their flat expressions did not acknowledge his arrival. Fairhurst squeezed past a woman carrying a tray with two bowls of soup and made his way towards them. Only then did they look up at him. Anatoly inclined his head a little and pulled his lips back to what passed for a smile.

'My friend,' he said, gesturing a hand to the empty chair opposite him and Yuri. 'Sit, please. We get some coffee.' Then he looked past Fairhurst and summoned a waitress with the click of his fingers.

Jumped up KGB prick, Fairhurst thought, sitting down, smiling as he shook both their hands. He flicked a glance at Anatoly's fine pinstripe suit then down to the gleaming gold pinky ring, with a dazzling yellow diamond glinting under the ceiling lights. He guessed he was in his mid-forties. How times had fucking changed. The Commie cunt probably grew up freezing his arse off in some poxy Soviet village in the back of beyond on a diet of pigs' trotters and cabbage, while every day they pledged their allegiance to the bloody Communist Party. But give these fucking peasants a few quid and a sniff of glamour and suddenly they were champagne Charlies throwing their money and weight around cities across the world. Fairhurst was good at concealing his thoughts, though – he'd been doing that all his life.

He had asked for the meeting because he needed to make Anatoly understand that things might get a little rough for him and his oligarch mates in the coming months. It was all about how he was able to sell it to them. But Anatoly sat gazing at him, his pasty complexion and hooded eyes giving him a tired, bored expression and it didn't fill Fairhurst with confidence. Next to him, big Yuri, eyes as black as coal, hands like shovels, lifted the cup to his lips and sipped. He too was well dressed in a dark grey suit, a ten grand Rolex watch peeping out from the cuffs of his white shirt. He wore a red tie, perhaps as a little nod to his Communist beginnings, though this bloated thirty-something had left all that behind a very long time ago. The waitress arrived and gave Anatoly a surly look that said she didn't like people clicking her fingers at her.

'What can I get you?' she asked.

'Coffee,' Fairhurst said. 'Cappuccino, thanks.'

'Black.' Anatoly glared at him. 'Two.'

'So,' Fairhurst said, after the waitress had gone, 'how is the property business these days, Anatoly? Last time we spoke you were trying to acquire two mansions in Holland Park. Did that go well?'

Anatoly nodded slowly. 'Yes. It did. The property business is booming, as you Brits would say. But we are also building our import business.'

'Importing?' Fairhurst asked, surprised. He hadn't expected this, but it had people-trafficking, gun-smuggling and drugs stamped all over it. 'May I ask what you are importing?'

Anatoly sat back and gave a little shrug, his lips moving to a sarcastic smile.

'This and that, my friend. Some mechanical parts for industrial use . . .' He waved his hand dismissively. 'Various things. We have several small businesses all beginning to grow across the country, from Moscow to Novosibirsk.'

Mechanical parts for what? Fairhurst wanted to ask. He

had to stifle the urge to smile. Maybe the bastards were bringing back the Lada biscuit tin car or something. But he had to sound interested.

'Well, that's all good. Investment and growth is everything. And your people have done that very well since having the freedom to move without the shackles of the old days.'

Anatoly nodded. 'Yes. And that is why we may be calling on your assistance in the future,' he said. 'Importing goods and containers from Eastern Europe is not without its problems. So perhaps we can talk soon on how we can smooth that passage.'

Christ. This was all he needed. It was bad enough that the Serious Fraud Office was picking apart the Russian oligarchs' investment in the London property market, but if they got wind that they were now moving into the importation business they would have a collective coronary.

'Yes, well, we can see about that in due course,' Fairhurst said, clasping his manicured hands on the table. 'But I asked you here, Anatoly, because I want to discuss something that I'm afraid will be problematic for the Russian oligarchs who are moving money around London . . . I—'

Anatoly put his hand up.

'Wait a second, my friend. First, I must tell you of a big problem we have at the moment.'

Fairhurst didn't like being silenced like this, but he thought he'd better listen.

'Really? What is the problem?'

Anatoly glanced over his shoulder then leaned forward, lowering his voice to a whisper.

'You know the Hatton Garden heist? The robbery?'

'Of course,' Fairhurst said. 'Who doesn't? Biggest, most daring raid ever in this country.'

'Yes. It was,' Anatoly said, his lips tightening. 'But the bastard robbers. They stole very valuable things from strongboxes that belonged to me and also to two of my business partners.'

'Seriously?' Fairhurst said, secretly delighted. 'I'm very sorry to hear that. Was it jewellery? Money?'

'Diamonds,' Anatoly said. 'Yellow diamonds.' He pointed to the diamond pinky ring. 'Diamonds like this are rare and are worth millions. One of them belonging to my friend was worth two million euros alone. Just one diamond.'

Fairhurst was genuinely shocked. He'd heard only what the police reports had said, that the strongboxes were plundered and valuable jewellery and other items were stolen. But the problem with strongboxes was that they were there for a reason – to hide wealth from the taxman – and they were there so that they could be accessed only by their owners. So the contents were never listed by anyone except the people who owned them, and so far, there had been no rush from owners to state exactly what had gone missing. Probably some of it was stolen before it even got to the strongboxes anyway, stashed away until it could be moved. Now it was all gone. And the police were nowhere near solving the case. Tough titty, Fairhurst wanted to say. But he managed to give an expression of concern and shock.

'I had no idea,' he said. 'As I said, we know very little of the contents. But that is truly terrible for your friends if they have lost such prized diamonds like that.' He wanted to say something like they would turn up, but he knew how ridiculous that would sound. The diamonds were probably being cut as they spoke, and were already more than likely to be out of the country. But he wasn't here to discuss any bloody missing diamonds. He had to break the news that some of them were about to get their collars felt. Fairhurst allowed the silence to hang for a moment, as though he was taking in the true shock of Anatoly's plight. Then he cleared his throat.

'Anyway, Anatoly,' he said. 'I'm afraid I have some news that is not going to improve your day.'

The Russians exchanged glances, then looked at him.

'You may have read the various reports in recent months that the Serious Fraud Office was looking into investments in London by non-residents – well, mostly focused on Russians. Oligarchs.'

Fairhurst couldn't very well say gangsters, but he let it hang in the air. Anatoly tightened his grasp around his coffee cup, but his expression didn't change. Sometimes you just couldn't tell what this bastard was thinking.

'Well,' Fairhurst went on. 'The files have landed on my

desk, and I've been ploughing through them line by line in recent weeks.' He paused, kept his hands firmly clasped on the table. 'I'm afraid to say that it doesn't look too good. There are areas of these reports that will merit a case for prosecution. And, as you know, I am Attorney General, and I have to oversee a move on some of these individuals.'

Anatoly's eyes screwed up a little as though he was confused.

'Move? What do you mean move?'

'Well . . .' Fairhurst wondered if he could really be this thick. 'By move, I mean prosecute. In court. The Director of Public Prosecutions will want to move on a case, and because of the extent of the evidence, I won't be able to advise against it.'

The silence went on for so long that Fairhurst could almost see the wheels turning in the brains of this pair of thick bastards opposite him. What the fuck did they think would happen if they were throwing billions around London, buying up half the city? Eventually someone was going to look at them closely. Sure, he had promised them that he would do his best to cover their backs. But things had moved on now. *He* had moved on. He was the Attorney General, not just the ordinary QC who had advised them four or five years ago. From what he had seen from the SFO's investigation, they had clearly overstepped the mark. Greed. And there was an inability on their part to understand how things happened in countries as corrupt as Russia. They just didn't get it.

'My friend. I understand you have a job to do. That you prosecute people.' Anatoly raised a hand and waved his forefinger slowly. 'But not us. Not the oligarchs who have invested in your country.'

Oh Christ, Fairhurst thought. I'm going to have to give it to them straight.

'No, Anatoly. Not in this country. Your oligarchs have invested in themselves. They have bought property here in London, but they have not bought it for the good of the city. They have bought it for themselves. And the documents I have looked at show no visible signs of taxes and inward investment that benefit anyone other than themselves.'

'But you told us you would have our backs,' Anatoly said, his voice going up an octave. 'That was your words five years ago. You told me, and my friends that night, and you had the other MP with you – your fat friend who is now the Home Secretary. You told us you would have our backs.' His pale face reddened a little. 'And, as you remember, you were well rewarded. Is that in the Serious Fraud Office report?' he hissed.

Fairhurst felt just a little off balance. Christ. He'd never been in any doubt all along that they were thugs, and he knew they would not take this news well. And yes, he even expected them to throw a little tantrum. But he steadied himself. There was no evidence anywhere of payoffs or of any of the time he spent in the company of those oligarchs on a smattering of occasions five years ago. They would just have to swallow the pill. Get on with it.

'Look,' Fairhurst said, 'I said I will have your backs, and I will try my best to do whatever I can. I promise you that. But you are going to have to sacrifice at least two of your people. There have to be prosecutions. I cannot do anything about that.' He glanced from one to the other. 'I came here to warn you, Anatoly. To mark your card in good faith, and to tell you that you must go now to your people and you must make decisions on what areas you can sacrifice. Because you cannot have it all your own way.'

Anatoly's eyes were blazing.

'My people will be very let down by you. This may not end well.'

'Anatoly,' bristling at the veiled threat, 'just calm down and have a think about it. And then when this all blows over, I can look at ways to help you smooth the way in your importing business. But as I said, you have to understand you cannot have it all your own way.'

They sat for an age in silence, the air prickling with brooding anger. Eventually, Fairhurst looked at his watch.

'I'm afraid I have a meeting in my office shortly, so I'm going to have to go. But we can talk whenever you want.' He put on his most sincere expression. 'I will do what I can. But it is time to make your friends understand that there have to be sacrifices.'

Anatoly didn't answer, and he didn't make eye contact with Fairhurst as he stood up. Neither did Yuri. When Fairhurst reached out his hand, they both ignored it, and sat quietly fuming. Fairhurst had no option but to turn away and walk out of the café.

CHAPTER TWENTY

The Counting House bar in Glasgow's George Square was bustling with early evening drinkers. Smack in the middle of the city centre, it was the kind of big roomy pub that was a handy meeting place, and many of the customers would be on their way out for the night or heading to the train stations nearby to go home. Cal and Tahir had managed to get themselves past the bouncer at the door, despite being underage, and they were sitting on high stools at the window onto the street, drinking pints of Coke. They'd been sent there by Jack to keep watch for the London mob. Jack had told them that some guy called Joey had been dropping info to Hannah about when thy were coming, where they were staying and what they were looking for. This Joey guy was going to phone and let them know if they went to a pub, so the Counting House was a good base to start from if they got the call. It struck Cal as a well risky strategy for whoever this Joey guy was, to be spilling his guts to the Caseys, informing on his own people. Cal had heard about how the Caseys had dealt with their own traitor a few days ago, who had apparently been passing information to this London crowd about Wolfie staying at the big house. That had cost Alex Mackie his life. Cal had only met Alex once or twice and he seemed sound enough, but the word was that he'd been up to his neck in hock and betrayed the Caseys for money. The fact that Alex simply 'disappeared' was spoken about among the troops, but nobody would ever have dared ask Jack about it. When Jack had pulled Cal and Tahir in yesterday, he'd told them they had a job to do. If the call came that the London mob were in the Counting House or anywhere else, they had to be ready. They were to listen, see what they could pick up, and if possible mingle with these pricks who'd travelled up earlier in the day. They were here to cause trouble, Jack had said, to get to Wolfie. He'd told both of them they didn't have to do the job if they felt uneasy. But that was the last thing Cal and Tahir were going to admit. Especially after their near death in Amsterdam, this looked like a cushy number. When Cal's mobile rang, it wasn't Jack's number that came up on his mobile, but Hannah's. He showed the screen to Tahir.

'Cal. It's Hannah. You're in the Counting House, I take it?'

'Yep. Been here about fifteen minutes. It's very busy,' Cal said.

'Okay. Good. You're in the right place.' Hannah said. 'I've just had a call from Joey to say they arrived in the bar about five minutes ago. There's five of them. They're at the bar now – at the far end from the door, he said. English accents, obviously. So if you can be anywhere close to the bar, you might pick them out. One of them has his head shaved, a big monster of a guy. Wearing a black sweatshirt. Can you see anyone who looks like that?'

Cal scanned the big round bar which was two or three deep in some places. But he spotted a group of guys at the far side. A big shaven-headed guy was standing with his arms folded as the others drank and chatted.

'Yeah. I think so. I see five guys now – far end of the bar. One of them head shaved. Black top. That might be them.'

'Okay,' Hannah said. 'I'll leave it to you. But listen, Cal. Be careful. Jack said to remind you that you're only there to see if you can pick anything up from them.'

'Yeah. I know what to do, Hannah. We'll be careful.'

He looked at Tahir and they both drained their glasses, then got off the stools and headed for the bar. As the place was busy, they squeezed their way past the throng until the closest people to them were the five guys. Cal watched as one of them tried to get the barman's attention, and he and Tahir stood against the bar. The bar staff looked under pressure, trying to cope with the amount of people. They stood for a couple of minutes and the bar staff kept passing the guy with his money outstretched and going for another customer.

'Fuckin' hell!' the guy muttered, turning to his mates. 'Good thing we're not fucking thirsty!'

His mates chuckled.

'Maybe it's your accent, mate. Try it with a Scottish accent.'

They all sniggered, and Cal smiled at them, then as one of the barman made eye contact with him, he put his hand up. The barman came across and spoke to Cal.

'What can I get you, pal?'

Cal could sense the guys were pissed off and knew this was his chance.

'Mate,' Cal said to the barman, 'this guy's before me.' He stood aside and gestured to the man next to him.

'Oh, thanks, mate.' He looked pleased.

As he reeled off the drinks order, Cal turned to the rest of the guys.

'Mental in here trying to get served, man.'

'Thanks, mate,' one of them said.

'We thought it was something we said,' another said.

'Nah. It's always like that. Sometimes you're lucky enough to catch the bar staff's eye. It's just your luck.' He glanced from one to the other, as the guy handed over the pints. 'You on holiday in Glasgow?'

'Yeah,' one of the guys said. 'Few days, bit of business and to take in the sights and stuff. Maybe a club or two. And a famous Glasgow curry.'

'Aye,' Cal said. 'They're the best in the world. When did you get here?'

'Couple of hours ago. Out for the night now.'

'Good,' Cal said. 'Enjoy yourselves. If you need any pointers in the city me and my mate know every corner of it.' He paused. 'And you might want to watch your backs in certain places. You don't want to be going to bars down the East End and just walking in. Better in places like this that are busy with all sorts.'

'Cheers,' the older guy said. 'That's good to know. We won't be going anywhere stupid. Where's the best place for a game of snooker for a couple of hours before we go to eat? Is there a snooker hall anywhere?'

Cal glanced at Tahir who had kept his mouth shut so far and was only smiling and nodding in all the right places.

'Snooker hall?' Cal said. 'Sure. There's a good place down on the Clydeside.' He gestured in the direction. 'Not far. You could walk to it, but it's a bit awkward if you don't know where you're going.'

'Cheers, mate,' the older guy said. 'You from the city yourselves?' He glanced at Tahir, and Cal could see the wheels turning in his head.

'Yeah,' Cal said. 'We live here. It's a great place. Lots to do. Where you guys from?'

'London. You ever been in the big smoke?'

'No. Not yet. Might go in the summer though.'

'You should. It's a fantastic city. You working here?'

'Aye,' Cal said. 'We work for an estate agent. Learning the trade.'

'Good job. You boys want a drink – seeing we jumped in front of you?'

Cal looked at Tahir who nodded.

'Two Cokes, please. But you don't have to.'

'Not at all, mate. Glad to. Friendly faces and all that.'

'You'll be fine in Glasgow. Nothing but friendly faces.' Cal was beginning to enjoy this.

Cal caught the barman's eye again and ordered the drinks which the older guy paid for. They chatted a little more about life in Glasgow and London, and Cal noticed that one of them was very quiet. He wondered if that was Joey, the informer. As the guys were almost at the bottom of their pints, the older one turned to Cal.

'So where is this snooker place then? Can you point us in the direction?'

Cal glanced at Tahir who said nothing.

'Sure. No problem. We go there a lot. We'll walk down with you if you want. Or we can just show you exactly where it is.'

'Good. You fancy a game of snooker, lads? Bit of rivalry between the Scots and the English?' the older guy joked.

'Definitely,' Cal said. 'A challenge. We'll beat you out the park.' He turned to Tahir.

'You'd put money on that, would you?' one of the guys said.

'Aye,' Cal said with bravado. 'My mate Tahir here is ace at snooker. Hurricane Tahir.'

They all smiled as Cal led them across George Square and down behind Ingram Street towards the Clydeside.

'You're on,' the older guy said, then stretched out his hand. 'By the way, I'm Nick.' He shook Cal and Tahir's hands then reeled off the names of the others – Billy, Dave, Mark and Joey.

'Cal,' he replied.

'Tahir.'

Cal couldn't believe how easy this was. He didn't know what he was going to do next, but he felt they at least had made a connection. These guys were either stupid or they must have thought that Cal and Tahir were just a couple of young lads with no agenda. They were wrong about that.

During the five-minute walk to the snooker hall, the chat was about football – Celtic and Rangers – and Cal talked about how mad the derby days were. The guys chipped in about the same in London with Arsenal and Spurs. To anyone listening they were a bunch of blokes heading for a game of snooker. He noticed that the Joey bloke didn't say much. Probably shitting himself in case he got rumbled.

Once inside, Nick paid for the table while another guy bought drinks. As two of the guys got the tables set up, Cal said he was going to the toilet. He was glad it was empty as he would only have a moment to make the call. He pushed the last call option and Hannah's voice immediately answered.

'Hannah. I've only got a few seconds. We're with these guys. Tell Jack we're in the snooker hall down at the Clydeside. Everything's fine. We're just talking football and stuff, and they said they were on a few days' break. So we're just playing helpful Glasgow boys.'

'Christ almighty!' Hannah said. 'Are you sure it's okay?'

'Yeah. No problem. Just tell Jack that's where we are. We'll stay here for a bit. I don't know what his plans are.'

'Okay. The first smell of any danger, then you guys get out of there fast.'

'Aye,' Cal said as he hung up.

Back at the snooker table, Tahir was cleaning up against big Dave. Nick stood on the sidelines drinking his beer and chuckling as Cal approached.

'You weren't wrong about Hurricane Tahir here. Fuckin' 'ell. This guy is potting everything like lightning. Every fucking thing he touches. Where's he from?'

Cal looked at him, deadpan.

'Glasgow. He lives here.'

'Yeah, but. You know. He don't talk like a Glaswegian. Is he one of them refugees or something? Asylum seeker?'

'Aye,' Cal said. 'He's from Iraq originally – he's Kurdish – but been here nearly three years now. We're big mates.'

'Yeah. Well I don't know where he learned to play snooker like that, but tell you what, that kid's got a future in the game if he fancies it.'

Cal smiled. 'Yeah? I'll tell him. He is really good. Don't think he's ever thought about going pro though.'

'He should.'

As Nick said it, Tahir potted the black ball, then placed the cue on the table. He turned to everyone and bowed.

'Game over.' Tahir smiled and winked to Cal.

The big guy went into his back pocket and pulled out a wad of notes, peeled a fifty off it and handed it to Tahir.

One of the other guys came forward.

'A hundred quid says I'll beat the shit out of you this game.'

'Fine,' Tahir said.

'What about a four ball?' one of the other guys said, looking at Cal. 'Can you play, mate?'

'Not as good as Tahir,' Cal said. 'But I can play.'

'Fine,' the guy said. 'That evens it out a bit. Me and Mark will play you for a hundred. You in?'

Cal looked at Tahir.

'You bet.'

Cal glanced at his watch as Tahir set up the table. The last four players in the hall on one of the other tables had finished and were downing the dregs of their pints and putting jackets on. Then, as they left, Cal glanced across at big Tam behind the bar – an ex pro boxer with a face to show for it – who managed the place. He was stony-faced, and he was standing with his arms folded. Tam's mobile rang and he picked it up and pushed it to his ear. One of the London mob leaned over the table and aimed a shot, the balls clacking and scattering, two of them going into pockets. Then suddenly big Tam came across the room and went to the big exit doors. Nobody seemed to notice as he closed them and slid the bolts. Then he went across to the table.

'Right, lads, that's it. We're closing now.'

'What?' Nick and everyone else turned to him.

'You heard. Place is closing now.'

Dave stepped forward.

'Fuck off, man! Place is closed! We just started a game.'

Tam looked at him with dead eyes.

'I said the place is fucking closing. Are you fucking deaf, you English prick?'

Dave lunged forward.

'You cunt!'

His words were barely out when the doors behind the bar burst open and in came three masked men.

'Right! No bastard move or you're dead,' one of them shouted as they rushed forward.

Nick was white to the lips, then the penny seemed to drop. He glared at Cal and Tahir as they backed towards the bar and the exit doors.

'You fucking pricks. You'll fucking pay for this.'

'Shut it, arsehole.' One of the masked men came forward brandishing his gun. 'The next person to open their trap gets this stuffed in it. You got that?'

Cal and Tahir watched from the back doors as the masked men closely circled the London mob, guns pointed at them. Cal had no idea who the men were, but knew they must be part of the Casey crew. Probably guys he saw every day who had other jobs with the organisation, but who he knew got used for stuff like this. Then he noticed one of them had long legs and tight black skinny jeans with black leather ankle boots. He nudged Tahir.

'Hannah,' he whispered. 'Fucking hell!'

The masked men crowded the London mob and pushed them at gunpoint in the direction of the doors behind the bar.

'Just keep moving,' one of the men said. 'Through the doors. Down the stairs.'

They shuffled together, ashen-faced, looking as though they expected to be executed at any second. Nobody spoke. Then they were shepherded down the back stairs and into the tiny back alley, where the doors of a white van were opened by two other men who Cal knew were Jimbo and Charlie who worked in security at Kerry's house.

'Right. In the van,' one of the masked men said. 'Quick. No fucking hanging about.'

Cal watched as Nick and the men looked at each other. Then Nick looked at Cal and Tahir and his eyes were black with rage as he mouthed, 'You cunts,' and drew a hand over his throat. One of the masked men punched him hard on the back of the head and he stumbled as he climbed into the back of the van. When they got inside and the doors were closed, they drove off at speed down the alley and out into the city which Cal had promised them was full of friendly Glaswegians who'd be happy to see them enjoy their trip. As Cal and Tahir turned to go back out of the other end of the alleyway, Cal looked up at the fading graffiti on the wall. A 'Glasgow Smiles Better' logo with a smiley face.

Hannah could smell the fear coming from all of the five bastards as the van sped out of Glasgow and down the motorway towards the A74 South. She knew where they were going. Jack had told her he, Danny and Wolfie would meet them at a rendezvous point down the A74 that was well off the beaten track. It was beginning to get dark. Hannah knew her face was wet with sweat behind the mask and she was dying to take it off. She saw Joey sitting across from her, his face grey with worry, and she wondered if he thought she had double-crossed him, but she knew he would have nowhere to go. He was fucked from every angle and he looked it. But she would explain to him when she got the chance that it wasn't in his interest to be spared any violence. The van sped on and half an hour later they were off a side road past Blackwood and then up a country road that led to an old quarry. Between the blacked-out windows and the darkness nobody knew where they were. Eventually they came to a fork in the road that led to a dirt track and up towards the headlights of another car. The van stopped and Hannah got out. Her father stood leaning his backside against the Land Rover. She could see the glint of a gun in his hand. Danny and Jack stood next to him, guns in hands. She wasn't sure if all of them would be executed, but she knew Joey wouldn't be. She'd already given Jack and Danny a clear description of Joey, so she hoped that they had a plan. The back doors of the van opened and the men were bundled out, stumbling, blinking in the headlamps. Then came the looks of shock when they spotted Wolfie.

'Well, well, if it isn't my old mates.' Wolfie stood up, squaring his shoulders. 'I hear you cunts have been looking for me.' He paused, then took a step forwards so he was directly in front of them. 'Well here I am. Fucking Lazarus. Back from the dead.' He glared at Nick. 'I'm your worst fucking nightmare, mate.'

Hannah could see the men shivering in silence, their breath coming out like steam in the freezing night air.

'You're looking a bit shit-scared, lads,' Wolfie sneered. 'You want to say some prayers? Bit late for confession, right enough, isn't it, you fucking amateurs.'

Somewhere in the distance a dog barked. Then came the shaky voice of Nick.

'Wolfie. Listen. It wasn't nothing personal, mate, I promise you that.'

Wolfie stepped so close to him Hannah could see the breath steam in Nick's face as her father spoke.

'Nothing fucking personal? You put me in a coffin and nailed me down and you say it's nothing fucking personal?'

'Look . . . We can talk about this. I'll tell Alfi we can't go after you any more. You're welcome to the fucking diamonds. They're yours.'

Wolfie grinned.

'Oh, I see. Pleading for your fucking life now, are we? Yeah, mate. You're right. The diamonds are fucking mine. That's what you get for being greedy cunts, and maybe Alfi has got that message by now.'

'Wolfie,' Nick said, 'listen to me. There's something you need to know. Some big Russian fucker is involved now and he's pulling out all the stops to find you. That's why we're here. We don't give a fuck any more about the diamonds. It was your plan, and fair enough, we tried to fuck you over but believe me there's big regret about that. We were prepared to leave it, then this big cunt comes to Alfi and tells him he needs to find you. Not just for the diamonds, but for some fucking documents that are missing.'

'That right?' Wolfie said as if he didn't know. 'Well. Thanks for that information, mate. And for that I'm not going to send you for a long swim in this quarry behind me. I might just give you a second chance.'

'Please, Wolfie. I have kids.'

'Fuck you, Nick. Fuck the lot of you.'

And with that, he stepped forward and kneecapped Nick. The sound of his screaming echoed in the wilderness and he buckled to the ground. The others stood wide-eyed as Wolfie went along the line and placed the gun on one knee of each terrified man. He fired again, kneecapping each of them and in turn they all screamed and collapsed onto the wet ground, groaning in agony.

'Okay. I want you to work out how you get out of here, and if you do make it, then take that message back to Alfi. Tell him he's fucked with me twice now, and it wouldn't be smart to come back.' He took a step towards Nick and stepped hard onto his bloody knee as Nick yelped.

'Oh, and tell him I'm now fucking loaded with more money than the little Sicilian prick could ever have dreamed of.'

Then Wolfie turned away from them and looked at the Casey crew. Danny and Jack nodded to the masked men, who went back into the van, except for Hannah. She pulled off her mask and looked down at the men. It was the last face they saw as they passed out.

CHAPTER TWENTY-ONE

Vic had driven for seven hours, stopping only briefly in a motorway café where he grabbed a coffee and some snacks to eat in the car. The further north he went, the safer he felt, because he knew that the frenzy of searching in the immediate aftermath of his and Juan's escape would have died down. Spanish police would put on a show of hunting an escapee down, but by nightfall they would have plenty of other crimes on their plate. By the time Vic had driven to the ancient village of Cuenca, an hour or so from Madrid, he was sure he was clear to rest up for the night. He'd talked to Sharon en route, and she'd agreed to fly up to Toulouse, a couple of hours over the French border, in the morning before he headed north for the ferry to UK. It was a bit risky, but he knew this might be the last time they could be together for a very long time. He'd be in custody within a couple of days of arriving in the UK and wasn't expecting to get bailed. But for tonight, he was happy to be alone and to relax in this isolated mountain village, perched high above a deep gorge. Nobody would ever think of looking for him here.

He'd booked into a small hostel run by an old woman who sat behind the counter in the chilly reception. She didn't even ask for his passport, but flatly asked for the room payment up front. When he handed her the cash, she pushed a key across to him, nodded, then turned and disappeared behind a bead curtain. It looked like he was the only guest in the place, and once he had had a long hot shower and a change of clothes in his tiny room overlooking the vast ravine, he put on his jacket and went out. The village was quiet apart from a few tourists wandering around, and the couple of restaurants that were lit up in the main square were mostly empty. He decided just to go for tapas in one of the bars, rather than sit in an empty restaurant in case waiters felt they had to make conversation with him, asking him where he was coming from and shit like that. Along the square he found a bar, peered through the windows to make sure it was quiet, and stepped inside. There was only one other customer in the place, an old man who sat reading a newspaper at a table in the corner. He didn't look up when Vic came in. The barman was leaning on the gantry, engrossed in his mobile. He dragged his eyes away from his phone, shoved it back in his jeans pocket and walked along the bar. He raised his head in that mildly bored way the Spanish did, but said nothing.

Vic asked in Spanish for a small beer. As the barman poured it, Vic studied the array of tapas behind the glass shelf on top of the bar. It looked like meatballs, pork stew, vegetables, and something pale on a skewer. He asked for a portion of each of them. The barman sighed as though the effort was intruding into his phone time, before spooning the food onto tapas dishes and shoving them into the microwave. Vic sat up on a stool at the end of the bar where he could look out onto the street. He took a long thirsty gulp of his beer and relished the feeling that a simple thing like a glass of beer could give him after weeks cooped up in prison.

He gazed out at the steady drizzle on the cobblestones, and for a fleeting moment wondered where he would have been if he hadn't met Sharon again that day in Fuengirola. He might have been on the other side of the world, reinventing himself, living an ordinary life with his past well hidden. He could even do that now – he had more money than he needed to escape and go missing. He knew how to do that too, but he wouldn't. He couldn't get Sharon out of his mind. But in the next few days, he'd be sitting in a prison cell in UK looking at a twelve stretch unless some clever lawyer could work a miracle. The ping of the microwave brought him back from his reverie, and the barman pushed two of the dishes in front of him along with some bread. He picked up the peculiar-looking grey-coloured food on the skewer and bit into it. Tasted like chicken or pork, but more chewy. He could see the barman looking at him from the side of his eye for a reaction. Vic gave him an enquiring look, holding the skewer up.

'Brain of the sheep,' he said, his face suddenly opening up to a grin. 'You like?'

'*Sí*,' Vic replied, then smiled back. '*Mejor que los testículos*.' Better than testicles.

The barman chuckled.

'*Mas cerveza*?'

'*Sí*.'

As the barman filled a fresh glass of beer, Vic was surprised to see a crowd of what looked like late-middle-aged tourists crossing the square and heading to the bar. This he didn't need. The door opened and they came in, plastic macs soaked and shaking their umbrellas at the door. They were merry and loud, and from their accents, Vic deduced they were German. He didn't pay much attention to them and continued with his tapas. The crowd of what seemed like couples on a group holiday were ordering drinks and thronged around the bar close to him. One or two of them nodded in his direction, but he made sure he didn't make eye contact with them. He ate his tapas, cleaning the dishes with the bread, and sipped at his beer. One of the men squeezed into the bar too close to him for comfort.

'Good?' he asked, pointing at the dishes.

'Yes,' Vic answered.

'You are on holidays?' the German persisted, despite Vic's obvious disinterest.

'Yes. Travelling.'

'Good,' the man said. 'We are too. From Germany.' One of the other tourists put a beer down in front of the man and he hoovered most of it in one gulp.

Vic nodded but said nothing. Christ. A drunk German asking fucking questions. He turned to the barman who gave a sympathetic shrug.

'You are English?'

Vic glared at him, wanting to say, Listen, Sherlock can you just fuck right off? But he didn't.

'Yes,' he said.

'Where are you going to after Cuenca?'

Vic didn't answer. He picked up his beer and took another long drink. Then he took twenty euros out of his jeans pocket and pushed it towards the barman. He waved the change away, much to the barman's delight. The German looked crestfallen that his new friend was ignoring him, then he suddenly looked annoyed.

'Enjoy your trip,' Vic said because he felt he couldn't leave without saying something.

The man stood watching him as he pushed past the rest of the Germans towards the door. Vic breathed a sigh of relief to be out in the rain away from nosy fucking Germans wanting to know his life story. He should go back to his room and sit the night out, but he wandered up towards another bar around the corner. One more beer in peace, he said to himself, just to drink in the atmosphere after a long day.

By the time Vic was leaving the other bar the village was eerily quiet. He passed by the bar he'd been in earlier and noticed that most of the German tourists were gone, apart from a couple of stragglers. He didn't linger and headed across the square towards the darkness of the tight back-street that led to his hostel. It was only a couple of minutes from his place to the square, but after walking along the almost blacked-out street, he still couldn't see the lights of his hostel. There were so many twists and turns in this medieval village that it would have been easy to get lost, but Vic was sure he'd gone the right way. He stopped for a moment, turned another corner, and headed into the darkness. He thought he heard footsteps but he know it must be his imagination because the village was more or less deserted a few minutes ago. He stopped, and could only hear his heartbeat. Then he walked again. Where the fuck was his hostel? He peered and in the distance he could see the lights of the big monastery hotel that had been behind him when he'd left the hostel, so he must have gone in the wrong direction. He turned, retraced his steps. He would go back to the square and start again. As he headed for the square he heard again the footsteps behind him. He stopped and stood tight against the wall, peering in the darkness.

'Hey, English!'

Vic glanced around, scarcely breathing. Then, from the darkness, the light of a mobile phone. The fucking ruddy face of the German tourist in front of him.

'What the fuck?' Vic said. 'What do you want, for Christ's sake?'

The German was unsteady on his feet, his rubbery lips pulled back to a sneer.

'I see you on television, English.'

His words hit Vic like a kick in the stomach. Fucking hell! He didn't answer. Stood bracing himself, not sure what he should do next.

'I saw your face today. In our hotel. On the news. English man escape jail in Spain along with Spanish man. Looks like you.'

'Well it's not me. So fuck off!'

The German shone the phone light in Vic's face, nearly blinding him.

'Yes. Is you. I know things like this. I'm retired now. But I was policeman in Germany, and I know these things.'

Vic moved to walk past him, but the crazy fucker now blocked his path in the tight street. Vic went the other way, and the German blocked him again. What the Christ was this guy trying to do? Make a citizen's arrest? Be a hero on the bus to Madrid in the morning?

'Get out of my fucking way,' Vic spat.

'Or what? Will you call the police?'

Vic didn't answer. He had to do something, because this drunk bastard was not going to let it go. Before he could stop himself, Vic lashed out and hit the German square in the face. He staggered back and fell, but Vic heard the thunk of his head on the cobblestones. He took his own mobile out of his pocket and shone the light on the German's face. He could see blood seeping out of the back of his head onto the ground, and he was unconscious.

'Jesus Christ, you stupid bastard,' Vic said, hoping he wasn't dead.

But there was nothing he could do. He crouched down and could see the man was still breathing, but if he tried to help him and pull him to his feet back to safety, he would get the blame for it and there would be cops all over him. He pulled the man up to a sitting position, and suddenly his eyes opened, blood still coming out from a gash on the back of his head. He was dazed, but he wasn't seriously injured. Vic pushed him against the wall and left him there. He didn't look back.

He kept his torch on and managed to find the right way back to his hostel, pushing open the door, glad the old woman wasn't around. He had to get out of here and fast. He went to his room, grabbed his bag, then tiptoed along the corridor and out into the street. He walked briskly to the car park, praying that he didn't hear any activity from the direction where the German sat. He hoped someone would find him soon, because if he lapsed into unconsciousness and lay there all night, he might be dead in the morning, and every cop from here to France would be looking for him. He got into his car and started the engine before easing his way down the winding streets out of Cuenca and onto the motorway. He'd have to find somewhere to sleep in the car, far enough away from here. He shook his head in disbelief as he hit the highway. So much for a sense of freedom.

Sharon watched Vic as he poured the remains of the bottle of red wine into her glass. The initial rush of excitement she'd felt when they met in the bar next to the hotel where Vic was staying had tapered off. Now they sat holding hands, like any other couple having a special night together. That this could well be the last ever night they would be together was unspoken, but both were more silent than they'd been before. There were no guarantees anywhere in their lives, Sharon thought. She had lived that way most of her life, and the only stability she'd had for any length of time had been when she was with Knuckles initially and had given birth to their son. But as the years wore on, and his crime empire had become bigger, the certainties in her life had grown fewer and fewer. And despite having been taken in by Kerry Casey and now being a firm part of her organisation, Sharon knew that any day it could all change. That was one of the reasons she had never declared her feelings for Vic. She didn't feel she had to say it, and she hoped that by her actions he would know the depth of her love for him. But even now she was sure of his love for her, there were no guarantees. Sure, they could be together far away from here on the other side of the world, with Vic's money and a new life with her son. But all the time, they'd be looking over their shoulders, waiting for the knock on the door from police. Vic was doing the right thing, giving himself up, but the thought of him being jailed for nine, ten or more years, made it so difficult to make promises. A prison term of that length could change him, and she could change too, having to lead her life without him. She'd asked herself all the way up here as she flew from Málaga to Toulouse – did she really want to spend the next ten years alone, visiting her man in prison? She'd done that with Knuckles. And that was what was facing her if she committed to Vic. On the other hand, he might walk free on a technicality, but they both knew how unlikely that was.

Vic put his hand on hers and she reached across and touched his face.

'I'll miss you,' she said. 'No matter what happens.'

'Me too,' he said. 'I thought about nothing else but being with you since I got arrested in Spain. I didn't think I would get the chance to do this.'

Vic summoned the waiter and paid the bill, then they finished their drinks and left the restaurant to walk to the hotel nearby. In the foyer, Sharon walked behind Vic as he led her into the lift and hit the button for the fourth floor. Then he turned to her, took her in his arms and pulled her close. He held her so hard and kissed her so passionately it took her breath away.

'Jesus,' Sharon said. 'This is what it felt like all those years ago, when we were trying to stay away from each other, but couldn't.'

'I remember, sweetheart,' he said, kissing her neck.

He took her by the hand as they went out of the lift and along the corridor to the bedroom. As soon as they got inside Vic pulled her towards him and they slammed into the back of the door as it closed. They weren't even going to make it to the bed. He kissed her breathlessly, and she could feel the longing in him as his hands clutched at her hair, then touched her face, as he looked into her eyes, his hands slipping down to her breasts and then to her thighs and she felt her whole body was alive and tingling as he pushed himself against her. She tugged at his belt and opened his trousers, and he groaned as she slipped her hand inside. He pulled up her skirt and gently massaged between her legs, and she ached with pleasure as he pulled down her pants. As she stepped out of them he dropped on his knees and put his head between her legs, devouring her. She was close to climaxing even before he stood up and lifted her buttocks and eased himself inside her. It was over in seconds and he called out her name and she felt the warm rush inside her.

'Sharon, I love you. So much.'

He picked her up and carried her to the bed. And they lay that way for a moment, half naked, breathless. Then moments later they slipped off their clothes, and just the touch of each other reignited the fire, and as he pulled Sharon on top of her, she eased him inside her again and she had had never known such pleasure as long as she lived. They slept with Sharon lying across his chest until the light began to spread across the morning sky. As she gazed out of the window while Vic slept, suddenly Sharon felt tears come to her eyes, because she knew she had never been loved like this so unconditionally in her whole life. When Vic woke up, he rolled onto Sharon and nuzzled her neck.

'Do we have time for one more?'

Sharon giggled and reluctantly slipped from under him.

'I think we'd better get moving. You need to be on the road.' She leaned over and kissed him as he lay staring at the ceiling. 'There will be other times,' she said. 'I promise.'

In the hotel car park Sharon waited while Vic threw his rucksack into the back of the car. For a fleeting moment it occurred to her that he might not go to the UK after all. He could just get in the car and keep on running if he changed his mind, and if he did, she couldn't blame him. He stepped closer to her and took her in his arms.

'So,' he said. 'That's it, then. Can't put this off any longer.' He hugged her. 'Christ, I'll miss you, darling.'

'I'll miss you too, Vic.' She felt choked as she held onto him for a long time. 'But I'll see you soon. Once you're in the UK, give me a call, and I'll get Kerry to send someone to meet you. She's got a lawyer standing by. I think Marty is coming down to be with you.' She paused. 'Are you nervous?'

He shrugged, looked at her. 'No,' he said. '*Que sera*, sweetheart. But I'll be back.'

'I hope so, Vic. But I'll come over as soon as I know where you are.'

'Will you?' He touched her hair. 'I'd love that. Last night . . . Well . . .' His voice tailed off. 'You know what I mean, darling. Don't let that be the last.'

'Of course not,' she said.

He held her face and gave her one more kiss, then turned away and opened the door of the car. Sharon stood watching as he drove out of the car park and away from her.

CHAPTER TWENTY-TWO

From the study, Kerry could hear Wolfie loudly joking with Danny and Jack as they walked down the hall. They sounded well buoyed up. The London mob had come to Glasgow and the Caseys had sent them back bleeding, their tails between their legs. That was how *they* did business, and when Danny had called her last night afterwards, he'd sounded triumphant. She should be too, for her troops seeing off hard men who'd come to harm them. In a few days, the news would also filter out once again across the city and beyond that nobody messed with the Caseys.

The door opened and they came in, Wolfie beaming.

'So, have you heard anything from our friends in the big smoke?' Kerry motioned them to the table.

'Not bloody likely,' Wolfie said.

'But have you seen the news on television today, Kerry?' Jack grinned. 'Just a short clip about police probing a brutal attack on four injured men found wandering along the A74 in the early hours of this morning. Looked like they'd each been shot in one knee.'

'Really? I didn't see that.'

'Yeah. They were picked up by a passing motorist who stopped to help, but the fuckers were armed and hijacked the poor bastard's car. He called the cops but by that time, no doubt, they were well down the road.'

'Well,' Wolfie said. 'They'll not be auditioning for *Strictly Come Dancing* any time soon. Fuckers!'

Everyone laughed, including Kerry, even if she would never quite take to how uplifted the men got after a spell of combat. Winning the fight was everything to her, but she was driven by more than just the battle – for her it was about the future. The end game was what she had been fighting for since the day she had taken over.

'So talk me through it,' Kerry said as the troops picked up cups and poured coffee before sitting down.

She listened as Jack started the story of how he'd instructed Cal and Tahir to watch and listen in the bar and see what they could pick up, but that they'd used their initiative and lured the London mob to their snooker hall.

'Tell you what, Kerry,' Jack said. 'I know you've got reservations about how you use these lads, given their age, but they really are top hands. Growing into the job big time.'

Kerry nodded, but it still niggled that she was putting Maria's son in danger on the frontline.

'Yeah,' she said. 'I hear what you're saying, Jack. But they didn't actually do what they were told last night. They went off the grid a bit, and if they'd been rumbled we might be talking about a completely different story today.'

'Fair dos,' Jack said. 'But they were smart, thinking on their feet like that, chatting these dickheads up. I think the fact that they were so young is what made the London crew think they were just innocents.'

'Yeah. You're right about that,' Kerry said. 'But the jury is still out on Cal and Tahir. I've got plans for them in the future. I'd like to look at getting them into the property business, learning the trade, maybe out in Spain. They're the right age to be looking into the future.'

There were a few nods around the table, but Kerry could see that right now not everyone in the room was looking at the long-term. They were happy to have pulled one over on Alfi Ricci, and were basking in a bit of glory.

'So what do you think Alfi Ricci will do now?'

'Who knows?' Wolfie said. 'From what we gathered from whimpering Nick, they were only here because this Russian geezer is putting pressure on Alfi to get his gear back. I'd take that with a pinch of salt, but I don't think it's over yet.'

'Well,' Danny said, 'we'll be ready for them if they come calling again.'

Suddenly Wolfie cleared his throat, and a huge grin spread across his face. 'And now that we're all together,' he said, glancing at Hannah and winking, 'the news just gets better and better.' He glanced at Kerry and Danny. 'I've had a call this morning from your old mate Manny Lieberman.'

'From Israel?' Kerry asked, surprised.

'Yep. Israel,' Wolfie replied. 'It's game on, my friends. Him and old Moshe have done a deal over there. They've only gone and sold the bleeding diamonds.'

There was a collective surprise and delight around the table.

'That's brilliant, Wolfie.' Danny gave him a thumbs up. 'So why did the pair of them bugger off to Israel?'

'Security, mate,' Wolfie said. 'According to Manny, since he made the call to Moshe, the two of them had been preparing to get out of Dodge toot suite. You know. Just in case there were some fuckers waiting in the wings when we handed the diamonds over.' He looked at Hannah. 'Which, as you know, of course, there was. Tell you what. We were lucky to get away with that in Amsterdam.'

'We were,' Kerry agreed. 'So, did he say any more? I mean, was the deal easy to do, or were the old guys under threat over there? Call me naive, but I'm a bit astonished that two old guys like that made a deal with you at all, Wolfie, when they knew where the diamonds came from and how much danger they were putting themselves in.'

'Yeah,' Wolfie said. 'That's why they got out of there and went to Israel, where they are well protected and have their own contacts to shift the diamonds. Of course they knew where they came from, and all the more reason to get rid of them fast. And, once they put some calls in, they could have sold the bloody diamonds twice over.'

'Amazing,' Kerry said. 'Great news.'

She didn't want to ask if Wolfie had been paid the money yet, in case he thought she was asking for the Caseys' cut. For the rest of the meeting they spoke about business deals that were being done in Spain and Kerry was glad to be telling them that the Caseys had bought up a string of estate agents after the Spanish owners were arrested for dodgy deals. The authorities would no doubt be scrutinising the business from now on, but Sharon had told her she was hiring some good people to run the businesses legitimately. There was plenty of money to be made in property without going rogue. And the hotel build was well under way, with builders talking about finishing the major bricks and mortar construction in the next few months. Things were looking good for the future, Kerry said. When the meeting was over, everyone left, except Wolfie and Hannah. As the door closed, Wolfie turned to Kerry.

'Kerry, I just wanted to say again how I'll for ever be in your debt for what you did for me and Hannah.'

'Not at all, Wolfie. If my father was here, he would have done the same – and he would have been having a laugh this morning at how it all went down last night.'

'Yeah, he would,' Wolfie said. 'But I wanted to just give

you some figures on the diamonds and stuff, and talk to you about your cut.'

Kerry didn't feel comfortable talking money with a man like Wolfie. It wasn't because the diamonds were stolen, though if she was honest about that she'd rather have not become involved. But it was the fact that he and Hannah had felt a bit like family since they'd arrived, the stories Wolfie'd told her giving her an insight into a world her father had lived in that she knew very little about.

'Talk to Danny about it, Wolfie,' she said. 'It's your deal.'

'No, no,' he insisted. 'I want to do right by the Caseys. So here's what I'm thinking. I haven't got the dosh in my account yet, but Manny says Moshe will move it in the next couple of days. It'll go into three accounts I have – one in Jersey and two in the Cayman Islands.'

Kerry couldn't help but smile at his delight.

'So,' he continued, 'Manny has told me that for all the gear they sold, I would get three and half million.'

Kerry felt her eyes widening.

'Seriously?'

'Yep. The cut for the old boys was just under two million. Fair enough. Couldn't have done it without them. But it's been a nice little earner for them, I'll say that.'

'Indeed,' Kerry said.

'So with the remainder, I was thinking that one and a half million would go to the Caseys for helping us out of a very big hole.'

Kerry nodded. It sounded like a lot of money, and as far as she was concerned, the Caseys had laid nothing out for it, so it was a win-win situation. Money for nothing. Well, almost nothing.

'I'm sure that's more than fair, Wolfie,' Kerry said, feeling a little awkward talking money.

'Great,' Wolfie said. 'And the thing is, Kerry, I've still got a fortune in gear down in London – stashed away until things die down. Then in time, I'll get the stuff and see if old Manny and Moshe want to do another deal. So I'm quids in everywhere I look.'

Kerry smiled as Hannah shook her head and rolled her eyes.

'Yeah, Dad,' she said. 'But you want to quit while you're ahead, old man, and get yourself somewhere far away.'

'Of course,' he said. 'In time.'

'Just one thing,' Kerry said, as they were turning to leave. 'The discs and the photographs. I'd like them. I have a plan for them. You okay with that?'

Wolfie stopped, glanced at Hannah, who shrugged.

'Then, Kerry, they are all yours, sweetheart. Do with them what you will.'

'Thanks,' Kerry said. That was all she wanted to hear.

CHAPTER TWENTY-THREE

'What a fucking mess!' Alfi Ricci paced the floor in his office. 'Look at the fucking state of you two. I mean how fucking naive can you possibly be? Talk about getting fucked right up the arse! Jesus!'

To be fair, Alfi did feel a bit sorry for Nick and Joey who had limped into his restaurant in crutches, their faces etched in agony. That was four men he was down, including the other two who were still in hospital. Kneecapped. For their own stupidity. When he'd got the frantic phone call from Nick the other night to say they were driving back to London in a stolen car, Alfi couldn't believe his ears. They'd only left yesterday morning for Glasgow where their job had been to get hold of Wolfie no matter what it took. Of course he didn't think it was going to be easy wading into Casey territory and trying to drag that bastard Wolfie from their clutches, but he assumed they had some sort of plan. Even if they did, they'd ballsed it up within four hours of arriving in that shithole Glasgow after being duped by a couple of fucking teenagers. When this got out, Alfi's enemies would be laughing their tits off. He was still trying to live down the story of how they captured Wolfie and were about to cremate the cunt when the doors burst open and in came Wolfie's fucking cavalry to the rescue. Four men he'd lost in that job, and now he had another four of his boys hobbling and out of action for Christ knows how long. At this rate, he was going to have to go down the bloody job centre for staff.

'It wasn't as straightforward as it sounds, boss,' Nick said, clutching his knee, wincing in pain. 'But we can try to work out another way to get to Wolfie.'

'And how the fuck you going to do that, when he's up there in Fort Casey?' Alfi asked, impatient.

'The daughter,' Nick said. 'That girl of his. Hannah.' He jerked his head at Joey who sank further into his seat. 'Remember, Joey here managed to let her get away.'

Alfi puffed. 'Oh, yeah,' he said, glaring at Joey. 'Don't fucking remind me of that. And how you going to get to her?'

Alfi stood over Nick, watching as he shifted in his chair, cleared his throat.

'Well, I was thinking . . .' Nick said.

'Oh, here goes,' Alfi rolled his eyes.

Nick ignored the jibe.

'I was thinking, Alfi, that there's a way we could get to

her.' He paused, took a breath. 'You know them bastards who did Wolfie's wife in? Remember? The bomb? They blew up her car as she turned on the ignition. Blew her to smithereens.'

Alfi nodded, remembering the horror of it all, and how it had almost broken Wolfie. His father's old mate had never really been the same after that, shrinking into the background, not taking on many jobs. It was a few years ago now, and Alfi remembered that Wolfie's daughter had only been about sixteen at the time. But years later she was convicted of hunting down one of the gangsters who'd planted the bomb and throwing him out of a twelfth-floor window. Alfi recalled the admiration that went around the London gangs for that. Nobody had even heard of the girl apart from that Wolfie had a daughter, and there she was, fearless and out for revenge.

'Yeah, so what?' Alfi asked. 'That was a long time ago. She's just out of jail.'

'Exactly. She was there the other night, as I told you. So she's obviously gone away to be with her old man.'

'Yeah,' Alfi said, glaring at Joey. 'Thanks to Superman here for letting her go.'

'Well,' Nick said. 'She's obviously a bit of a hard ass, and I'd bet that she's not finished yet with the geezers who killed her mother. You know it was the Townsends who did it, don't you?'

Alfi looked at him.

'Of course I fucking know it was the Townsends. It was Charlie who took the swan dive, wasn't it?'

'Yeah. But big Larry is still on the go. Runs a car showroom out in Romford. Front shop for ringed cars. Insurance jobs, apparently. But also a lot of class cars an' all.'

'Yeah. So what you saying?'

'Well now that Hannah is out of jail, I'd be surprised if she was going to just leave it at that. Wolfie knew it was the pair of them Townsends who did it, so I'd say that Hannah bird might be biding her time before Larry gets his comeuppance. In fact, probably if she hadn't got caught up with Wolfie on the run from us, she might even have been after Larry by now.'

'Dunno about that,' Alfi said. 'Is she really going to go after him when she was banged up for years for doing his brother? She's the first person the cops would be looking for.'

'Maybe, but I'm sure there's more than her would like to see Larry Townsend's ugly mug splattered all over the floor.'

Alfi nodded.

'Yeah. That's for sure. He's a right arsehole, that Larry. You know he beat a young lad up so badly a couple of years ago, the lad is in a wheelchair with brain damage?'

'No,' Nick said. 'I didn't know that. What happened?'

'Oh, some barney over the boy doing a bit of double dealing. You know how the Townsends' garage does hookey insurance jobs? Well, seemingly the lad opened his stupid trap. I mean a hard slap might have been enough. But that fucker Larry is coked out of his nut one night and he kicks the living shit out of the boy. Not that I give a fuck about any of them, but what's your point, Nick?'

'I was thinking: what if we could find a way to get Hannah down here and pave the way for her to punch Larry's ticket and get off scot-free?'

'And how you going to do that, Einstein? Your forward planning hasn't exactly been wonderful so far.'

'We could find a way to get to Hannah. Let her know that Larry is there for the taking. He's vulnerable if he's on so much gear. So a word or two in her ear might bring her here.'

'Then what?'

'Then we fucking grab her. Hold onto her. Put the word out to Wolfie that we've got her, and if he doesn't come across with the goods, then he'll be going to her funeral.'

'Yeah,' Alfi almost laughed. 'Like Wolfie's funeral!'

'Well, no. We'd organise it better.'

'And how we going to get to her?'

'I haven't figured that out yet. But there has to be a way. Even if we get the word to the Caseys and hopefully Hannah will get that.'

'But what if she's not even planning revenge on Larry? Maybe she's rehabilitated after all that time in jail.'

'No way,' Nick said. 'Her mum got blown up by these cunts. You don't get rehabilitated after that.'

Alfi thought for a moment, then he spoke. 'Yeah. I suppose that's right. Okay. Let's see if we can get our heads around that. Might be more bother than it's worth, and it might go tits up again. But meantime, those fucking Russians will be breathing down my neck any day now.'

Nobody answered.

'Okay. Get the fuck out of here now and let me think straight.'

Alfi watched as the two of them got to their feet and hobbled towards the door of the restaurant. Stupid and all as Nick could be sometimes, he might just have a point about that Hannah bird.

Joey sat in his room in the hostel and finished the remainder of his Chinese takeaway. The night manager of the hostel had taken pity on him as he'd struggled to get through the front door in crutches. Luckily his room was on the ground floor, but it was at the end of a very long corridor, so it was taking him ages to get there. Jan had come from behind the reception to help him, and as she'd supported him to his room she'd asked if he'd had dinner. He was starving and in too much pain to even struggle to the nearby café, he'd told her, so he was grateful that she went out and brought him in some food. She even bought it from her own pocket. He was so touched and depressed that he almost burst into tears when she handed it into him. Now as he lay back on the single bed, his leg raised on a pillow, he reflected on the verbal kicking they'd got from Alfi. It was to be expected, he supposed, after what happened. Even now, he still couldn't believe those two young boys had set them up so cleanly for the Caseys. He wasn't sure what hurt most though: the pain that surged through him when the bullet went into his kneecap, or the fact that it actually happened. He didn't know what to think. He'd betrayed his own team to let Hannah know where they were, and had effectively set them up. The last thing he expected was to be shot like a dog. He couldn't believe that Hannah was even there to witness it. Obviously she hadn't been able to say anything to help him while it was all happening, or it would be signing his death warrant. But he thought she might have at least phoned to say something afterwards. He chided himself for being so naive. He'd been used and that was all. He was stupid to think that Hannah was any kind of friend, even if she had shown him kindness that first time he'd encountered her. He picked up his phone, and scrolled down until he saw her name. He was on the verge of deleting it, promising himself to grow up and forget any notion that she was his friend. He was about to push the delete key when the phone rang.

It was Hannah. He let it ring six times, then before he could stop himself he answered.

'Joey,' she said. 'Are you all right?'

Silence. What was she playing at?

'I'm on crutches. Thanks for that, Hannah.'

'Come on, Joey. You know there was nothing I could do.

If you'd been the only one not injured serious questions would have been asked by Alfi. You know that. And in any case, it happened so quickly, I didn't even know what Wolfie was going to do.' She paused. 'Actually, I thought he was going to bump you all off and dump you in the quarry.'

Silence.

'So,' Joey said. 'Am I supposed to thank you for that?'

'No. But I hope you know that it had nothing to do with me. It all went a bit crazy.'

'Yeah. Well I'm in a lot of pain.'

'I know, there's nothing I can do. But I might be coming down to London soon, so maybe we can meet up?'

'Down here? Why?'

'Just some things I have to do. Nothing important.'

'You want to watch your back. Alfi Ricci is on the war-path. Says these Russians are breathing down his neck because he hasn't delivered Wolfie or his gear, so everyone is looking for blood.' He paused. 'Oh, and by the way, Nick was suggesting to Alfi that they should try to lure you down here on the promise of getting you close to Larry Townsend, you know, for revenge. Nick says they could do that, then grab you and that would bring Wolfie running. Just marking your card.'

'I'm not too worried about that, but thanks for the heads-up.' She paused. 'But look, if there is anything I can do I will. Okay?'

'Yeah. Whatever. I have to go.' He hung up, huffy.

CHAPTER TWENTY-FOUR

Vic Paterson was back. As he drove off the ramp from the ferry at Dover, he felt a mixture of relief and dread. All the way from Spain, through France until he got to the ferry terminal in Calais, he'd been watching in his rear-view mirror, his gut dropping every time a police patrol car appeared. If he'd been stopped anywhere in France, he would probably have been handed back to the Spaniards pronto, but now, whatever happened, he was back home. He drove into the motorway service station off the M1 and went to the café. As he stood in the queue for food, Vic's heart sank by the minute. The adrenalin rush of the escape and being with Sharon had gone, and now he was looking at where he would be this time tomorrow. This was his last opportunity to walk away from all this and take his chances. He took his mobile phone out of his pocket and scrolled down to Sharon's number, picturing her smile, her eyes dazzling with indignation that afternoon when he met her in Fuengirola for the first time in nearly fourteen years. He put the phone back in his pocket, slid his tray across to the checkout and paid for his food. Then he went across to a table far away from the other customers, the sales reps, the families on their way about their ordinary lives. In another world, maybe with a different start in life, that might have been him, a family man raising his kids. He had never regretted it, until now for some reason. Something about looking at another world that was out there, one that he'd never really been a part of, because most of his grown-up life was about making money and staying one step ahead of the cops, or the other villains trying to cut you up behind your back. He stared down at his food and picked at it with a fork. He'd been hungry long before he got off the ferry, but suddenly the hunger had vanished. He pushed his plate away and took a long drink from the mug of black coffee. Then he took out his mobile again, scrolled down to Sharon and pushed the key. She answered after only one ring.

'Vic! You're okay? I've been worried sick.'

Hearing the concern in her voice made Vic smile. The thought that if he walked away he would probably never see Sharon again made his mind up.

'I'm good,' he said as breezily as he could. 'Well, as good as a man can be who's wondering what his sleeping partner will look like this time tomorrow.'

'Aw, Vic. I'm so glad you made it this far. And I know how

you must be feeling, pet. But you've got to just keep your chin up. It's not over till it's over.'

Vic smiled at her optimism, even if he didn't share it.

'So what happens now, sweetheart?' Vic asked. 'Do I just sit tight?'

'Okay,' Sharon said. 'I talked it all through with Kerry yesterday, and she's talked to Marty Kane. He's on his way to London, and he'll meet you and he'll have the QC with him. He'll talk you through the script, then you . . .'

Her voice tailed off, and Vic could hear she was struggling to talk.

'Come on, Shaz. It's okay. Listen, sweetheart. I can do this.'

Silence. Then after two beats he could hear Sharon clear her throat.

'I know, Vic. But . . . but I just feel so . . . well, that I got you into this.'

'Come on now. Nobody got me into this, Sharon. I got myself into it. I knew what I was doing. And I made a shitload of money out of it, that I'll be spending once I get out.'

He wanted to say, With you, Sharon, but he didn't want to put that kind of pressure on her. He was putting on his bravest face, but he knew he might be an old man by the time he got out of jail. He didn't expect her to wait for him.

'Okay, Vic. This QC Marty has got on our side is shit hot and the first thing is, he's going to make sure that you don't get extradited to Spain. Marty says he's confident you'll be kept here. Then it's a question of wait and see.'

Vic saw the long months on remand, the days and nights, the dull, depressing, frustrating routine. He swallowed hard.

'Okay, make the call then, Sharon. Tell me where to go and I'll head for London.'

Silence for a couple of beats and he could hear her breathe.

'Okay, I'll do it now.' She paused. 'And I'll come and see you as soon as I can. I promise you. I will. I . . . I've thought about you non-stop since Toulouse. Jesus, Vic. I miss you.'

Vic felt his throat tighten a little. It would have been easier if she'd been matter-of-fact or joking in her usual way, keeping herself behind the wall. He wasn't used to hearing her like this.

'Me too, sweetheart. I miss you.' He paused. 'I love you.'

The silence was deafening and Vic was about to hang up when he heard her.

'I love you too, Vic.' Then she hung up.

By early evening, Vic was on his way to Belmarsh high security prison. He sat in the back of a police car in handcuffs, the crackling of the police radio the only noise in the car as the two young uniformed cops spoke very little during the hour-long journey.

He reflected on his meeting a couple of hours earlier with Marty Kane and the QC James McKain. It had been as positive as it could have been. He liked Marty, who shook his hand warmly when they met in the lawyer's office in

Canary Wharf, and he'd told him that Kerry Casey passed on her highest regards. She was grateful, he said, for everything he had done for them. The QC had sat behind his desk, very matter-of-fact, explaining the situation in regards to extradition, telling him there would be an official request from Spain in the next few days once the UK police informed them that they had their prisoner. He said he had been looking at this over the past couple of days and he was confident that the Brits would not want to give him up. The police said they had an informer – an insider who witnessed the load-up of drugs and everyone involved, and he was giving names, including Vic's, in return for freedom. But the crucial point that gave them hope was that there was no actual evidence of drugs or possession, because the drugs seemed to have disappeared. He said his defence would be that there may not even have been drugs in the truck, and that he was only hitching a lift. But it might not work. They would no doubt pursue conspiracy to smuggle drugs or something that they could concoct and take to prosecution. He was very direct about the drugs charges and said if it went to trial and he was found guilty, he could be looking at a very long prison sentence. He said that in the coming weeks or months, he would face an approach from the police for him to inform on people. They would offer him a deal that might get him out in a few years, depending on what he told them, and what names he could give. If he cooperated and his information was good, then he might even be entered into the witness protection programme, where he would start a new life, probably abroad. Vic listened, glancing at Marty whose face was impassive. The way the QC was explaining it to Vic made turning grass sound like an attractive prospect, and Vic had to keep himself from smiling at the very idea of it. Nothing would make him grass on the Caseys, or Sharon, or anybody else for that matter. He'd done time before and kept his mouth shut, and he would do that now.

The police car pulled into the road towards Belmarsh. Vic knew this prison well. He had never been inside it, but he'd had mates over the years who had served time here on remand and on long sentences. The security was as tough as it got. Even when you appeared in court for a plea, there was no way the police cars carrying you could be hijacked. There was even an underground route from the jail to Woolich Crown Court. As they got out of the car, the young coppers eased him out of the back seat and he stood looking up at the imposing building silhouetted against the night sky. Vic swallowed hard. He squared his shoulders, Sharon's voice ringing in his ears telling him she loved him. He could do this.

Hannah didn't tell her father that she wasn't going with him until the last minute. She knew he wouldn't take it well. But she also knew that he loved her too much to make an issue of it. She was thirty years old, for Christ's sake. She could do what she wanted, she told herself. But still she felt guilty. When she'd broken the news to him a couple of days ago, as he was packing up, he hadn't spoken for fully five minutes. She felt awful. From the day her mother had been murdered, she'd known just how precious she was to her father. She was all he had to come home to, and even through the difficult teenage years as he'd dealt with Hannah's anger and rebelliousness, she had never felt anything less than cherished. And she would never want to hurt him. But Wolfie's plans did not fit into Hannah's world – not at the moment, and maybe never. Buoyed up with the fortune in his various hidden accounts, and knowing that he may be hunted down if he stayed in the UK, Wolfie was for the off. He was heading for the Cayman Islands to live out the rest of his life away from everything that had surrounded him for most of his life. There was nothing back in London, or anywhere in the UK for him, he'd told her many times over the years. He'd only stayed in the UK because of Hannah, and he'd hoped now both of them could make a fresh start. And in her darker days, when Hannah had been languishing in her prison cell, the thought of getting as far away as possible and reinventing herself had been attractive. It still was. But it was for another time. Not now. Not while she had unfinished business. She hadn't told her father what that was, but she knew he wasn't daft.

They sat in the café in Glasgow Airport where Wolfie was

about to get on a flight to Paris, then the Cayman Islands. This was really happening. All those dreams of this new life were about to come true. Wolfie looked great as he sat dressed in his dark blue jeans, loafers and white open-neck shirt. With his silver slicked-back hair, he looked every inch the successful retired businessman. All that was missing was the tan, and he would catch up on that shortly, he'd joked with her earlier as he'd said his farewells to the Caseys. But Hannah knew that behind his soft grey eyes, he was troubled. And she also knew why. He pulled his chair a little closer to her and touched her hand.

'Listen, sweetheart. Why are you *really* staying here? What's keeping you in the UK?'

Hannah had been waiting for the inquisition. Her father had seldom asked about her private life since she had been a teenager and was dating whatever new boy she'd brought to the house. But the only time he had asked her for the truth had been when she was arrested for murder. She'd admitted what she had done. That was a long time ago, and he'd spoken to her in the prison cell where she was being held on remand, and he'd hugged her and wept as he'd told her it was his fault – everything was his fault. If he hadn't crossed those bastards on the business deal, her mother would still be alive. Hannah hadn't shed a tear as he'd crumpled in front of her. She'd told him not to worry, that whatever happened she could cope with it.

'Dad,' she said, 'I've got friends here, and some people

I have to say goodbye to. Stuff like that. I've got some things to wrap up.'

Wolfie nodded slowly, looking her in the eye.

'Things to wrap up,' he said. He took both her hands. 'Hannah, please tell me you're not thinking of going after that bastard. He's not worth it. You've had your revenge. It nearly killed me seeing you in jail like that. But you have to put all that behind you now. You know that.'

Hannah hadn't answered for a moment, she knew she was going to have to lie to him.

'I'm not going to do anything stupid. I'm never going back to jail again. Ever.' She looked away from him. 'But I've just got a few things I need to do, and some people to see.' Then she smiled. 'And very soon I'll get on a plane and come and join you. I'll be honest with you, Dad, I might not want to stay in the Cayman Islands for ever, but I do want to go there and see what's on offer – if it's the kind of place where I could have a future that suits me.'

Hannah hoped that painting the positive picture would distract him from questioning her more closely. But he was still troubled.

'You know that bastard Townsend is really nobody these days. Okay, he owns some businesses down there in London, but he's not the big shot he hoped to be. And he's coked out of his nut – so I'm told. I keep tabs on people like him.' He paused. 'And don't think I haven't wanted my revenge on him either. I did. But there's no point.'

Hannah sighed and tried to look frustrated.

'Dad, I told you. I've just got some stuff here, then I'll join you.' She spread her hands. 'Now can we just drop it?' She looked at her watch. 'Come on. You'd better get checked in.'

Wolfie said nothing as they both stood up. He had very little luggage, only a small check-in bag. He was going to buy some stuff at the airport, then a new wardrobe once he got there. They walked from the café along the busy concourse to the queue for business class. Only a few people were there, and Hannah stood with him for a moment.

'Well,' she said finally. 'This is it, Wolfie.' She smiled.

He smiled back.

'C'mere.' He put his arms out and she stepped into them. They held each other tight and she could feel the same heartbreak of parting that she'd felt the morning she'd been arrested.

Hannah felt a little choked and she stayed with her head on his shoulder until she swallowed her emotion. Then she broke away.

'Now make sure you call me at the airport in Paris before you get on the plane. I'm so excited for you, Dad.'

Wolfie said nothing, his lips tight with emotion as he hugged her again.

'I love you so, so much, my darling. I'm going to miss you. These past few weeks being with you have been the best I've felt in years. You'll always be my little girl. My baby, Hannah.' He sniffed. 'So please, promise me you won't hang around the UK long.'

'I promise,' she said. 'I'll see you very soon.'

With that, she turned away, and she could feel him watching her all the way to the automatic doors, where she turned around and waved at him and could see the tears in his eyes.

CHAPTER TWENTY-FIVE

For most of the morning, Kerry had been embroiled in her old life, ploughing through newspaper articles online, hoping to find some kind of update on the Walker family who she'd represented all those years ago when they sued the pharmacy company and lost. For so long she'd placed the memory of defeat at the back of her mind. The last time she'd spoken to James and Marilyn and their daughter Lilly was in a café next to the London civil court, at a loss for words trying to console a tearful Marilyn. Kerry felt she had failed them, even though she suspected that one of the vital witnesses who'd changed his statement had been got at by the pharmaceutical company. There was no point in pursuing that, and there was no point in building up any false hopes for the family. The case was over, and Kerry had moved on. She never forgot them, but that had never made up for her failure.

Sifting through the articles now brought back the image

of Quentin Fairhurst, QC, triumphant as he'd strode past her. How sweet it would be, she thought, if she could get revenge on him after all this time. From the moment Kerry had seen the damning photos of Fairhurst and the Home Secretary, and the DVDs stolen from the bank heist strongbox, the thought of revenge was never far away. She'd been too busy to even consider it in recent days, and was actually still too busy now. But she found that wading through documents and old newspaper cuttings of the case absorbed her all morning. The last cutting she found was from a year ago, saying the girl, Lilly, was now a teenager. It was James and Marilyn telling their story to a local newspaper of how on so little benefits they could not cope much longer at their home in Brighton and faced having to put their paraplegic daughter into care. Kerry promised herself she would find a way to help them, to change their lives. She made a note of their address. She put the cuttings to the side of the table when she heard a car down in the yard and looked at her watch. Marty Kane was coming in as planned to brief her on the situation with Vic Paterson. A couple of minutes later there was a gentle knock on the door of her study, and Marty walked in. She was pleased to see him looking less strained than he'd been in recent weeks. He'd told her that his son Joe and his wife had abandoned their idea to move down to England after Fin's kidnapping, and at last the iciness between Joe and him was beginning to thaw.

'Marty,' Kerry said, as he walked across to the long table in the study. 'How was the journey up from London last night?'

'Plane was late,' he said, sitting down and placing his briefcase on the table. 'So I didn't get to the house until after ten.' He sat back and sighed as Kerry pushed an empty mug towards him, then a coffee pot. 'I'm glad I'm not addressing a jury this morning.' He poured himself some black coffee and put the mug to his lips. 'In fact, let's face it – these days I'm glad every morning I'm not addressing a jury.' He smiled. 'I'm enjoying standing back a bit, Kerry.'

'So you should do, Marty,' she said. 'You've seen the insides of enough courtrooms to last you a lifetime. And I'm glad, too, you've a bit more time on your hands – it was great to be able to ask you to go down and see what the score is with Vic Paterson. So how was it? What's he like as an individual?'

Marty shrugged a little.

'Always hard to see what a person is like when they're about to get banged up in jail like that. But he came across as quite affable. Bit of a hard case, I suppose, and looked to be coping with it all quite well.' Marty reached across to his briefcase and clicked it open. 'But I'm afraid we didn't have very pleasant news to give him – well, his brief had to give him.' He pulled out a folder, sat it on the table. 'According to the detectives briefing the Crown Prosecution Service, they have Vic bang to rights.'

Kerry screwed up her eyes, confused.

'But how can that be? I thought all they had was CCTV of him in the truck and nothing to actually prove he was doing anything other than hitching a ride.'

Marty nodded.

'Yes. That's what we all thought – including Vic. When the Spanish cops spoke to him in jail they didn't say much except that he was on a CCTV camera in Santander docks in the truck.'

'Why didn't Spanish police move in then and raid the truck?'

'Well, from what we hear, there was a decision by the DEA to wait until the truck actually got to the UK as they wanted to see where it was headed, obviously in the hope of snaring more of the smuggling gang – maybe get a lot more bodies in jail.' He paused. 'But whoever was tracking the truck managed to lose it, or the truck lost them. No idea of the background, but the DEA lost track of it for long enough that they weren't sure where it was.'

'Jesus,' Kerry said, remembering that Vinny had told her that they had lost track of the shipment. 'So the cops bungled it up?'

'So it seems,' Marty said. 'But that doesn't get Vic off the hook, I'm afraid.'

'How come?'

'Well, you'll recall the chaos down in Manchester and the shoot-out. There were all sorts of things happening, and during that time, Vic got away. I remember there was an assumption that the driver of the truck was killed – is that not what we thought?'

Kerry put her hands out in a who knows gesture.

'Actually, I'm not sure where that came from, Marty. Maybe it was an assumption that he was killed, or I think at least injured. I really don't know, now you come to mention it, and these past couple of months everything has kind of moved on from that day, as you know. I'm not sure anyone knows what happened to the driver. We didn't even know where Vic was until he suddenly contacted Sharon from the Spanish jail.'

Marty nodded slowly. 'Yes. That's the thing. Because it turns out that the driver was not killed, and that he's not only very much alive, but spilling his guts to the DEA on the entire operation.'

'You're kidding!'

'I kid you not, Kerry.'

'Jesus! How did that happen? I mean, how did the cops get a hold of him?'

'It turns out that in the middle of the gun battle, the bold Carlos – that's the driver's name – got shot in the arm, but managed to roll out of the truck and make his escape. So he was seen wandering not that far from the scene with blood pouring out of him, and was picked up by cops who'd been called by a local shopkeeper.'

Kerry shook her head.

'Christ almighty! So he's an injured man in a foreign land, not really in a position to make himself scarce. Then police arriving on the scene after the shoot-out picked him up, assuming he was caught in the crossfire?'

'Yes. Once they'd checked his ID they found he was the driver of the truck, and by the time he was taken to hospital the DEA were all over him.'

'So where is he now? In jail?'

'No. Apparently in some secret place under the protection of the DEA. He's told them everything – the location where the truck was loaded with the cocaine, and he's dropped a few names of Colombians on the Costa del Sol who were involved. He's even mentioned Pepe Rodriguez, but of course as we know he's already history. So the DEA are pumping him for everything. But at the end of the day, he's only the truck driver, so it's not as though he knows everything. But he knows that Vic was sent to be with him on the truck and tell him where it was going. He's implicated Vic in the smuggling operation, and that's bad.'

Kerry hadn't seen this coming. Sharon would be distraught when she found this out, as she'd been pinning her hopes on the case against Vic not being strong enough.

'And how did Vic take this when he was told all about it?'

'We didn't give him this level of detail yet, as he's just turned himself in, but he knows it's not looking good. The QC is going back to see him tomorrow, then he'll give him everything,' Marty said. 'But Vic knows what this means. He's not long out of jail himself after a long sentence, so if this sticks, then he won't see daylight for a very long time.'

'Christ! This is terrible, Marty. Vic was doing this to help us.'

'I know, Kerry. It's going to be very difficult. It was always going to be hard as it was, him being in the truck carrying a massive shipment of cocaine, but the brief might have found a way through that. But when you've got someone prepared to go on the line pointing the finger at him, then it's a different matter. It's not looking good. By the end of our interview with Vic, he was more calm, and just saying he was hoping we could do something. But once he gets the full picture from the QC, he's smart enough to know how hopeless this is.'

'So what's the next step?' Kerry asked. 'I take it the CPS will build up the case and that will be it?'

'Yes,' Marty said. 'Might take a couple of months. And remember, the police don't actually have the cocaine in question. They will have done tests on the truck and they'll be able to prove cocaine was there, but they don't actually have it, so that will be one aspect for the defence to pursue. But this driver is giving a lot of detail and apparently there might even be photographs of the cocaine being packed into the truck.'

'Photographs? You have to be kidding! Who takes pictures of drugs being loaded into a truck?'

Marty spread his hands, incredulous.

'Who knows, Kerry! Some daft down-table Colombian who wanted to send snaps to the folks back home to show he was a big shot.'

'Jesus! I don't believe this!'

They sat for a long moment in silence. Then Kerry spoke.

'Marty, you know we have pictures of Quentin Fairhurst in compromising positions. And a DVD. And also of Henry Callaghan getting bungs, and with women?'

Marty didn't answer. He looked at her, then took his rimless specs off and polished them with his tie before putting them back on.

'Kerry,' he said, raising his index finger, 'don't even think about going there.' He shook his head.

'But, Marty! Fairhurst is a corrupt bastard. I told you. I knew him years ago from a case I unfairly lost to him. I'm sure they bribed or blackmailed a key witness who changed his statement at the last minute.'

'What has that got to do with anything, Kerry – a case you lost to him? Are you looking for revenge?'

Kerry puffed out a frustrated sigh.

'Maybe I am,' she said. 'But we have evidence that could bring him, and also the Home Secretary, down. We could ruin both their lives, and rightly so.' She paused, part of her knowing how ridiculous this sounded to a pragmatic legal brain like Marty's. But it didn't sound ridiculous to her. 'Maybe if he knew something is out there that could destroy him he might look at the CPS case against Vic and make it disappear.'

Marty almost laughed.

'Oh, Christ, Kerry! Are you talking blackmail here? God almighty! I don't even want to say that bloody word out loud.'

'Okay,' she said. Kerry stood up, paced the room a little, then turned to Marty, her hands outstretched. 'Fair enough. I completely hear what you are saying. But listen. Just say there was a situation where Fairhurst was made aware that damning information existed that could ruin his career and his life. Just for the sake of it imagine that. Can you see how he might buckle if someone put it to him that this would be made public if he didn't agree to what was being asked? To make the case disappear?'

Marty shook his head.

'Christ, Kerry! You *are* talking blackmail here. You're actually talking about blackmailing the Attorney General of Her Majesty's Government.' He put his hands on his head, perplexed. 'And you think he's just going to roll over? He's not. He will have the full force of the law down on whoever attempts to blackmail him. You're talking ten or twelve years in jail here.'

Kerry folded her arms. She'd known Marty would react like this. From the moment she'd seen the photos and DVD of Fairhurst only one thought had been in her mind – revenge. She could simply have made sure the photos and tapes got sent to a national newspaper and ruined him. But using them as a gun to Fairhurst's head to intervene in Vic's case seemed to her a perfectly reasonable scenario. Of course it would be impossible, ridiculous, stupid, and all of the things Marty was saying. But a little voice somewhere inside her told her that it might even work.

'But what if he *did* buckle, Marty?'

'He won't buckle.'

'We can't just leave this to the QC to try and get Vic off the hook. We owe him.'

'We don't owe him a ten-year stretch for blackmail, Kerry. Please. Tell me you're not seriously thinking about this.'

Kerry let out a long slow breath. Yes. She was seriously thinking about this. She was seriously thinking of the look on Fairhurst's face when he was shown the damning evidence that would ruin him. After a long silence, where Marty sat rubbing his face with his hands and shaking his head, Kerry spoke.

'You know,' she said, sitting down, 'everything is looking great for the Caseys these days. We've moved on – the way we always wanted it, the way my father always wanted it. That whole business with the Colombians, and the cocaine we took from them, we've turned that into success for us, and because of that we can work towards the end game.' She gestured with her hand. 'Everything we have here was built from crime, but that's over now. We're pulling out of everything and leaving people loyal to us in charge of their own turf. The Caseys are becoming more legit with every deal we sign, with every property we buy. The future is looking great and we can turn away from all this violence and murder and shit that we've had to swim in for years – well, my father had to long before me. It was his goal to go straight, but Mickey with his drugs dragged him in the shit.' She sighed. 'I've had it with this, Marty. I'm taking the Casey organisation to a better place. But I'm not going to leave a foot soldier like Vic Paterson behind, who has given us so much, when he wasn't even part of the family. That's not how I do business.'

'I hear it all, Kerry,' Marty pleaded. 'And I'm proud of everything you say. Your father would be proud that finally you can live the dream he had for all of you. But why risk it right at the end by placing yourself in a situation where you could lose everything?'

Kerry said nothing for a moment, then she looked Marty in the eye.

'Because you know as well as I do that my father wouldn't have let someone loyal to him rot in jail if there was a chance that he could help.'

'Sure,' Marty said. 'I agree. But leave it to the lawyers, Kerry.'

Kerry didn't answer. She knew by the worried look on Marty's face that he realised he had lost the argument.

CHAPTER TWENTY-SIX

Hannah walked through the gates of the cemetery and stood for a moment in the silence, soft rain falling on her face as she looked up at the gloomy afternoon sky. She gazed along the path lined with headstones, grey and granite, all the way up to the high point where she knew her mother lay buried. She shuddered at the thought of her mother's beautiful face rotting away beneath the cold, damp earth. The last time Hannah had trudged this well-worn path had been just before the cops picked her up and charged her on suspicion of murder. She'd come here then, to stand by her mother's graveside, because in her heart she had nowhere else to go. She wasn't remorseful for killing one of the bastards who had planted the car bomb that killed her mother. Far from it. And she wasn't finished yet. She wasn't looking for some spiritual approval from her mother's grave, because she felt she had done the right thing. But there was just a need to be close to her and standing there remembering was as close as she could get.

Now, as Hannah walked up the path, her hands dug deep into the pockets of her raincoat, there was a heaviness in her chest that she had not felt for a very long time. Perhaps it was because she'd said goodbye to her father, or maybe the adrenalin-fuelled few weeks she'd had was wearing off, and loneliness was creeping in. Now that her father had gone, it underlined the feeling that she was adrift on her own. Six years in prison had seen many of her friends fall off the radar and fade away. Only one or two dropped her the occasional line or visited. It was the other prisoners who had become her friends, a kind of family, and she'd formed ties which had given her contacts on the outside if she needed anything. One of the women she'd grown close to was Jess Tomlin, serving eight years for plotting the murder of her husband so she could get her hands on his money. Jess had told her he was a no-good waster, who ran prostitution and people-trafficking rings, and had raked in a fortune selling girls on to gangmasters who would keep selling them on until they were worthless, or dead. Jess had shown her the scars on her back where he'd burned her with a red-hot poker after she'd set several girls free from a flat where they were being held and forced into prostitution. She'd said it was worth it, and that she'd planned her revenge from that moment. Her husband had been found riddled with bullets in a flat he'd used for secret rendezvous with his mistress. But someone along the line had grassed to the police that Jess was behind the murder. The killer was never found but Jess was convicted of conspiracy to murder – though not before she'd emptied her husband's bank accounts and stashed the money away. It was Jess who had given her a name to contact – Terry Colby – in London if she needed help, and Hannah had already been in touch with him. She'd asked him to check out the movements of Larry Townsend, the second-hand car dealer who ran two garages in Romford. Townsend had never been far from her thoughts all through her prison sentence. He was the second man who'd planted the bomb that killed her mother, and it was his brother Charlie that she'd thrown off the balcony. Payback for this bastard was long overdue.

As Hannah stood at the graveside she could see herself back in the moment when it all happened with her mother. She could hear the sirens, she could see the flashing lights of the fire engines and police cars as they arrived. She could see the burnt-out mangled wreckage of what was left of her mother's car as it lay smouldering in the rain. For those first few sleepless weeks after the emergency services picked up the remains of her mother from the ruins, those images were all she could see every time she closed her eyes. She was haunted by them, but even more haunted by the fact that it should have been *her* in the driving seat that morning. Hannah had been taking her mum out for lunch that day to get her out for the afternoon following a bout of flu. She'd just passed her driving test and had wanted to drive her mother's car, but her mother assured her she was fine and that she had to get back in the saddle, as she put it. She'd hated being under par, and lying low with any kind of ailment had never been part of her mum's make-up. She was always on the go, full of energy and determination. So Hannah had agreed, and as her mother went out to the car, she had gone into her bedroom to pick up her handbag. The explosion had shaken the whole house, windows blew out, and Hannah dived to the floor. Frozen with fear, she instinctively knew it was a bomb. She looked out of the window as shards of metal, that had been sent high into the air, cascaded back downwards, crashing onto the street. Then came the inferno as the tank exploded. Neighbours ran from their homes, and Hannah sprinted out of the house and through the thick black smoke. But she couldn't see her mother. There was nothing there, and as she was buckling over coughing and passing out, she felt strong arms dragging her back to safety. Then the police, ambulance and fire brigade arrived. Hannah could hear herself scream, 'Mum!' as she passed out.

Standing at the graveside, the horror flooded back as vivid as it had been that day, and Hannah felt the warm tears on her cheeks as she remembered her father's grey face when he arrived minutes later. She would never forget that. She had never even seen him cry. But this wasn't crying. He was wailing, piercing screams that brought him to his knees, neighbours weeping over him as they tried to comfort him. From then on, there was nothing left in Hannah's life but the quest for revenge.

Hannah had arranged to meet Terry Colby in the café close to her flat in Canary Wharf. She'd only been back in her home for a couple of days and hadn't ventured far, instead enjoying the quiet space to work out her next move. She hadn't been able to think of the future in any real sense, as all she'd been thinking about was how to go about this next business. She knew it was risky hooking up with this Terry Colby character as she didn't know him from Adam, but she trusted the word of her old prison mate Jess that he was sound and would look after her. Right now she didn't have a lot of options, and she didn't want to go recceing Townsend in case she was clocked. Aleksy, the Polish man who ran the café with his wife, had welcomed her with open arms when she walked in, and it had made her feel good to be back. The café was busy with lunchtime workers from the nearby offices, and she sat at the back facing the door, hoping she would recognise Colby from the customers coming in and queuing at the counter for takeaway food. She was on her second mug of tea by the time she checked her watch. He was already ten minutes late. Hannah tried not to let her heart sink. She had never been good at relying on others, and all her life if she'd wanted something done she'd done it herself. But she didn't want to make any mistakes this time in case she ended up back in jail. She sipped her tea and gazed through the windows as the sky cleared and the sun broke through the clouds. Whatever happened, she would deal with it, she decided. Her mobile pinged with a message and she pulled it out of her pocket. She smiled as an image of her father came up on her screen, sitting at a beachside bar raising a bottle of beer, the ocean glistening in the background. The caption read, 'Hurry up, sweetheart! I miss you! You're gonna love this place!' Hannah swallowed the lump in her throat and looked away from the screen towards the door. As she did, the door was pushed open and a tall figure in a tan suede bomber jacket walked in. She watched as he stood for a moment, his gaze sweeping the place as customers eased their way past him and out of the door. He didn't look like he was planning to join the queue. This had to be him. Then their eyes met and he gave her a long look and made his way across the café. He walked towards her, hands in the pockets of his jacket, his dark hair untidy and a couple of days' stubble on his cheeks, good-looking in a kind of rough but sexy way. Hannah immediately batted the thought away.

'Hannah?' He looked down at her, dark eyes questioning.

'Yep.' Hannah smiled up at him. 'Terry?'

'That's me,' he said, a half smile as he pulled a chair back and sat down.

'How you doing?' Hannah reached across the table and they shook hands. 'Thanks for coming.'

This was *her* show. His handshake was firm and warm. When they released, he smiled and sat back, his eyes locking hers as though he read the signs.

'Good to meet you,' he said. 'Any friend of Jess's an' all that . . .'

'You go back a long way, she told me,' Hannah said, feeling the need to get to know him a little.

'Oh yeah,' he said, smiling as he pushed a hand through black hair flecked with a little grey. 'Like a whole lifetime, me and Jess. We've been best of mates since we were about five years old – next-door neighbours in Bethnal Green – inseparable, we were.' He shook his head and looked at Hannah. 'How is she? I mean, how is she really in that fucking place?' He paused. 'When I go to visit her, I get this feeling that she's all full of the chat and stuff but I can see in her eyes what she must be going through. Know what I mean? The hurt and stuff. That's six years she's done now. Might be eligible for parole next year, so that's keeping her going. But it must be hard. It's a helluva long time to have been banged up in jail.'

Whatever else he was, Colby was a real friend, Hannah thought. Jess had told her that he was the only person who ever visited her in jail, and that all the fair-weather friends she had made over the years married to that bastard of a husband had melted away like snow off a dyke. But Colby was always there. She wondered if he was secretly in love with her.

'It is tough,' Hannah said. 'No doubt about that. But Jess is very resilient. I mean, when I got in there, I thought I would go nuts looking down the barrel of a six-year stretch, but I very quickly made friends with Jess. She was good to me. And you know, to be honest, I think I made more friends inside than I've ever had in my life.' She smiled. 'Christ! What does that say about me!'

He nodded. 'I can imagine though. Never been inside before myself, so I don't know. But I suppose you just got to rely on each other.' He paused as the waitress came and took their order. 'But well, you got through it, and I'm sure Jess will get there too.'

Hannah wondered if Colby was the killer who'd done Jess's husband, but as Jess had never mentioned who it was that pumped her brutal man full of bullets, she let the thought go.

'So,' she said, 'Larry Townsend. Let's talk about this bastard and look at what's next.'

'Okay,' he said. 'Here's the lowdown on everything I've got to know about him over the past couple of weeks.' He pulled his mobile out of his jacket pocket. 'I've got pictures an' all. I know his movements from the moment he leaves the house until he gets home at night. Sometimes he doesn't get home. Gets shacked up with some bird in Hackney.' He scrolled his screen and held it towards her to show a picture. 'That's the fucker there. He's a right coke-head. Dealing but putting plenty of his own stuff up his nose. Put it this way, it would be doing the world a favour getting rid of this piece of shit.'

Hannah nodded as the waitress put the cups on the table.

'Yep. And the sooner the better.'

CHAPTER TWENTY-SEVEN

It had taken some convincing, but Kerry knew nobody would stand in her way. She was the head of this family, and if she was hellbent on doing something nobody would stop her. So when she'd told Danny and Jack of her plan to go to London and confront Quentin Fairhurst the first thing they'd said was to talk to Marty Kane before making a move. When she told them she already had and he'd advised against it, they'd pleaded with her to think again. But she knew that they would accept her decision. Despite the warnings that she might end up in jail, Kerry had said it was her choice. She'd take the chance. In the end, she accepted their insistence to hook up with Billy Hill in London, who would look after her just in case anything happened. Billy had been an old associate of her father, and it was him who had shifted the Colombian's cocaine for the Caseys, in return for a cut of the profits and a small stake in their Costa del Sol hotel.

Billy had picked her up at Heathrow Airport in his blacked-out chauffeur-driven Merc and driven her to the Mayfair hotel. They'd gone for coffee in the hotel lounge once she'd checked in, and they sat opposite each other with the fake wall fire glowing and crackling.

'So are you doing all right, Kerry?' he said, glancing at her stomach. 'I mean, health-wise and stuff, with you being pregnant an' all?'

'Yes.' Kerry was a little amused at Billy's frank question. 'I'm feeling well enough so far.'

'Great stuff. That was a right scare down in Manchester though, with you getting shot. We was all worried sick about you.'

'Thanks, Billy,' Kerry said, feeling touched at his kind words. But she wanted the conversation away from her. 'So you've just about retired now? Putting your feet up, are you?'

Billy had made a small fortune from selling on the cocaine the Caseys snatched from the Colombians, and he was now almost out of the business altogether. As agreed at the time he had a share in the Caseys' hotel complex over on the Costa del Sol, but he was very much in the background.

'More or less, Kerry,' he said. 'But I'm looking forward to the hotel being finished. Might spend a bit more time at my place on the Costa del Sol playing a bit of golf and relaxing. I think the hotel is going to be a massive success for you. And fair dos to you for pushing it all the way. Your old dad would be proud.'

Kerry smiled. 'I think so. We've a bit to go yet. But Sharon tells me that the property and restaurants we bought up over there are beginning to look really good on the books.' She paused, thinking how lovely it would be to be living in the sunshine with her baby. 'I might even end up over there myself in time. I like the idea of bringing up my baby in a different world to where we are now. I spent a lot of time there as a teenager, so I still miss it a lot.' Kerry drank her tea, trying to picture how life would be, but her heart was sinking because she still didn't know if Vinny would be a part of it.

'So,' Billy said, 'what do you want me to do when you go to see this politician geezer? I must admit, I'd love to be a fly on the wall when you slap those DVDs and pictures down in front of him.' He gave her a roguish smile. 'Fucking bigger criminals than the rest of us, these bastards. An' that's the truth.'

'Yep,' Kerry said. 'It sure is.' She wanted to confront Fairhurst on her own. 'I think it would be best if you are somewhere not too close. I mean, if he does agree to meet me, then I want it to be just him and me. He knows me from way back, so I'm hoping he'll agree to meet me for a coffee or something. I'm going to make contact with his office in a little while. I'd like to do this today, if it's possible. But I think it's best if you're not around when I actually meet him.'

'Sure.' Billy nodded. 'We'll work it out once we know.

Whatever you think is best.' He wagged a finger. 'But if there is a sniff that the old Bill are going to come and cart you off, then I'll be ready to do a runner with you.'

Kerry found herself smiling at Billy's cheeky charm.

'Let's hope it doesn't come to that.'

Later, Kerry was in her room, lying back on the pillows, checking her laptop to make sure the phone number she was about to ring was the correct one. She'd used one of her old legal contacts to give her the best number at the Westminster offices where she could hope to track down Fairhurst. She swung her legs out of the bed and stood up, crossing the room to the window where the traffic snaked up Mayfair. It was now or never. She didn't feel nervous, but was focused and ready. She scrolled down to the number and pressed the keypad. The clipped tones of a woman answered 'Department of the Attorney General's office.'

'Hello,' Kerry said. 'I'd like to speak to Mr Fairhurst please.'

There was a short pause and Kerry could picture the indignation on the face of the secretary who probably protected her bosses like an armed soldier.

'Who is this please?'

'My name is Kerry Casey.'

'From where?'

'It's a personal call,' Kerry said, in tones just as clipped.

'Oh. Is Mr Fairhurst expecting it?'

'Perhaps you could just let him know that Kerry Casey is on the phone and would like to speak to him.'

'Are you from the media? Because there is a media office.'

'No. I'm a lawyer. Mr Fairhurst knows me.'

Pause.

'And may I tell him what this is in connection with?'

'No. You may not.'

Pause. Kerry could feel the mounting frustration of the overprotective PA. Eventually she spoke.

'If you hold on, I'll see if Mr Fairhurst is in the building.'

Kerry rolled her eyes. Clearly Fairhurst was in the building and was probably only a few feet away from her in his office. She hung on, half expecting her to come back and ask for more details. But to her surprise it was a male voice that came down the line.

'Kerry Casey.' The voice was laced with sarcasm. 'Can this be *the* Kerry Casey?'

'The only one I know, Mr Fairhurst.'

'Well, well, Kerry. The last time I saw you was in a court case a million years ago. As I recall, you left a little huffy about losing, dear girl.'

'Glad you remember me then,' Kerry said, deadpan. 'It was a long time ago, but I still remember it very well.'

'Hmm,' he said. 'So to what do I owe the honour of your call, Kerry? Surely you're not in trouble with the law, are you?'

She could hear him almost chuckle.

'No. Not at all.'

'It's just that your name popped up, strangely enough, when some of the people here were looking at criminal empires throughout the country, and newspaper cuttings were on my desk about the Casey family. Now run by Kerry Casey. Surely that can't be you.'

Kerry hadn't expected this. The last thing she thought was that he would know anything about her, as she'd disappeared from his radar such a long time ago.

'Well, you can't believe everything you read in the papers, as you know.'

'Yes. Quite. But is that you? That Kerry Casey? A criminal family in Glasgow?'

He was toying with her, and she knew if he'd been given intelligence on her for whatever reason, then he would know it was her unless there was another Kerry Casey running a criminal empire who was a lawyer.

'It is a family business. Far from what is written in the press.'

'I'll take your word on that, Kerry,' he said. 'I did always think you were an honest girl, and if I may say so, chucked in at the deep end in that court case where you and I went a few rounds together.'

'It was a difficult case,' she said. 'And sad how it ended, but that's another matter. I—'

He interrupted. 'So, Kerry. What can I do for you?'

'I wondered if we could perhaps meet up for a chat and a drink. I'm in London passing through on my way further south to meet friends, and I wanted to run something past you.'

There was an ominous silence.

'Kerry, do forgive me, but you could hardly say we were the kind of friends who run anything past each other. I don't even know you. You didn't even accept my invitation to dinner that day after the court case, and to be honest, had you done that, it could have been the start of a great new career for you. I saw something in you as we battled in that court case. You lost, but that was it. You had some mettle about you, that's for sure. But I don't see how I would want you to run something past me. Are you looking for legal advice? Surely you have plenty of associates for that?'

Kerry let it hang for a moment. Then she spoke.

'No. Not legal advice. But I have some information that I think you would like to be aware of.'

'What kind of information? Is it a matter for the police?'

'I'm not sure.'

'Now you are intriguing me.'

'So will you meet me? Even for a coffee or a drink. As I say, I have something that I think you should know about.'

'What kind of something?'

'I don't want to say over the phone. Seriously. This is important for you. If it's possible we could meet briefly in the next day?'

'I'm going away tomorrow for the weekend – a family thing. Long planned. I'm not free really.'

'How about this afternoon? Early evening?'

'God, you're a pushy lady, are you not?'

'As I say, I think this is important for you.'

She heard him sigh, and then a long moment of silence before he finally answered.

'Okay. Just for sheer intrigue. I'll meet you in Westminster at five thirty. There's a decent wine bar across the bridge – the Red Lion. I only have a half hour, so whatever you have to tell me has to be brief. I honestly am not even sure if I should be doing this, but I'm remembering you now quite vividly and how lively you looked that day, and how sad too. Okay, for old times' sake and all that, I can spare you half an hour.'

'Fine. I'll be there.'

Kerry hung up before he could say any more. Christ. That was as bizarre a conversation as she'd ever had. She knew she was flying by the seat of her pants, calling Fairhurst up out of the blue like that, but it was a case of trying to make contact. It couldn't be done through a third party, and what she had to tell him had to be done with just her and him in the room. She almost smiled to herself, thinking of his arrogance, and how the bastard was so ego-driven that he probably entertained the notion that she was propositioning him. How wrong he was.

*

Billy Hill picked Kerry up from her hotel and drove her to Westminster. They arrived early as Billy wanted to case the place first, and make sure he could grab himself a seat near to where Kerry would be, though far enough away so that he didn't attract any attention. The pub was off Westminster Bridge in a side street, shaded and quiet, but with a few leftover lunchtime people or early evening people in for a drink. The long mahogany bar was more like a bodega with wines from all over the world and food on the counter. Kerry chose a spot where she could see anyone coming in the front door. Billy was across from her, three tables away, on a comfy chair reading a copy of *The Times*. With his silver hair and in his pinstripe suit he looked as though he could be one of the old lords over from the House for a spot of lunch and a break. Kerry ordered some sparkling mineral water and a pot of tea. She looked at her watch. It was almost five thirty. It was growing dark outside, the place was getting busier, but there was still a clear view from where she was sitting. She thought of Sharon, and how when she'd told her of her plan, she'd said how much she'd love to have had a ringside seat for the showdown. She checked her watch again and looked at the door as three men came in one after another. They all looked like civil servants or lawyers, the dark suits of the grey men she'd seen in courtrooms and offices when she worked as a lawyer. But one of them was middle-aged, tall, handsome, with a hint of a tan, and wavy dark-silver hair slicked perfectly.

Quentin Fairhurst. Game on. Kerry got to her feet as she could see him looking around the room. Then he saw her. He turned to the men who were with him and said something – they went to the bar and he strode across the room towards her. Kerry knew she should feel nervous but she didn't. It was like one of those moments when she'd been anxious before a case, and then as she stepped into a courtroom or stood up to address a jury the nerves just slipped away. She was ready for this. Fairhurst stretched out a hand as he reached her, a smile on his face.

'Well, well,' he said, shaking her hand warmly as he flicked a glance up and down her body. Kerry had dressed in a black wool sweater and skirt and long boots as she'd known he would do this – she remembered him being a lecherous bastard. 'The famous Kerry Casey. And don't you just look lovely. In fact even lovelier than I remember you. And you with your own empire, as the papers say.'

'Flattery,' she said, 'will get you everywhere. And as I told you, don't believe everything you read about me.' She paused and looked him in the eye. 'Quentin Fairhurst. After all these years. Who'd have thought we'd be in a London pub together just a stone's throw from where you run your own little empire across the bridge.'

They both smiled at each other but it was the ready-to-pounce smile of wolves eyeing each other up to see who was ready to attack first.

'Let's have a bottle of wine,' he said. 'I've had a bloody

long day.' He waved the waiter over. 'And Kerry, genuinely. I'm glad to see you. You look fantastic. How about a nice bottle of Sancerre?'

'Please, not for me. I'm only on the water. I've a busy day tomorrow, lots of travelling and some people to see later.'

'Oh, that's a pity. And since you dragged me out here with this intrigue, I was looking forward to having a few drinks with you, maybe even organise dinner if you're up to it.'

'We'll see,' she said. 'If not tonight, then another. No alcohol for me today though. But you feel free. Seriously.' She thought that he'd need a stiff drink once she dropped the bomb in front of him.

The wine arrived in a sweating bucket of ice and the waiter opened it and poured a small glass out for Fairhurst which he took. Fairhurst then directed the waiter to take the bottle to his colleagues across the room in the corner. When he'd gone, Fairhurst put the glass to his lips and took a decent glug. Kerry noticed his wedding ring and manicured fingernails. His suit had dark pinstripes and was topped off with a crisp white shirt, pale blue tie and highly polished black Oxford shoes.

'So, Kerry,' he said, 'I just want to say that, well, I know it was a very long time ago, but I did feel for you and the family in that court case. Sometimes it happens like that. Sometimes a case falls and one feels that it should not have happened. You fought a very brave and hard case. I have huge respect for you for that.'

'I should have won though. You know that. The witness who was on our side suddenly turned and nobody could explain that. It seemed wrong.'

He looked her in the eye.

'Yes, but that can happen sometimes too, for all sorts of reasons. But the way we live is that we get on with it after the verdict. That's how it is. '

'I know,' she said. 'And I accepted that.'

'But you never fought another case like that again. I checked you out and couldn't understand it. You were doing conveyancing, divorces – all that crap. You're better than that, Kerry. You had integrity.'

She shrugged. 'I still have integrity, Quentin. But I just got disillusioned.'

'Poor show, really. You could have gone all the way.'

'Like you?'

'Yes, if you want to put it like that. It's all about determination, picking yourself up and driving on. That's what got me where I am now.'

'In a very powerful position. The most powerful position.'

Kerry stopped herself there and could see he was eying her suspiciously.

'So, what is this important information you want to impart to me?'

Kerry clasped her hands in front of her on the table and leaned forward.

'A man called Vic Paterson. He's in jail on remand. Major

cocaine haul. You'll know all about it because there is an extradition battle going on with Spain as they want to prosecute him over there.'

He narrowed his eyes, his brain ticking over.

'Hmmm. Yes. I know of the case. Not reached me yet in any major way. It's with the Director of Public Prosecutions. But the man is in jail – Belmarsh, I believe. We'll be claiming that one, all right. No way are the Spaniards getting the glory on it.' He paused. 'But what's your point?'

'Vic Paterson is a friend of my family. And he's innocent.'

He put down his glass and chuckled.

'Oh yes, I'm sure he is. Same as the rest of them who pitch up to the UK with a cargo of drugs. What the bloody hell, Kerry? Am I really here to talk about a bloody criminal? Please tell me you are joking.'

'No. I'm not joking, Quentin. Vic Paterson is not guilty of this.'

'Yes. Then he'll have a chance to defend himself in a British Court. So your point is?'

'It's up to you.'

'What do you mean it is up to me?'

Kerry reached into her bag and pulled out the white envelope. She put her hand inside, took out one of the black and white photos and looked over her shoulder and around before sliding it face down across the table to him, face down. He looked at her, his face like flint. Then he picked it up and turned it over. Kerry watched as the colour drained from his face. He twisted his neck a little and kept staring at the photo as though in disbelief, or perhaps remembering the actual scene. He said nothing. Now she was pushing across the second photo. It was of the Home Secretary and some young girls. He picked it up, again, his face impassive, but she could see the muscle in his cheek tighten. His tongue darted out to moisten dry lips. She could see him breathing harder. Then the third picture of the money changing hands. He picked it up, stared at it unblinking. Then he put all of them down on the table.

'There's a DVD too that you're the star of. Do you want to see it? The Russian gangster who is handing over the money is a man called Anatoly. But I'm sure you know that.'

Kerry watched as he didn't answer. He picked up his drink and threw it back, taking a breath through flared nostrils, the colour back in his face now, looking red and intense. He leaned across to her and whispered, 'You're trying to fucking blackmail me with staged pics, you little, lowlife vixen?'

Kerry didn't answer but held his gaze and their faces were so close to each other she got a whiff of the Sancerre on his breath.

'Not staged, Quentin. I think you know that.'

He took a breath, his lips tight.

'One phone call and you'll be in a bloody cell in half an hour. You are actually attempting to blackmail a member of the British government. Are you seriously that naive?'

Kerry spread her hands.

'I'm just letting you know that these photographs are out there.'

'Where did you get them?'

'I understand they were stolen from some strongboxes during the diamond heist. I've no doubt this is the first time you've seen them. But, your Russian your mate Anatoly is all over the place looking for them. He's got some sidekick called Yuri rattling a few cages.'

'I don't know what the fuck you are talking about. I don't know any Russian, and I know these pics are staged.'

'But they're not. You can see the date on them, when they were taken. They're all provable. In a court of law if it should come to that.'

He sat for a long moment saying nothing, then his shoulders sagged.

'And what do you want?'

'Vic Paterson's release. On a technicality. That's up to you. You're good with technicalities.'

'Not a chance.'

'It's up to you.'

'I can call my colleagues over and they will have you arrested right now.'

'Go ahead. These aren't the only copies, by the way.'

He fixed his tie in his jacket, finished his drink and leaned forward.

'I know what you are, where you came from, you bloody

gangster. You're a fucking criminal, and you think you can come down here from that shithole in Glasgow where you run drugs and protection rackets, and threaten to shake the corridors of power? You are in for a shock. A huge shock.'

Kerry gave him her best bored look.

'You won't have much time to make up your mind, Quentin. So I'm going to give you a day or so to talk to your mate, the Director of Public Prosecution, who I'm sure will be guided by your advice. It's up to you.'

'You're going to jail for a very long time.'

'Fine,' Kerry said. 'We can write to each other, because you'll be there too, you snooty prick.'

Fairhurst stood up and turned his back on her. She watched as he went across to his minions enjoying the wine and they immediately stood up. They were out of the pub in two seconds as Kerry sat and pushed out a very long sigh, then caught the eye of Billy Hill. He got up and went across to her.

'Looks like you played a blinder there, Kerry. Now let's get out of here before the cops arrive to arrest you.'

Kerry stood up, squared her shoulders and marched out of the bar. That had all felt much better than she'd even imagined.

CHAPTER TWENTY-EIGHT

The pub in Romford was filling up with the Friday night crowd, either on their way to clubs later or in for a drink after dinner. The music was blaring and the lights low. It was three deep at the bar. Hannah and Colby had followed Townsend from his showroom down the road to the bar. They'd sat in Colby's car as Townsend's Merc pulled up and he'd climbed out of the passenger side. They'd watched as the burly doormen shook his hand like he was some kind of big shot. Townsend stood with them for a moment, smoking a fag and sharing a joke that appeared to have them all in stitches. From where Hannah was sitting he looked as if he was high as a kite. They waited a few minutes after he went inside, then got out of their car and walked across to the pub.

The place was bouncing. At one side of the bar was a hen party with a gang of girls, barely wearing dresses, tottering on heels and done up to the nines. They were passing a giant penis balloon from one to the other, hooting with laughter. Most of the tables were full of guys out for the night, suited and booted, drinking beers and shots, alternately eyeing up the totty at the bar and turning to check out newcomers every time the swing doors opened, admitting another battery of revellers. Hannah and Colby managed to find a free podium table close to the window where they could stand and observe Townsend at a distance at the bar. His jacket was off by now, his tie loosened and his sleeves rolled up as he and the guys that surrounded him drank from bottles of Moët in silver ice buckets. The DJ at the far side of the room was playing thumping music so loud Hannah could hardly hear herself think. Six years in jail must have aged her, because she couldn't imagine herself willingly going into a place like this in a million years. She told Colby she would go to the bar, and squeezed her way through the throng. She was dressed in a tight black dress that showed off her curves, a leather biker jacket and black ankle boots. She gradually eased her way down to the end of the bar where Townsend was holding court around a podium along with three or four blokes who hung on his every word. She hoped to catch his eye. Once she was a couple of feet away, she glanced in his direction and saw that he was staring at her. She locked eyes with him just for a second and pulled a bit of a smile as she eased her way through two men and squeezed up to the bar. The bar staff were rushed off their feet, and they were all over the place trying to serve. She stood next to the group of blokes who had let her squeeze in between them and could sense they were eyeing her up. One of them was standing a little too close for comfort and she could feel him slightly pushing himself against her. From the corner of her eye she saw his mates sniggering.

Hannah turned around slowly so that her lips were at the bloke's ear. 'You try that one more time and you'll get a boot in the fucking balls, mate.'

The guy's face fell and he blushed a little, then stepped back.

'Sorry, darlin'. Was just trying to get to know you.'

Hannah glared at him, then turned to the bar where she finally caught the eye of a barman. She ordered two large gin and tonics. While she waited to be served, she dug twenty quid out of her bag and stood, keeping her distance from the blokes. Suddenly, Townsend was at her side, as the barman slid the drinks across to her.

'Let me get that for you, miss.' Townsend took a fifty quid note out of his trouser pocket.

She turned and looked him in the eye, for a moment not knowing quite what to say. She hadn't expected this.

'Thank you,' she said. 'That's very kind of you, but I'm okay to pay for my own drinks. I'm over there with my friend.'

Townsend ignored her as she attempted to hand the money over, and the barman also ignored her and took his money.

'It's just a drink, sweetheart. No problem.' He turned to glare at the men standing close, who took a step back. 'I just thought maybe you needed a bit of taking care of, with all them lads looking like they were horned up next to you.'

Hannah smiled. 'Thanks. But I can take care of myself.' She took her drinks from the bar. 'And thanks for the drinks.' She nodded across to where Colby was standing but not looking at her. 'I'm here with my friend.'

Townsend glanced over, then back at her.

'Oh, right. That your old man then, love?'

'A friend,' she said.

Townsend moved back a little but not far enough for her to squeeze past him.

'I've not seen you here before,' he said. Then looking around the bar, he added, 'And among all the birds in here, you look a cut above the rest. I can tell.'

Hannah gave her best coy smile.

'Well, thank you kindly.'

She moved to get past him.

'Look, er . . . I'm Larry. Nice to meet you.'

'Emma,' she said.

'Emma. Lovely to meet you. Like a breath of fresh air in here. Tell me. You don't live round here, do you?'

'No. Just visiting.'

'Okay. Enjoy your drink.' He was about to turn away, when he touched her shoulder. 'Listen. Do you fancy having a drink some time? Dinner maybe? Lunch?'

Hannah tried to look taken aback.

'Larry. I don't even know you. Thanks. But no thanks. Now, I'd best get back.'

'Okay.' He fished out a business card from his jacket pocket. 'Here's my number. If you're ever in the mood for some good nosh and champagne and a few laughs, give me a shout. I'd love to get to know you a bit more. That's my place – car showroom. I sell top quality, I do.'

She took his card and slipped it into her bag.

'Thanks. I'll keep that in mind. I've been away for a while, and now that I'm back I might be in the market for a decent car,' she said enthusiastically. 'Enjoy your night, and thanks for the drink.'

Polite but firm. She could see that Townsend wasn't used to birds knocking him back like this. And Hannah knew he was hooked right in.

As they drove away from the bar, Colby turned to Hannah from the driving seat. She clocked his eyes swiftly take in everything from her cleavage to her ankles.

'He was watching you all the way across the room,' Colby said. 'You definitely pulled there, mate.'

She stared straight ahead. Somewhere just under her focus on the job in hand, Hannah felt a little twinge of desire for Colby after he'd looked at her the way he did. But she would leave it at that. She hoped he wasn't about to say he couldn't blame Townsend for fancying her, because that was not a conversation she wanted to have right now. Colby was here to help her nail this bastard, not flirt. But despite that, she liked that he noticed her.

'Yeah,' Hannah said. 'I think he took the bait all right. He's the kind of arsehole who probably just clicks his fingers and the girls fall at his feet. That's the impression I got.' She turned to Colby, half smiling. 'But I was cool with him.'

Colby smiled and he shot her a sly sideways glance.

'Yep. That would ramp it up a bit,' he said. 'You didn't give him your number, did you?'

'No. But he gave me his card.' Hannah opened her handbag and pulled out the business card. 'Says he sells top quality gear. I told him I might be looking for a decent car.'

Colby chuckled. 'Oh, well done! But I'd bet his cars are about as top quality as the shitty coke he pushes, no doubt.' He turned into the main road back to London. 'So what now? You going to call him tonight?'

'No,' Hannah said. 'Not tonight. That would be too soon. He's getting jagged up in there on Moët with his mates, so I'll let him simmer a little then I can plan it properly.'

Colby nodded, then turned to her.

'So. What now? Are you going home, or have you got any plans for tonight?'

Hannah couldn't help but smile.

'Oh, yeah,' she said. 'Course I have. After six years in the nick, my life on the outside is just a social whirl.'

For a moment they said nothing, and Hannah was

wishing she hadn't said that. And she hoped Colby hadn't picked up the hint of desolation in her voice. The truth was she was all dressed up with absolutely nowhere to go. She was on her own. She could go back to the empty flat, but somehow it underlined her loneliness more than ever. She could get a takeaway and watch the lights across the river spreading across the city, while drinking enough wine to make her want to sleep.

'Look,' Colby cleared his throat. 'If you've no plans, do you fancy having a bit of dinner? I know a great little Greek place not that far from my flat in Fulham. Food is none too shabby.'

She turned to him.

'You have a flat in Fulham? You selling top quality cars too?' she joked.

They both chortled and the atmosphere was suddenly lightened.

'Yeah. Well. Believe it or not, my old grandad left me it in his will when he popped his clogs five years ago. He bought it when he was in his twenties and Fulham wasn't the haunt of the rich Tory boys it is now. My grandad was a bespoke tailor. Trained in Savile Row when he was a nipper and branched out on his own. Made a lot of money, he did.'

Hannah was surprised and intrigued that Colby had a background like that. She'd assumed he was from a hard upbringing, same as his mate Jess.

'Oh, right,' she said. 'Fascinating. So what you doing on

the wrong side of the tracks, if you don't mind me asking?'

'No. Course not. Funny old life,' he said. 'Why don't we go for a bite to eat and I'll tell you a few stories?'

'You got nothing else to do?' She paused, cursing herself. 'Sorry. I don't mean that the way it came out.' She wasn't doing very well in the flirtation stakes here, even if she wasn't supposed to be trying.

Colby shrugged. 'Sure,' he said. 'I've got a few things I could be doing, but I'd prefer this. You and me, having a decent bit of nosh and a laugh. You're good company, you are, Hannah. Not what I expected.'

Hannah laughed. 'Oh. What did you expect?'

'Dunno really. Some angry bird, all bitter and stuff after six years in the nick.'

Hannah pushed back her hair and smiled.

'Oh. I give good bitter, actually, if truth be told.' She smiled. 'I love Greek food though. Dinner it is then. And you can tell me a few stories. I might have a few to tell as well.'

Something akin to butterflies pulsed in her stomach. She was feeling out of her depth in male company after all those years in jail, and she didn't quite know how to handle it. *Just go with the flow for the moment*, she told herself. *Relax. It's only dinner. He's only being kind.*

'Great.' Colby turned onto the main road and headed for the dual carriageway and back into the city.

*

Zorba's restaurant was pretty, in vivid shades of cobalt blue and white, like the kind of Cretan tavernas where Hannah remembered spending lazy afternoons and long nights in what now seemed like another life. A huge mural of a turquoise blue sea crashing onto a sun-kissed beach adorned the main wall, and just the sight of it brought a flood of memories back to her, when life had seemed full of possibilities and endless fun. They were shown to a small table in a whitewashed alcove at the far end of the restaurant where the lighting was low and cosy. It was beginning to feel like a date, Hannah thought, and much as she wanted to keep any of that nonsense out of proceedings, she couldn't help but enjoy how at ease Colby was in her company. It was obvious he was used to wining and dining women, and as he sat back and rolled up the sleeves of his crisp, white linen shirt, Hannah hoped he hadn't noticed her running an eye over him. When the waiter came they ordered a couple of gin and tonics to kick off, and a bottle of wine with dinner. When the drinks arrived, Colby raised his glass.

'To freedom,' he said, clinking Hannah's glass. 'And to you for surviving.'

Hannah smiled. 'And to absent friends,' she said.

Colby nodded. 'Yeah. When Jess gets out, we should have a night together.'

'I'd like that,' Hannah said.

By the time they'd got through the starters and were onto the red wine, Hannah was beginning to feel relaxed and was enjoying Colby's company. If it wasn't for the fact that they had earlier been recceing a man whose days were numbered, then they would have looked like any ordinary couple on a night out. But Hannah was acutely aware that she had a job to do. She took out her mobile, and Townsend's business card, and keyed in the number.

'You phoning him now?' Colby looked surprised.

'No. Texting him,' Hannah replied, keying in a message. 'Keeping him interested. I'm just saying it was nice to meet him, and hope he's enjoying his night.'

Colby smiled. 'Bet he texts you back and asks where you are.'

Seconds later, Hannah's mobile pinged, and she smiled as she turned the screen around to show him the message: 'Where are you?'

'You've obviously done this before,' she joked.

Colby laughed. 'No,' he said. 'Would never be that direct, but dicks like Townsend – that's all they know. Steam right in there. No class.'

Hannah didn't look up from her phone as she answered her text, then turned the screen to Colby. Her message read: 'Having dinner with my friend.'

Colby sat back and folded his arms. He lifted his glass to his lips and smiled. Hannah's mobile pinged again, and she read it out.

'"Enjoy your night. Would be good to see you again soon. You're one hot woman".' Hannah chuckled.

'Very subtle,' Colby said. 'Don't be surprised if he sends you a picture of his cock before the night's out.'

'Perish the thought.' Hannah laughed and took a sip of her drink.

A couple of moments later, her mobile pinged again, and this time it was a message asking to meet her. Hannah texted him back and told him she'd get in touch very soon.

'That should keep him panting,' Colby said.

Hannah then put her phone on silent and slipped it back in her bag.

'Okay. Well that's cooking along quite nicely.' She sat forward, looking at Colby. 'So. You were going to tell me a few stories. What about your grandad and your family? I thought you and Jess were brought up on the council estate?'

'Yeah,' Colby said. 'We were. In the same block of flats. My old grandad disowned my mum when she got pregnant with me because she refused to marry the boy who'd put her up the duff. So she went off on her own, and scraped a living working as an office cleaner and a million other shit jobs to make ends meet.'

'And did your grandad never see you even after you were born?'

'No. He was one of those old bastards who would never admit he might have been wrong. It broke my mum's heart, it did. She got in touch with him from time to time, sent him pictures of me, you know, my first day in school, my first communion – all that crap. But the old fucker never even replied. So by the time I was a teenager, she just stopped contacting him. Completely lost touch.'

'What about your grandmother?'

'She died when my mum was a teenager, before she got pregnant. So he was on his own.'

Hannah watched as Colby downed the rest of his wine and refilled their glasses. He was telling the story in a matter-of-fact way, but beneath the slight bravado, she could see it had hurt him.

'Were you never tempted to get in touch with him, as you got older?'

Colby was silent for a moment, and Hannah knew she had touched a raw nerve. He shrugged and suddenly looked sad.

'Yeah. My mum died suddenly. Heart attack about six years back. Pretty awful really, and she was only fifty-one. Maybe as she'd got older she might have tried to get in touch with him again, but she never got the chance. So, the day before the funeral, I went to his house and knocked on the door.' He shook his head. 'Who knows what I was thinking. I suppose I just wanted to let him know that his daughter was dead, and I actually wanted to tell him he was an old cunt for just shutting us out of his life. But when he answered the door, none of that happened. I could see straight away that he knew who I was – you know, from the photos and stuff years earlier – he would know.

But he didn't even invite me in. I told him that his daughter had died and the funeral was the next day. He fucking just stood there, seemed like for ages, perfectly still, saying nothing. Kind of gazing into middle distance. Then a fucking tear came out of the old bastard's eye, and he nodded his head and said, okay, and stepped back in the house and shut the door on my face.'

'Jesus! That's awful,' Hannah stopped herself from reaching across the table to touch his hand because she could see calling up the memory was painful to him.

Colby sighed. 'Yeah. It was. You know what? I actually cried after I walked away that night. It was like – here was this man who I didn't even know, who I'd never even met, and yet I wanted to go back and put my arms around him because I could see he was hurting. But at the same time I wanted to shout at him for being such a bastard to my mother, pushing her out like that.' He took a breath and shook his head. 'Anyway. He never turned up at the funeral, and I never saw him again, until the lawyers contacted me and said he was dead and he'd left me his flat. There was no letter from him or anything, just the word "Sorry" in a document he had given them. Christ almighty! Talk about stubborn old fucker!'

'That's such a sad story, Colby,' Hannah said.

Colby ran a hand through his hair and squared his shoulders a little, as though shaking off the ghosts.

'Yeah, well. All part of the shit life throws at us, isn't it.

And here we are.' He took a breath. 'Anyway. You've had a bit of a raw deal yourself, I'm sure.'

Hannah nodded. 'Yes. Though it was a good life until my mum got killed. All kind of fell apart a lot for my dad after that. And for me. You know the story.' She looked at him. 'And the story continues, as you see.'

Colby drained the last of the wine into their glasses, and signalled to the waiter for the bill.

'We can split this,' Hannah said, smiling. 'It's not like it was a date.'

Colby laughed. 'No, no. Let me buy you dinner to celebrate your freedom.' He locked her with his dark eyes. 'Tell you what though, Hannah. It was a good night. Sorry for going on about my sob-story background, but you did ask.'

'Not at all,' Hannah said. 'It says a lot about you.'

'Yeah?' Again his eyes met hers. 'And what does it say?'

'Well. When I first met you, I thought you were a Jack-the-lad kind of figure, but there's more to you.' She paused. 'It's been good to get to know you a bit. And the food here beats that old prison grub by a country mile.'

Hannah looked at her watch. She knew Colby's flat was nearby, so she wanted to make sure she wasn't in a situation where she'd be invited in for coffee – or anything else – even though the idea of it might have been fine in any other situation.

'I'll need to get a cab back across to my flat,' Hannah said. 'I'll just flag one outside.'

Colby looked at her a little too long, and she waited for him to say something. But he didn't.

'Sure,' he said, and paid the bill in cash. 'Let's go then.'

Outside, they stood in air that felt cold and crisp after the warmth of the restaurant and atmosphere. Hannah zipped up her jacket against the chill. Colby stood, hands in the pockets of his jacket, and for a few moments they stood gazing at each other in silence. Then he looked beyond her.

'Here's a cab. I'll flag it down for you. Do you want me to come with you? Make sure you get in safe? I mean, after what you told me about the guy in the flat the day you got out of jail.'

Hannah was sorely tempted, but she smiled.

'Nah, you're all right. I'll be back in no time. And thanks for dinner. It was a lovely night, and I haven't had one of them for a long time.'

'Sure,' he said. 'I enjoyed it too. You give me a shout tomorrow, once you talk to old lover boy then, will you?'

Hannah smiled as the taxi drew into the kerbside.

'I will.'

Colby opened the door of the cab, and as she went to get in, he leaned across and pecked her on the cheek, and gave her a one-armed kind of hug. It took her by surprise and it was over in a second, but long enough for her to catch the scent of him and feel his skin on hers.

'Text me when you're home safe, Hannah, will you?'

She didn't answer, and got into the cab and gave him the

thumbs up. But before she was a hundred yards down the road a wave of loneliness washed over her, and part of her wished everything could be so different, that she wasn't going home alone, that she had gone to the Cayman Islands with her father. And part of her wished that she wasn't planning revenge on a complete stranger. But she shook herself from the gloom by the time the taxi pulled up outside her building.

CHAPTER TWENTY-NINE

Hannah stepped out onto the terrace of her flat overlooking the Thames. She shivered a little in the chill as she stood gazing out at the fading late-afternoon light. She checked her watch. Colby would be picking her up shortly to take her out to Larry Townsend's car showroom in Romford. When she'd phoned Townsend yesterday, she'd told him she was keen to have a look at some of his cars. She'd bitten her tongue as she'd listened to his used-car-salesman bullshit, immediately reeling off models that would suit a 'gorgeous woman' like her. Christ, he was such a prick! He told her not to worry about a deposit, and that he could arrange finance pronto. Then he'd been silent for a couple of beats after Hannah told him she would pay cash. She could almost see him salivating. This was easier than she thought. So why was she suddenly feeling a little depressed? she asked herself. She'd waited six years for this payback. Six years. All the time she'd been in jail, it was revenge that had kept her going. She had never felt any remorse over shoving the bastard's brother to his death. She'd paid lip service to the social workers and shrinks who worked with prisoners to rehabilitate them; telling them she regretted what she'd done – but it was all a lie, because she'd never regretted it, not even once. And the moment they'd opened the doors to freedom, she'd known this was where she wanted to be – seeking revenge. Once this was over, she could start to live again. It was just nerves, she told herself, that were making her have this nagging self-doubt that had suddenly begun flooding her head in the middle of the night. She hadn't slept well and had woken up with a blinding headache. But she'd gone for a four mile run along the river, and by the time she'd got back, the thoughts had gone. She pushed them away again now. Today would be the only chance she had to put this behind her. She heard her mobile pinging, went back into the lounge and picked it up from the coffee table. It was a text from Colby. He was outside. She took her handbag from the sofa and opened it, checking the small pistol for the umpteenth time to make sure it was loaded and ready. Colby had acquired it and given it to her. She'd decided not to share with him the drama of Amsterdam, and the fact that she was totally comfortable handling a gun. She slung the bag over her shoulder, left the flat and got into the lift in the hallway, then walked out of the front door. As she climbed into the passenger seat of

Colby's car, she saw him eyeing her short denim skirt and tight black top.

'You ready for action then?'

She shot him a confident glance.

'Yep. Ready as I'll ever be.' She said it more to convince herself than him.

The car showroom was just as tacky as Hannah had imagined, and both she and Colby burst out laughing as they drove past to have a quick look at the set-up. Above the massive glass frontage was the bright red gigantic sign, *Larry's*. Then some lavish dots and another fancy sign: *The only car dealer you will ever need.* Jesus! But, surprisingly, there were a few classy-looking BMWs and Mercs on the forecourt, and a couple of big blacked-out SUVs – so his clientele were more high-end than the average punter looking for an old Ford Focus with low mileage at a bargain price. Colby pulled the car into the kerbside just a short walk from the showroom. As he switched off the engine, he turned to her.

'You all right, Hannah?' Colby said. 'You've not said much on the journey.'

Hannah glanced at him then out of the windscreen. She didn't want to have a conversation.

'I'm good,' she said. 'I'm focused. I don't say much when I'm like that. Just focused on the job ahead.'

She flinched when he touched her arm briefly.

'Hannah,' he said. 'Listen. If you're not sure, or having

second thoughts, then we can just drive away now. Because once you're inside that place, it's the kind of environment where you want to be in control and sure of yourself.'

Hannah didn't answer for a long moment. Then she turned and looked him in the eye.

'I'm good, Colby,' she said and meant it. 'I'm ready.'

Again the silence for a moment. She opened the car door.

'Okay,' Colby said. 'Good luck.' He paused. 'If you need me, you know what to do.'

Hannah nodded but said nothing. They'd arranged that if there was any sign of trouble, she was to press the speed dial on her phone and let it ring twice. Colby was hanging around, but she wanted to make sure she didn't need to call for help. Get the job done and get out of there was her plan.

Townsend was out on the showroom floor chatting to one of the salesmen. He had his back to Hannah when she came through the automatic glass doors, but the salesman's eyes widened when he saw her, and Townsend immediately turned around. His face beamed with delight, as though he couldn't quite believe his luck that this striking bird had just walked into his den. He flashed a five-grand-perfect smile and strode towards her. Hannah stood tall, hoping to Christ he wasn't going to throw his arms around her.

'Emma! Sweetheart!' he said, using the false name she'd given him. He stretched out his arms towards her. 'Are you a sight for sore eyes on a miserable Friday afternoon!'

He took hold of both her hands.

'Good to see you, Larry,' she said. Then she glanced around the room and looked impressed. 'Quite a set-up you've got here, I must say. Some really smart cars.' She eyed the bright yellow Alfa Romeo Spider convertible close to her. And she wondered if he actually moved any of these cars or if they were just a front to wash the money of some thug higher up the shitty food chain.

'Yeah,' Townsend said, stepping across to the Alfa Romeo and opening the door. 'We only deal in quality here, darlin''. Keeps the riff-raff out, if you get my drift.'

Hannah nodded, smiling so hard her jaws hurt. She got his drift all right. And he had riff-raff stamped all over him, from his stiffly gelled hair to his shiny petrol blue suit that fitted him just a little too neatly. That kind of fit was fine on Daniel Craig as James Bond, she thought, but on Larry Townsend it made him look like one of those coked up boxing hoodlums you saw on televised fight nights, throwing chairs around the crowded arena. But she hid her disdain well. And in any case, Townsend was so caught up that she was actually here, he wouldn't have noticed anyway.

'You like the little Alfa?' he said, gesturing for her to have a look. 'Go on. Sit in it, Emma. See if it feels right. She goes like the clappers, this one. And turns a few heads in the process – bit like yourself, if I may say so.'

Hannah eased herself into the car, conscious that he was

watching her skirt ride up her thighs as she slid into the bucket seat.

'Hmmm. Nice motor,' she said, smiling up to him. 'Convertible too. Would be a real pleasure, Larry.' Then she swung her legs out and stood up. 'But might be a bit flash for me, to be honest. I'd probably be more interested in one of your SUVs. I might even plan a long trip in it. And they've got plenty of wellie too, haven't they?'

Townsend looked thrilled that she was so on his hook as he walked her across to a big red SUV with blacked-out windows. He opened the door and she sat inside.

'This is more my style,' Hannah said. 'But I bet it's a fortune.' She smiled to him. 'I mean I've got money that was left to me, but I'm not a millionaire, Larry.'

Townsend wagged a dismissive finger.

'Don't you worry your pretty little head, sweetheart. If you fancy this, then we can have a look at the figures, and I'll make it happen for you. That's what I like to do when a client comes through that door who knows what they want.'

Hannah smiled then got out of the car and stood next to him. He took a step closer to her and lowered his voice.

'Tell you what, Hannah,' he said, looking into her eyes. 'Our boys are just wrapping up here, and on a Friday night I give them a few quid to go down the pub, and if I can join them, I do. But since you're already here, why don't you come into my office and we can have a little chat.' Again with the smile. 'And I'm sure I can rustle up a glass of bubbly to celebrate the weekend ahead.'

Hannah gave him her best I'm-all-yours smile.

'Sounds like a great idea to me.'

'Great. I'd like to get to know you a little better, and maybe if you feel like it, we can go out and have a bit of dinner later.' He put a hand up. 'I mean, no pressure or anything.'

'Sure,' Hannah said as she followed him across the showroom to the hallway leading to an office with a sign that read, 'The Boss'. Classy.

Once inside, Townsend slipped off his suit jacket and draped it around the big padded recliner behind his desk, then went to a fridge across the room and brought out a bottle of Moët, holding it up to her for approval.

'That'll do nicely.' Hannah smiled.

He took two champagne flutes out of a glass cupboard and put them on a large mahogany coffee table on the other side of the rather grand-looking office. He expertly popped the cork and poured the bubbles into two glasses, handing one to her. Then he raised his glass and clinked hers.

'To new friends. And may all our tomorrows be better than our yesterdays.'

Hannah tried not to grimace at the clumsy sentiment.

Then Townsend suddenly looked a little brooding, as he shook his head.

'My old dad used to say that every New Year's Eve at

midnight, before he got completely hammered and fought with everyone in the bleeding house.' He shook his head. 'And you know what? Our tomorrows only got better when he popped his clogs.'

'Yeah,' Hannah said, sipping her drink. 'You can pick your friends an' all that. But you're stuck with family.'

She needed to change the conversation from families.

'So, how long you had the showroom?' she asked.

'Oh, about ten years now. There was two of us in the beginning. Me and my brother, Charlie. But he's gone now.' He looked at her, then out towards the window into the street. 'Died. Well. Bumped off, actually.'

'Oh,' Hannah said, feeling a little nip of anxiety in her gut. Let's not bring back any memories. She didn't want to talk about this.

'Yeah. Chucked out of a fucking window at the high flats he lived in. Some nutcase bird.' He paused, and took a breath, as though trying to shake himself out of the memory. 'Anyway. All in the past, and the killer got jailed. So fuck all that. It was all a bit mad in them old days, it was. But it's different now. I'm a successful businessman.'

'I can see that,' Hannah smiled, taking a glug of the drink.

Townsend put his glass on the table, and went across to his jacket pocket. He took out a wad of notes.

'Excuse me a moment, darlin'. I'm just going to weigh the lads in and send them off for the night. Maybe join them in the pub later. But I like them to know that I look after them. That's what being a boss is all about.'

'Of course,' Hannah said. 'So do you have security at night to look after your cars on the forecourt once you close up?'

Hannah was wondering if some heavies were about to come in the door once the salesmen clocked off.

'Yeah. But not till around nine. Once it's dark.' He opened the door. 'Back in two ticks. Enjoy your drink.'

As soon as he left, Hannah took a long breath and let it out. Keeping up appearances was not as easy as she'd hoped, now that she was actually in here and about to be on her own with this guy. She knew he would probably make a pass at her in the next fifteen minutes, and she knew she'd be able to handle him. But she had to clear her mind and think straight. She wondered where Colby was. Not that she needed him right now. She could hear the laughter of the sales guys along the corridor and could imagine that Townsend was bragging that he was about to make a sale over the desk of his office once this bird got a few drinks in her.

When he came back in, he ushered her to sit on the black leather sofa and he sat on the edge of it, close, but far enough away. He knocked back the remains of his drink, and poured another, offering Hannah a top-up, which she refused, saying she'd save it for later. She listened as he talked about how making it to the top of his game had not been an easy journey, and that there were things he had done in his early days that he wasn't proud of. Hannah tried her best to show empathy, saying they had all done things they regretted, and that was part of growing up. But all the time, the image kept flashing into her head of the carnage after the car exploded with her mother in it outside their home. She swallowed her anger as she listened, hoping to Christ he wasn't actually going to confess to her, right here on this sofa. Why was he even telling her this shit? A silence fell between them, and Hannah wasn't sure if it was because Townsend was suddenly a bit depressed remembering his past or that he expected her to tell a few stories of her own life. Then he suddenly reached across and took hold of her hand, gazing at her face.

'You know something, Emma,' he said. 'When you walked into the pub that night I couldn't take my eyes off you. I thought for a minute I recognised you.'

'Recognised me?' Hannah said, her voice an octave too high. She cleared her throat. 'One of those faces, I suppose. Maybe you get around the city a lot. I lived in Spain for a while when I was younger. Do you go down to the Costa del Sol? Though I think if I'd ever met you, I'd have remembered, Larry.' She squeezed his hand a little then took it away and picked up her drink.

The gesture of affection seemed to please him and he smiled back.

'Yeah. I do, actually. I spent a couple of years down the

Costa del Sol a few years back,' he said. 'Had to get out of here fast and get myself below the radar for a while, after a bit of trouble here.' He paused, swallowed. 'I mean, after my bruv got done in. There was a lot of cops and stuff. Too many questions.'

'Oh, right,' Hannah said, not really knowing what else to say.

She glanced at her watch. It was almost half six and the salesmen were well gone by now. It was just the two of them. Townsend slid across the sofa to her so that their knees were touching. He placed his hand on her knee and caressed it a little. Hannah glanced down, then away, as he moved his fingers a little higher towards the bottom of her denim skirt. His hand stayed there for a few moments, his fingers gently touching that part of her inner thigh. She felt uncomfortable, but she let it go, trying to work out when to move. Her handbag was next to her, and she reached across and touched it for reassurance. Townsend drained his glass then put it down on the table, and slid closer to her so that he was almost pinning her to one corner of the sofa. His breathing quickened, as he took Hannah's face in his hand, caressed it gently, then traced his fingers down to her cleavage. She felt a little frozen as he cupped her breast in his hand, squeezing it, at the same time moving his other hand up her thigh until his fingers reached her pants. Then, before she could stop him, he was on top of her so fast it was as though he'd choreographed this move to perfection. It took Hannah off guard as she felt him on top of her, grinding into her with his erection pushing against her groin, and now his mouth was all over her neck and chest. She tried to wriggle free, push him away, but he was very strong and solid. Christ almighty! This was not how it was supposed to play out. She was supposed to be in control here. She hadn't expected this to move so fast. He was breathing hard now, and pulling her legs apart so that he was now grinding in between them, groaning and gasping.

'Larry!' Hannah pushed him. 'Stop. What the fuck are you doing?'

He didn't take his mouth from her chest and was pulling her top up.

'Giving you what you want, Emma, darlin'. You know you want it, don't you? I could see that in your face from the first time I saw you.'

'Larry, stop! Fuck's sake!'

Hannah tried to wriggle free, but she was getting nowhere and it was making him more excited. He was so strong she was beginning to panic. She tried to push him back but then he flipped her onto her stomach and pushed her face into the sofa. She was suddenly powerless, barely able to breathe. Jesus Christ! Now he was straddling her, one hand pushing her face down, the other pulling up her skirt and yanking down her pants. Then she heard him unbuckling his belt and the zip in his trousers go down.

'Larry, stop! Fuck's sake! Stop it!'

'Shut up, you fucking bitch.'

He was pulling her buttocks apart and pushing himself onto her but she struggled as hard as she could. Then suddenly she felt a punch on the side of her temple and for a moment she felt the room swim as he tried to push himself inside her. She lay, breathless, panicking. She turned her head a little and saw her handbag wedged into the back of the sofa. She managed to free one hand and reached across and into the bag as Townsend tried to thrust between her buttocks. She felt the cold metal of the pistol in her hand. She quickly pulled it out and with every breath of strength she had she turned it towards him and fired into his shoulder. He stopped immediately, went limp and collapsed off her and onto the floor, clutching his shoulder, blood pumping out.

'You fucking bitch!' he said, shocked. 'You fucking shot me, you cunt.'

'Fuck you, Townsend! You were trying to rape me, you filthy bastard.'

Hannah struggled off the sofa, pulling up her pants, and got to her feet, tears of rage stinging her eyes. She kept the pistol pointed at him.

'Right. Okay, Emma. Listen. Calm the fuck down. I'm sorry. I'm sorry. I thought you were up for it. I . . . I was wrong. Please. I'm sorry. Put the fucking gun away before you hurt somebody.'

Hannah stood over him as he got to a sitting position. She shook her head.

'You haven't a fucking clue, have you?'

'What?' He looked confused.

'You have no idea who I am, do you? Have you actually got even an inkling who I am?'

'What the fuck are you talking about?'

Hannah kept the gun on him. She was composed now, fear turned to cold-blooded anger.

'You said you thought you recognised me. Do you have any idea? Think back, you prick. About your brother. About how he died. You said he was chucked off a balcony. Think back.'

Hannah watched as the realisation suddenly dawned on him, his flushed face now white with fear.

'Oh fuck! You're her? You're that Hannah Wolfe. You can't be. She's in jail.' He looked at her, his face etched with fear.

'Not any more,' Hannah said with a snarl. 'She's out.'

'Please. Listen. I can explain,' he pleaded.

'Explain what. How you put a fucking bomb in my mother's car?'

'It wasn't like that. It was for . . . It was meant for . . .'

'My father. You think that makes it better, you murdering piece of trash?'

'It wasn't our fault. We were forced into it by someone else. It was to do with Wolfie. They wanted to get him.' He was on his knees. 'Look. Emma . . . Hannah. Please. Just calm down. Let's talk about this. I can make this up to you. I've lived with this for years, what we did.'

'Really,' Hannah said. '*You've* fucking lived with it.' She cocked the gun.

There had been moments in the last twenty-four hours, in fact even the last two hours, where she hadn't thought she could do this. Where she thought that she could be bigger than this, that maybe there was some history on this story and that she was now six years from her initial revenge and she could walk away. But the last few minutes had decided it. He was a thug and a rapist, as well as a murderer. There was a special place in hell for bastards like this. She took aim at his chest and fired, watching the shocked look on his face for a second before everything stopped in his life and he keeled over onto the floor, turning the cream carpet crimson with his blood. She picked up the champagne glass she'd been drinking and shoved it into her bag – so her fingerprints were nowhere. She'd already checked that the car lot didn't have CCTV cameras. Only the other car salesmen in the showroom who saw her might be able to identify her if it came to that. But by that time she'd be long gone. She put the gun in her handbag and walked out of the office. The showroom was dark and eerily empty and she went across to the fire exit doors and pushed them open with her shoulder and stepped out into the drizzle. She choked back tears of fear and anger, and also a wrenching sadness somewhere inside at how it had come to this. Then she saw Colby's car roar up to the kerbside and pull over. She opened the door and jumped in as he sped off. She burst into tears.

CHAPTER THIRTY

Kerry sat in the back seat of Billy's Mercedes listening to the banter between him and Dave, his driver-cum-bodyguard. Since they'd left London heading for Brighton, they'd been regaling her with stories of days gone by when her father was a young man, making his name among the gangsters and rogues who ran London back then. She'd learned more about her father in the past few months from these conversations and Wolfie's stories than she'd known all her life. Her father had never come across as a hard man or a villain to her as she was growing up. He was just her dad, who adored her, who never scolded her and who protected her. Kerry had always known there was money in the family, and she suspected it was illegal, but the extent of the criminality had surprised her – even though she knew it shouldn't, given how she was now leading her own life. But always, anyone who spoke of her dad talked of the man who did everything for his family, and who hoped for a future that would be without guns and robbing and protection. The irony was never lost on her, especially as she'd just blatantly blackmailed the Attorney General into allowing a drug smuggler to go free. As they left the main motorway and cruised down the country roads towards the seaside town, Kerry wondered what would happen next with Quentin Fairhurst. She was fairly confident that he would not send the cops out to pick her up, because that would involve too much explaining from him. Even though he would convince them that this was blackmail pure and simple, he would know the police would always think that there was no smoke without fire. So the only thing he would have left was to inform the Russians, who owned the photographs, and tell them that the pics they had taken to blackmail him and the Home Secretary were now in the hands of bloody gangsters. But that was a tricky one too. So she was content to sit tight, and hope that the next news she got was that Vic Paterson was going to be freed on a technicality. But for the moment, Kerry was on an errand that she hoped would change the lives of one family.

She hadn't phoned the Walker family to tell them she was coming and what her plan was. She didn't want to give them the chance to say no. They might still say no, but she hoped that by being face to face with them, she would convince them that this was the right thing to do. She took it that they were likely to be at home, as they were full-time carers for their daughter and didn't go out much because of the upheaval it would involve. The last article she'd read in the newspaper said they were trying their best to raise money to keep their daughter from going into a care home, as they were finding it difficult to cope in the house they were living in. Kerry had hired a private investigator to keep an eye on them and report back to her how they were living, and it looked like they did very little but stay at home. Now they drove into the small housing estate a couple of miles outside of Brighton. It was a pleasant area, full of manicured gardens and houses that were small and semi-detached or terraced. Kerry checked the address again from the note in her pocket and as they scanned the numbers she spotted number twenty-four.

'There it is,' she said. 'The one with the old blue car outside on the street.'

They drove past first, and Kerry glimpsed small windows and a narrow-doored, semi-detached two-storey house with a postage stamp patch of well-kept lawn in the front. She felt a little nervous. She knew they would remember her, as they'd grown close in the months running up to the court case, but they'd had no contact since. She hoped they weren't bitter or angry with her, though James had seemed accepting at the time, broken-hearted as he and his wife were about the verdict. The Merc turned on the small roundabout at the top of the road and came back down and parked outside the house.

'I don't know how long this will take, Billy,' she said, opening the door. 'Could be a little while.'

'No worries, Kerry,' he said. 'We're not going anywhere. We're here for as long as it takes. Good luck, darlin'.'

Kerry got out of the car and walked up the path. She pushed the bell and heard it chime inside. She waited, excited and nervous at the same time. After a few moments, the door opened and a woman stood before her. Kerry looked up at her, recognising her from all those years ago, her face a lttle older and more weary than she recalled.

'Marilyn?' Kerry said, smiling. 'I'm Kerry Casey. Do you remember me?'

The woman's mouth dropped open in shocked, then bewilderment.

'Kerry Casey? From . . . from . . .'

'Who is it, Marilyn?' a male voice shouted from inside.

The woman glanced over her shoulder then back at Kerry.

'It's . . . It's . . .' She shook her head and bit her lip. 'Come in, Kerry.' She took a step back into the hall and opened the door wide.

Kerry stepped inside and for a moment they stood saying nothing. Then Marilyn's lip trembled and her face crumpled. Instinctively, Kerry put her arms around her and could hear her sobbing onto her shoulder.

'I'm so sorry,' Marilyn sniffed. 'It's . . . Just . . . Just seeing you. Oh, Kerry!'

'It's okay, Marilyn. I'm sorry for just landing on you like this, but I didn't want to phone first.'

'It's okay, it's okay,' Marilyn said, quickly recovering her composure. 'It's great to see you.' She glanced over her shoulder and down the narrow hallway, where Kerry could see a wheelchair at the end, and the compact kitchen beyond. The house seemed even smaller inside. Then suddenly from a door off the hall, James appeared and stopped in his tracks, stunned.

'Christ almighty! Kerry Casey?' He paused, peering. 'Is it? Is it you, Kerry?'

Kerry smiled broadly, delighted that at least they were glad to see her.

'Yes. Yes, it's me, James. I'm so sorry to barge in on you.'

'Not at all,' he said. 'Jesus. I can't believe it. After all these years. Come in, come in.' He beckoned her down the hall. 'It's just a shock, but great to see you. Are you in the area working?'

'No,' Kerry said. 'I wanted to talk to you about something. And I wanted to see you rather than anything else.'

They both looked at each other, suddenly worried.

'Oh,' James said. 'We don't owe you money, do we, Kerry?' He glanced at his wife, who bit her lip.

Kerry smiled and threw her hands out to dismiss the very idea.

'No, no, for God's sake! Of course not!'

'That's a relief,' he said. 'Because we ain't got much.' He

turned to his wife. 'Go and put the kettle on then, love. And Kerry can come and see our Lilly.' He lowered his voice. 'Before we go in there, she's not been great lately. So difficult for her. And a rough time with not being able to get out or do any exercise. She's just getting over a chest infection. We do everything we can, but we're struggling. But don't let her see that. She'll be thrilled to see you. She asks about you sometimes, and she still remembers everything about the case. Though we try to put it to the back of her mind, it keeps coming up. She feels we were robbed.'

'You were,' Kerry said. 'Absolutely robbed. And I was powerless to do anything about it.'

'Well. That's a long time ago. Come on.'

Marilyn went into the kitchen and Kerry followed James into the living room. An adjustable hospital bed took up most of the room at one side, and various utensils and bags and clothes were folded neatly in a corner next to it. The young girl sitting on a padded chair at the fireside looked up. She was so different from all those years ago, her hair shorter, face a little fuller and she looked like she'd put on a lot of weight. Kerry couldn't help noticing her swollen ankles, obviously from lack of movement. But the eyes were the same she remembered, bright and full of determination. Lilly's mouth dropped open and her face lit up when she saw Kerry.

'Look who's just fallen out of the sky and landed on our doorstep, Lilly.'

Lilly looked shocked and a smile spread over her face as she raised her hands in disbelief.

'Kerry! Kerry Casey!' She turned to her father. 'See, Dad! I told you she would come some day, didn't I? I knew you'd come. I wrote to you. Did you ever get my letters?'

Kerry's heart sank. She had never seen any letters. She'd left the job so swiftly after the case and moved on.

'No. Sorry, Lilly. I left the job. I didn't know you wrote. I'm so very sorry.'

Kerry turned around to see tears in James's eyes. She smiled and stepped forward and bent down to hug Lilly. She smelled fresh and clean and warm, and right there and then a wave of emotion swept over Kerry and she had to fight back tears. All those years and nothing had changed for this family betrayed by the system and left to fight on their own. She wished she had stayed on to take the fight to the next level, but she'd been so deflated and defeated after Fairhurst and the way it turned out. She stayed hugging her for a few moments, then pulled back and looked at her.

'Hello, Lilly. So many times I've thought about you.' Then she stopped the catch in her throat. 'I'm so sorry I didn't get in touch for all these years, but I didn't want to prolong things, keep up hopes for you because I knew this was something that I couldn't win. It's so hard to beat these big pharmaceuticals who throw so much money defending themselves against cases like yours.'

Lilly shook her head and smiled. 'We didn't win, Kerry. But we're still here.' She pointed to a pile of books in a small trolley-cum-desk. 'Look! I'm studying. I'm studying at the Open University. I'm going to be a lawyer, Kerry, just like you.'

Kerry swallowed back tears. This girl, with all the odds stacked against her, pushing herself like this. All this time Kerry felt she had failed her, and yet she was saying she was inspired by her. She had never felt so humbled in her whole life.

'Oh my God!' Kerry said. 'This is wonderful. I'm so thrilled for you.'

Marilyn came into the room with a tray, on which there was a teapot, cups and biscuits and set it down on the coffee table.

'Please,' she beckoned to Kerry, 'sit down. It's been so long. Tell us about your life. Are you still a lawyer?'

Kerry sat down. How do you tell people who have been inspired by you and who believed in you that you are now the boss of a gangland family who has sanctioned killings and drug smuggling, who has blackmailed and sold millions of pounds of stolen cocaine?

Kerry puffed out a sigh.

'Well, no,' she said. 'I don't practise any more. It's a bit of a complicated story.'

'Oh,' Marilyn said. She glanced at her husband, then at Lilly, who looked a little crestfallen.

'But I'll tell you about it,' Kerry said. 'Or some of it.'

Kerry sat back on the sofa with everyone's eyes on her and over the next half hour she found herself telling them the story of the last few months, with them shocked and saddened and mesmerised. Then, when she'd told them as much as she wanted, she stopped, drained her cup and placed it on the table.

'Wow!' Lilly said. 'That is some story.'

Kerry looked from Lilly to her parents. She was about to speak, when James put his hand up.

'You won't find anyone judging you in here, Kerry,' he said. 'Sometimes life throws things at you and all you can do is pick yourself up and get on with it. So don't worry. You will always be the woman who cared about us and who showed us such kindness.'

'Thank you,' Kerry said. She took a breath then added, 'I saw the story about you in the newspaper – I know it was a year ago, but I only just saw it, and that's why I came down. How are things now for you?'

Suddenly everyone looked grim faced and fell silent.

'We're not going to lie to you,' James said. 'If you saw the newspaper article, you'll know it wasn't good then. And it's worse now.' He glanced from his wife to Lilly. 'The level of care Lilly needs, and this house,' he spread his hands, 'well it's just not the right environment and we're struggling. So we're looking at where we can go from here.'

Kerry knew from the article they were talking about the

care home for Lilly. She looked at Lilly, who flushed but swallowed.

'But it's not going to be too bad, Kerry,' she said, trying to put on a brave face. 'I mean, we've talked to the home and they said I'll be able to continue with my studies. I mean . . . I mean . . . I'll still be able to get visits from Mum and Dad.'

From the corner of her eye, Kerry could see Marilyn trying to hide her tears behind her mug of tea. The room fell silent and the air could have been cut with a knife.

Finally, Kerry spoke. 'Listen.' She gazed at each of them in turn. 'I'm here because I want to put something to you.'

Everyone looked at each other, then at Kerry.

'I have come into a whole lot of money that really is so surplus to what I need, and in fact it was something that I didn't even have to earn, or anyone who works for me had to do much to earn. It's just . . . how can I put it? A windfall.'

'You mean like a lottery win?' James said, eyes wide.

'Yeah,' Kerry said. 'That's it. Like a lottery win.' She swallowed. 'And I want to give it to you. To make your lives better.'

James's mouth opened in shock as he glanced at Kerry, then Marilyn. Nobody spoke. Kerry thought they were thinking it was drug money.

She continued, 'I knew I was coming here and I wanted to say to you that there is this new small estate being built nearby, closer to the sea. Great big houses, really terrific, and might suit you down to the ground. I'm sorry, but I took the liberty of asking them if they could change the design of one to suit a person with Lilly's needs and they said yes, they could do that.'

Marilyn looked at James.

'We've seen that estate, but all of those houses are over half a million pounds, Kerry.'

'I know,' Kerry said. 'But how amazing would it be to make that your home? And it would cost you nothing. You just go there, get it furnished and live in it and enjoy it. You'll have plenty of money to do it. And Lilly won't have to go to any home.'

Silence. Kerry sat waiting.

'You mean you would just buy this for us?'

'Yes,' Kerry enthused. 'And more than that. I will make an investment into your bank account that gives you a salary and will also help pay for the level of care Lilly needs. And a specially converted car, and all the other things that should have been given to you at the time if you hadn't been so robbed by the injustice of that bloody court case. Everything.' She paused; they all looked shocked and disbelieving. 'Oh. And there's a specialist doctor in Germany who might be able to look into Lilly's situation and help get her moving a bit more. It's a long shot, but worth trying. There will be money for that.'

Silence. Then eventually, 'But . . . But . . . where is this money coming from? I mean. Did people . . . di–'

Kerry interrupted him.

'No, James. People didn't die, if that's what you're going to say. Okay, it's money that came to my family because of old connections. That's all I can say. But nobody died. Nobody is going to jail or anything like that. The money is just there. And we don't need it, but you do. It's that simple. I came all the way down here to ask if you would accept it. Just think of it as a lottery win.'

The silence was so long and the air so thick with tension that Kerry was beginning to think that they were going to say no. These were decent people who wouldn't pick up a bus ticket from the ground they were so law abiding. Eventually, James looked at his wife then at Kerry.

'Well,' he said. 'We must be due a big win on the lottery by this time.' He smiled and shook his head, then he went across to his wife and they hugged each other, crying. Then they went across to Lilly, who was already sobbing, wiping her tears.

'Is it really going to happen, Kerry?'

Kerry hugged her. 'It's really happening now, Lilly. It should have happened years ago.'

Kerry felt overcome with exhaustion when she got into the car, and she knew it was partly because of her pregnancy but also just the stress and adrenalin of the last couple of days. But she felt good about what she'd done for Lilly's family. Nothing would ever compensate for the impact of the drugs on Lilly, and the years the family had spent struggling to try to stay together. But at least the money would be a way forward for them, and Lilly was the kind of girl who would make the very best of what she had. Kerry admired the girl so much, and felt that in her position she could never have been that strong and determined. She would spend the night in the hotel and go back up by road tomorrow with Billy driving her. He'd arranged to take her to dinner. She lay back, enjoying the sun breaking through the clouds. Her mobile rang, and she hoped it would be word that Fairhurst had buckled and released Vic Paterson. But she didn't recognise the number. She put the phone to her ear.

'Kerry Casey?' A male voice.

'Who is this?' Kerry's voice was sharp.

No answer for a couple of beats, then the sound of a throat being cleared and a voice.

'This is Alfi Ricci. We haven't met.'

Shocked, she glanced at Billy who had turned around.

'No. We haven't met. Which is just as well for you.' She mouthed 'Alfi Ricci' to Billy whose eyes popped.

Again the silence.

'Kerry. I know you're in London. I have some information I think you should know about.'

Kerry's mind was trying to process what this was all about. She'd had no dealings whatsoever with Alfi Ricci, and only knew him from what Wolfie had told her of how he'd betrayed him after the diamond heist.

'Listen, Alfi Ricci, if that's who you are. I don't know you. I don't know how you got my number. So maybe start by telling me that.'

The sound of a deep, nervous breath.

'Kerry, I know you're new to this game, but there are leaks in every organisation.' He paused. 'I'm not playing games with you. You need to know that you're in danger.'

'Goes with the territory,' Kerry snapped back. 'Ask your mate Wolfie.'

Silence.

'That was unfortunate. But I can't talk about Wolfie. I'm phoning you to warn you that there's a hit out on you.'

'From who?'

'Russian prick. Yuri. He knows you fenced his yellow diamonds for Wolfie, and you've got his DVDs and pictures. Thing is, Kerry, you stole his leverage. I think he was planning to blackmail someone with those pictures.'

'You seem to know a lot. So why you phoning me?'

'Because I know that this bastard won't stop until he gets you.'

'That's how it always is, is it not?'

'Yeah, but you can stop him, Kerry. You can eliminate him yourself.'

'Christ. You're talking like a Bond villain, Alfi. Get to the point.'

'Okay. Right. He asked me to get in touch with you, track you down and arrange a meet with him. Hand over his discs and photos. Then he'll call it quits. He doesn't care about the diamonds. He'll call off his dogs.'

Kerry had put the conversation on loudspeaker, and Billy was open mouthed, dying to butt in, but she waved him to stay quiet.

'The Russian is not in a position to call the shots. He has nothing.'

'No. But he has firepower. He has thugs all over the shop. Glasgow isn't a million miles away. And he will find a way to get to you, Kerry.'

'So what's in it for you?'

'I'm a bit short on manpower to deal with the Russians – thanks to Wolfie and his mates. So I can set the Russian up for you. Then you can get rid of him yourself.'

'You mean do your dirty work?'

'Meet me halfway on this. Yes, it would help me. And I will be forever in your debt if you remove this prick from the face of the earth. I will do anything for you.'

'You mean before he removes you.'

Silence.

'Well, yes. If you put it like that.'

Kerry sighed. She was tired of the killing and the fighting and the guns. She put her hand to her stomach. She wanted things to be different for this little life. But if Alfi was right, she would be followed by the Russian mobsters until they got her. Sometimes you have to face down your enemies. She'd done it before, and she could do it again.

'So do you have a plan, Alfi? I mean, your forward planning isn't exactly top drawer, is it?'

He ignored the sarcasm.

'Yes. I have a plan. I arrange a meet with him, and you can take it from there.'

'When are you thinking about?'

'I know you're in London. So before you go back to Glasgow.'

Kerry glanced at Billy, who rolled his eyes back.

'I don't trust you. Not one iota.'

'I know. I can understand that. I can come and meet you if you want?'

'That won't make me trust you any more, but fine.'

She reeled off the name of the hotel and told him to be there within the next two hours, then hung up. She turned to Billy.

'Just when you think there are no more surprises, eh?'

'We should do it, Kerry. The Russians are bastards in London, and they are powerful. Ricci's a slippery fucker too, but he's obviously shitting his pants about this. Listen: I have plenty of bodies who can deal with this, no problem. We can take the Russian out – and Ricci too, if you want.'

Kerry didn't answer. She massaged her forehead and closed her eyes as the driver headed off the motorway and into the streets of London.

CHAPTER THIRTY-ONE

Hannah hadn't slept much, her dreams fitful and full of anger. It was still dark when she woke up, and she lay there in the quietness of the early morning, reflecting on the previous night. She'd gone to pieces, sobbing and shaking, when she'd got into the car after putting a bullet in Townsend. Colby had said nothing as he drove at high speed until they were well away from the car showroom and on the road into London. Then he pulled over on the hard shoulder, stopped the car and put his arms around her. She wept on his shoulder as he held her tight, murmuring, 'It's over, Hannah. It's over.' She'd allowed herself to be comforted by him because right at that point she didn't know if she could actually stop crying, and if she was actually breaking down, because everything had overwhelmed her, or if it was because the brute Townsend had tried to rape her. But eventually she'd composed herself and they'd driven to her flat. He'd insisted on coming in with her, and when they were inside, he'd made tea as she sat at the kitchen table feeling as though she was in a stupor. Then afterwards, she'd opened a bottle of wine and they'd sat drinking as she'd told him what had happened.

In all the time since her mother died, and even when she was sent to prison, she had never felt this grief-stricken, or suddenly broken, and she found herself pouring all of that out to Colby. He listened, and didn't judge her when she told him she had no regrets about killing Townsend. When he suggested that she shouldn't be alone overnight, she'd told him not to worry, that she wasn't going to top herself. That had made both of them smile, and she had been glad he'd suggested staying, because she hadn't wanted to be alone. They drank more wine, ordered a takeaway and sat at the dining table gazing out over the Thames, comfortable in long silences and in each other's company. When it got late, she'd showed Colby the spare room, and before he'd gone in and closed the door, he'd put his arms around her and given her a hug that felt as though he was a friend who cared for her, and she liked him even more for that.

Hannah was brewing coffee and pouring fresh orange juice into a glass when Colby strolled into the kitchen, shirtless, hair ruffled and with a touch of stubble – looking far too desirable for someone who had just tumbled out of bed. For the first time in as long as she could remember, she was enjoying seeing someone in her home first thing in the morning. There was a little niggle of regret that Colby wasn't going to be featuring in her future plans.

'Morning,' she said. 'There's coffee. We can go out for breakfast – the Polish café?'

Even though there had been nothing between them last night, she still felt a little awkward, and knew that it might become even more awkward if Colby hung around the house long. She hadn't expected to like him as much as she did, and part of her wished she could get to know him a little better. But she was planning to spend the next couple of days organising her flight to the Cayman Islands and was looking forward to joining her dad. She was going to start living again. She wasn't even sure if she was ever coming back to London. But more than anything, she had to keep herself really busy, because if she was busy, she wouldn't get time to think of last night, of Townsend, of what he had tried to do to her, and how she had left him bleeding to death on the carpet. She could deal with what happened, if she didn't dwell on it.

'Perfect.' He crossed the kitchen and turned on the cold tap, taking a glass out of the cupboard and filling it with water.

Hannah couldn't help but watch his long, muscular back as he downed the water, then fixed himself a coffee.

In the Polish café, Hannah and Colby ate croissants and drank more coffee. Colby ordered bacon and scrambled eggs, and Hannah watched as he hoovered it up. When he'd finished, he sat back, dabbed his mouth with a napkin, and looked straight at Hannah.

'So, how are you, Hannah? I mean, after everything last night with that bastard.'

Hannah hadn't expected this and she bristled a little.

'I'm all right.' She pushed her hair back, looked at him, then at the table. 'To be honest, I'll deal with it in my head. That's how I do things. I just get on with it.' She really didn't want to go over it, to talk about it, or even to think about it. 'I'm not being funny or anything, but I have to put it in a box somewhere in my head and lock it up.' She paused, noticing that he looked a little embarrassed that he'd even brought it up. 'But, thanks so much for being there last night. I needed you.'

She couldn't believe she had actually said that. She had never told anyone in her life that she needed them, even if she did. She felt her face redden a little and picked up her coffee and swirled it around as a distraction. They sat in silence for a moment, then Colby spoke.

'So, this is it then? You're off to the Caymans in a few days?' He looked away then back at her. 'You know what though? I kind of wish you weren't going so soon, and that's the truth.' He paused, half smiling. 'That's probably not something you want to hear, but I feel, well, I feel we kind of clicked, if you know what I mean. I like being with you.' He paused, huffed. 'I never opened up to anyone about my grandfather and background before. But I felt I could with you.'

Hannah didn't know what to say. She felt exactly the same way, but she didn't want go there. She looked at him.

'I know what you mean, and I honestly liked being with you. But, who knows? I just got out of jail and . . . and . . .' She paused. 'Well, after everything yesterday, my head is a bit all over the place. I just want to get out of this place, far away, spend some time with my dad and see where life takes me.' She paused. 'But I do wish I could see you again. Spend more time together.'

She meant what she said, and hoped he understood that. Colby said nothing, and they sat for a while that way, then eventually he made the first move. He looked at his watch, then stood up.

'Well, let me buy you breakfast at least.' He smiled down at her, his blue eyes sharp in the light.

He went to the counter and paid, and she picked up her bag and followed him. They both went outside and stood for a moment in the cold morning. Colby looked at his watch again.

'Right. I'll be off then.' He paused. 'I probably won't see you before you go, Hannah, so look, I really wish you all the happiness in the world. You deserve it.'

Hannah felt a sudden pang of emotion in her chest as she looked at Colby, and she could see how much he cared about her.

'Thanks for everything,' Hannah said. 'And I promise you the next dinner is on me.'

She stepped forward, and he bent down a little as he put his arms around her. They hugged tight and stayed that way for a long moment, then Colby released her. He scanned her face, then he kissed her on the lips, a soft brief kiss, and they paused, both looking into each other's eyes as though they didn't know what to do next. Then he kissed her again, this time longer, and she could feel the warmth of his mouth on hers, and it felt so natural that she wanted it to keep on going. But then Colby ran his hand through her hair and let her go.

'Next time,' he said softly, as he took a step back.

She nodded, but said nothing as he touched her face one last time, then turned and left. She watched him for a few moments as he went, wondering if he would turn around. But he didn't. She looked up at the sky as the rain began to fall, then turned and walked towards her flat, feeling deflated and suddenly so alone. But she quickened her step and snapped herself out of it. There was much to be done before she went to the Caymans.

CHAPTER THIRTY-TWO

It was lock-in time after lunch in the jail, and Vic lay back against the pillows on his prison cell bed staring at the ceiling. Prisoners were off the blocks and locked in their cells for two hours every day while prison staff had their own lunch break. Some lags detested it, but Vic had trained his mind to cope with it and used the quiet time to keep his head positive. But every now and again, the thought that if his case went to trial he'd most likely be in here for at least a ten stretch filled him with dread. Today was one of those days. He'd woken up very early this morning with a sinking feeling, and he had had to talk himself into getting out of bed and facing the day. He'd seen people go to pieces in jail and he wasn't one of those who would ever let it get to him.

But over the last couple of days, he hadn't been able to get Sharon out of his mind. She hadn't been able to come and visit him over here, but he'd spoken to her on the phone a few days ago, and she'd told him the lawyers were throwing everything into getting him out. If he could even get bail, he considered he might disappear, but the court probably knew that too, so he'd be stuck in here till his trial. He closed his eyes for a moment so he could picture Sharon in his mind, that first time they'd met in Spain a few months ago, and he could pinpoint that moment with the sun at her back in the café and the way it lit up her eyes, and he'd realised he'd fallen in love with her. Stupid as it may have seemed, he couldn't stop himself, and the last time he'd seen her after his escape from the jail in Spain, he'd got the impression she had feelings for him too. And he still had the memory of her voice telling him she loved him on their last phone call.

He must have drifted off, because the next thing he heard was his door being clicked open and he turned his head to see the big Geordie screw standing over his bed.

'Paterson!' he said. 'Siesta's over, lad! Get up! You're wanted in the guv's office.'

It took Vic a moment to come to, then he quickly got to his feet, rubbing his hands over his face.

'Must have dropped off,' he said. 'The guv's office? What about?'

'No idea,' the screw said. 'Would you like me to tell him you're not fucking available?'

Vic sniffed and shot the officer a sarcastic look. 'I'm ready.'

He followed the guard along the corridor and noticed that all the cells were still locked, so he was baffled as to what was so urgent that he had to see the guv at this time. He hoped to Christ it wasn't to tell him that the Spanish police were at the front door to take him back over there. They went down the steel staircase, along and through three sets of locked doors and into a long hall where a line of offices lay behind closed doors. The guv's office was at the end. He'd only met the guv once, when he was doing his rounds, and he was a miserable-faced bastard with an expression that looked as though somebody had just shat on his desk. The screw knocked the door and a voice told him to come in. Vic followed the screw in and they both stood in front of the guv. He looked up when they came in, then sat back and for a moment said nothing, just made eye contact with Vic.

'Paterson!'

'Sir!' Vic said it through gritted teeth. He fucking hated having to call these pricks sir.

The guv looked down at some papers on his desk, then up at Vic.

'You just got lucky. You're out of here.'

There was a second when Vic felt light-headed. Did he just say 'you're out of here'? He narrowed his eyes.

'Sir?'

'Yes. You heard. You're out. Charges dropped.' The guv shrugged. 'Don't ask me why because I don't know. I've just had the phone call, and the paperwork delivered.'

Vic could feel his legs shaking and he took a deep breath and folded his arms. He wanted to say 'fuck me!' out loud, but that might have been an admission of guilt, so he just allowed himself a smile.

'Really?' he said. 'Now? I can go? I didn't hear from my lawyer.'

The guv spread his hands.

'What? You want to fucking argue about it? Have you fallen in love in here or something?'

For the first time, the guv actually smiled. He stood up and pushed paperwork across his desk.

'Sign at the bottom. Then GTFO before anybody changes their mind.'

Vic steadied his hand enough to get his signature on the paperwork, then turned to the guard. He couldn't understand why if charges had been dropped he wasn't being held as an escapee from Spanish jail while the Spanish authorities filed for extradition. But he wasn't about to ask questions. It might be a mistake. His stomach was doing somersaults and his heart was pounding.

'Thanks, sir,' Vic said.

The guv stretched out his hand and smiled.

'I'm out of here myself in two weeks, and I might be even happier than you are right now,' he said. 'Good luck to you. I know you're a fucking rogue. But today you're a lucky one.'

Vic could barely believe his ears that a man in his

position was talking to him like this, but he smiled broadly and said nothing. Just get the fuck out, he told himself.

After the signing of more papers and being handed back his belongings, passport, clothes, wallet, complete with credit cards, the screws sat behind the big glass frontage as they buzzed the main door open. Vic stood there watching it slowly slide across, every inch giving him a glimpse of growing freedom. He could feel them all staring at him. The door opened fully and he got a blast of the chilly air and breathed it in long and deep. Holy fucking Christ almighty! This was really happening. He pulled on his jacket and buttoned up as he stepped through the door. He was free.

Vic drove down the ramp and off the ferry in Santander. He knew he was taking a chance no matter which way he chose to get out of the UK and into Europe. If he'd pitched up at any airport, chances were that his ID would have flashed up on a security screen as being in custody on drugs charges. He could have stayed in London a few days to make sure the statutory details were changed to show the charges had been dropped and he was a free man. But he was afraid that any further digging might reveal that he was actually still on the run from Spain. He hadn't even waited long enough to have a chat with his lawyer on where he stood legally now that the UK had dropped the charges. Were the Spanish authorities still going to try to charge him? Or would they chase him down on a charge of breaking out of jail? Either way, and despite the risks of leaving the UK right away, Vic couldn't wait. As soon as he was far enough away from the prison he'd phoned an old mate, telling him he needed a car to disappear. In two hours his mate arrived with a car, some clothes, and two grand in case he needed fast cash. Vic was so grateful he had a genuine lump in his throat when his big mate gave him a bear hug as they parted, promising to hook up once it all died down. By the time Vic got to Southampton, it had been too late for the evening ferry, so he got some kip in a cheap hotel, and got on the early morning boat. He was shattered when he arrived in Spain, but he had a long way to go and only one thought in his mind.

Sharon. His stomach was actually turning over like a teenager on his first date. He hammered down the motorway, hoping that by now his UK lawyers might not have been told that the charges had been dropped. If they had, their first phone call would be to Kerry Casey. And Vic knew her first call would be to Sharon. He wanted to surprise her, but as he burned up the miles, there was just a niggle asking what if Sharon didn't want him? He would deal with that when the time came, he told himself, but the thought that she'd be as thrilled to see him as he would be to see her, kept him going – that and the black coffee. There's no way he would make it in one night, so hours later he stayed in a pension on the outskirts of Seville.

*

Sharon was driving back from the hotel complex, having spent the morning with the builders and interior designers. The place was going to look magnificent – the restaurants, bars, foyer and outside areas. And the bedrooms and suites with sumptuous furnishings and decor were definitely not for the package holidaymakers. The Caseys had thrown millions into this, and once it opened, it would become a landmark on the Costa del Sol. Kerry had told Sharon that the hotel would be a monument to her father who, even in his wildest dreams, could never have imagined something like this. The estate agents, bars and restaurants dotted along the coast were also beginning to look good, and every time Sharon spoke to Kerry, she was pleased that she had only good news to give her. It only seemed like last week when they were all dug in and under siege from the Colombians, and in her darker moments, Sharon sometimes lay awake at night thinking of those agonising hours when Pepe Rodriguez's thugs kidnapped Tony, and also her near-murder at the hands of his henchmen. She had indeed come a long way from the depressed woman she was living with Knuckles Boyle. It was like another world, and the way she was living these days made her get out of bed every morning full of hope.

Only problem was that she felt guilty over Vic Paterson. She was hearing from Kerry almost every week about lawyers battling it out over his case, and the latest call had been to tell her of her plan to blackmail Fairhurst. She hadn't heard from Kerry how it had gone but she would give her a call once she got a moment. She knew she should have security with her, but things had been so smooth lately she hadn't bothered to bring someone with her today. She had been enjoying the occasional trip into the village or to a beachside café for lunch, risky though it seemed, since everything had calmed down.

She took the slip road to Cabopino and drove along the coast road, then parked at the harbour. She went into the quayside and sat down, enjoying the activity around the boats moored there, with owners or workers cleaning and painting their vessels – the first real signs of the beginning of the end of winter. It was still early on, but the sky was blue and there was heat in the sun. She looked at her watch. She had a couple of hours to kill, so she would have lunch here. She called security to let them know where she was, just in case. She knew they would come out here and sit nearby and maybe even join her. It was the only company she kept these days, and she enjoyed their stories of their lives. But the truth was, she was lonelier than she'd ever been in her life, wondering where she would be this time next year. She ordered a glass of sparkling water and sat back and closed her eyes, listening to the sails clink against the metal masts. The waiter arrived to take her order and she asked for a smoked salmon salad. As she waited for her lunch, she saw her security man arrive, and give her a wave as he parked his car. Her mobile rang and she glanced at the screen before automatically picking it up. Vic? She was immediately on edge. Someone must have stolen his mobile. Christ! They could be watching her. She shot a glance around the harbour, empty apart from an older couple having coffee in the café two along from her. She was about to get up and go straight towards the security guard's car, when she heard a voice behind her.

'You patching my calls or what, Shaz?'

Her stomach did a backflip. That was Vic's voice. But how could it be? She turned around, and there he was, standing squinting in the sunlight, his face eyes full of the mischief she had fallen for all those years ago.

'Vic! Fuck me!'

He smiled and laughed. 'Well, sweetheart,' he beamed, 'if you put it like that . . .'

He opened his arms and she stepped in, breathless, dizzy and almost unsteady on her feet. They stood like that, holding each other tight as though if they let go they would both disappear. Then they kissed, full of longing, and Sharon looked up into his eyes feeling the tightness of emotion in her chest.

'Christ, Shaz, I love you so much, you have no idea how many times I've thought about this moment.'

'I love you,' she said as they kissed again, and Sharon held onto him, promising herself that this time she would never let him go.

CHAPTER THIRTY-THREE

Kerry had changed the plans and agreed to meet Alfi Ricci in his restaurant on her terms. For Kerry that meant watertight security involving Billy Hill's men posted in every area in and around the restaurant. Although Ricci had assured her that it was not necessary, that the Russians only wanted to meet her to discuss the possibility of coming to an agreement over the discs, Hill said it was a stick-on set-up. So he had men outside, across the street, in the kitchen and in the backstreet. If the Russian mob wanted to get to Kerry then they would need to come out of the woodwork, because there wasn't an inch of the place that wasn't covered by armed men.

She sat at a table with Billy Hill at her side. Alfi Ricci had greeted them with a firm handshake and motioned them to the long table at the back of the restaurant close to the kitchen. He'd looked a little taken aback when another three of Hill's men had arrived moments later, and Hill told them they were with him. If Ricci objected then he didn't show it and directed the men to take a seat somewhere. Two were by the door and one sat a couple of tables away from where Kerry and Hill were sitting opposite Ricci. The restaurant was eerily silent, apart from the clatter of pots in the kitchen and the muffled voices of staff preparing for the lunchtime customers. A television high up on the wall close to the bar was showing Sky News, but the volume was so low nobody could hear it. Kerry glanced at it from time to time, more as a distraction from the tense atmosphere than actually paying much attention to the news. They were drinking coffee, and Ricci had attempted to make small talk about his father being an old friend of Kerry's father. Kerry was unimpressed but wasn't about to get into an argument over old friends with the man who had told his henchmen to put Wolfie in a coffin. It was left to Billy Hill to make the chat about London and how much it had changed over the years. Ricci kept looking at his watch. The meet with Yuri and his sidekick was for eleven thirty, and it was now gone past midday and no show. Every time he checked his watch, he glanced at Kerry and Hill and gave a little shrug, as though he couldn't understand why the Russians would be late.

Kerry just wanted to get the hell out of there and get back to Glasgow. She really didn't need to be spending time on this. She glanced up at the news, almost zoning out, when suddenly she narrowed her eyes, peering at the screen.

Breaking News: Bodies of two Russians found dead from gunshot wounds in Kensington flat owned by billionaire Russian oligarch.

There was a reporter doing a piece to camera outside the building, and several police cars lining the street and cordoning off the area. Two fire engines were on the scene and firemen were coming out of the building wearing breathing apparatus. Residents were milling around outside as the camera panned the street.

'Look!' Kerry said, instinctively reaching across and nudging Ricci. 'On the television. Sky News.'

Ricci looked bewildered but turned around to face the television, then quickly got out of his seat and went to the bar. He picked up the remote control and pushed up the volume. Suddenly the restaurant was filled with the voice of the Sky reporter.

'Police are saying very little other than to confirm that two men were found dead in the flat from gunshot wounds, and that the men who lived in the flat were Russians. They said at this stage of the investigation they are not able to name the men, but it is being treated as murder. Teams of forensic officers have been in the flat in the last couple of hours after an elderly neighbour raised the

alarm when she smelled smoke coming from the flat. Police will not say if there are any suspects at this stage, but only admitted that it appears to have been an attempt to set fire to the flat either during or after the murders.'

The news bulletin then returned to the studio where some expert was talking about the amount of Russian money swirling around London these days, apparently from oil-rich oligarchs, but that in reality a lot of it was from Russian gangsters.

'Fucking hell!' Ricci said. 'That's the place they took us to. That's it! In Kensington!'

'What you talking about? Who took you?'

'Fucking big Yuri bastard. He's the enforcer for some guy called Anatoly. Christ knows who they are, but it's their diamonds and their DVD that bloody Wolfie stole. Fuck me! I don't believe what I'm seeing!'

'What do you mean they took you there?' Kerry asked, confused.

Ricci glanced at her, then back at the television.

'They took me and Nick there. Kidnapped us, they did. They took us right into the underground garage area and they were going to fucking waterboard us because we couldn't tell them where the discs were. They didn't believe us that we didn't know. That's why we were chasing Wolfie down, Kerry. These guys mean business.'

'Well, not any more they don't,' Kerry said. 'If these guys are the two Russians you're talking about.'

'But who the fuck could have the balls to bump off Russian gangsters?' Ricci asked.

Kerry glanced at Hill, and for a moment it crossed her mind that he had been doing his homework and perhaps sent a hitman to get rid of the Russians.

'Don't look at me, Kerry. I've got nothing to do with it, I promise you. But if it is them guys, then, fuck 'em.'

Kerry looked at Ricci, who was pacing the floor.

'Tell you what though,' she said. 'Whoever has done this knows what they're doing. This is a hit, all right.'

'But who would bump off a couple of bigshot Russians like this? I mean, none of the hoods around here would do that. There's too many Russians to take on for someone to do that.'

Kerry said nothing. Her instinct told her dark forces were at work here, and that maybe Quentin Fairhurst was behind it. But she didn't mention it, because the idea that a member of the government could be behind the murder of two Russian gangsters was far too fanciful. Or was it?

'Right,' she said, looking at Hill. 'We're out of here. If this is the Yuri character or anyone related to that mob, then I'm not sitting around waiting for any fallout.' She stood up. 'Let's go, Billy.'

Ricci turned to them.

'But what about me?'

'What about you?' Kerry asked.

'What if they come after me?'

Kerry managed to keep her face straight.

'Well, Alfi. That's your problem.'

Kerry and Hill were about to walk past Ricci when he stretched his hand out to block their way.

'But I thought we could work together, Kerry. Me and the Caseys. We could do a lot for each other.'

Kerry turned around.

'Yeah. Sure. Like the way you worked with Wolfie?' She shook her head. 'The Caseys don't deal with guys like you, Alfi. There is no room for you in our organisation.'

And with that, Kerry and Hill strode out of the doors, their security following behind.

Across the city in Westminster, Quentin Fairhurst sat at his desk, stirring sugar into his espresso. It had been a rough few days. But it was over now. He was watching the news on Sky as they reported on the murder of two unnamed Russians. But Fairhurst didn't need their names. His phone would ring at any moment and it would be the Home Secretary hyperventilating that the police had given the names of the dead as Yuri and Dima, enforcers for Russian billionaire Anatoly.

CHAPTER THIRTY-FOUR

Kerry hadn't felt so exhausted in a very long time. The last couple of weeks since she'd returned from London had been busy with meetings, organising and planning the next step for the Caseys. She couldn't believe how swiftly things had moved after her confrontation with Quentin Fairhurst. Within a week of their meeting, Marty had called her to say that the brief in London had told him that Vic Paterson had already been released. Even the QC couldn't make sense of it, but he was told there was a technicality over drugs not actually being present in the truck, as well as the credibility of the informer. Marty had never asked Kerry about the meeting with Fairhurst, because he'd expressly told her not to do it, but he would have guessed that she had blackmailed him. He had simply said to her when they last talked that he hoped this wouldn't come back to haunt them.

Kerry lay in bed, listening to the rain on the windows.

Sharon was arriving from Spain today with her son and Vic. She was looking forward to finally meeting Vic, and there was to be a celebration dinner at the house later with Danny, Jack and Marty and a couple more close associates. She was planning to make her announcement after dinner, that she was stepping back in the next few weeks. The business empire was thriving in every area where the Caseys had gone legit, especially in Spain, and Kerry had decided she wanted to make her home there before her baby was born. How any of that would fit with Vinny's life she didn't know, and right now she wasn't even sure how much they would be in each other's lives. She knew that she wanted him, but she couldn't ask him to give up his work. It was something she would discuss with him when he got back from wherever the hell he was. Her hand automatically went to her stomach and she was thrilled that soon she'd be able to feel tiny movements of her baby inside her. Not for the first time, she wished her mother could be here to be with her through this. She sat up on the bed. There was no point in wishing for things that couldn't happen, so she would just do as she always did and get on with it. As she was about to go into the bathroom for a shower, her mobile rang on her bedside table. She picked it up, but there was no name on the screen.

She stood up and walked towards the window.

'Is that Kerry Casey?' It was a male voice she didn't recognise.

'Who's this?'

'I'd like to speak to Kerry Casey please.'

'This is Kerry, but who is this?'

'Kerry. My name is John Sullivan. You don't know me. I'm a policeman. I worked with Vinny Burns. Undercover.'

Kerry's stomach dropped. He'd said 'worked'. Past tense.

'What do you mean "worked"?' Kerry blurted. 'Has something happened to Vinny?'

Silence. Kerry could hear her heartbeat.

'Are you there? What's going on?'

'Sorry. Look, Kerry, I shouldn't even be speaking to you. But Vinny told me a lot about you, and I know how he felt . . . and–'

'Wait! Where's Vinny?' Kerry couldn't stop herself interrupting. 'Why are *you* phoning and not him?'

Silence. Then eventually, 'Kerry. Vinny is missing.'

The words echoed around her head.

'Missing? What do you mean? When?'

'I can't talk long on the phone. But Vinny was working undercover in Spain. With me. We were working with the Spanish cops and the Drug Enforcement Agency on an undercover operation. I can't say much more than that on the phone. But Vinny was supposed to meet me and he didn't turn up. That's just not like him. No phone call. No messages. Nothing. That was ten days ago.'

'Christ! Someone's kidnapped him?'

'Looks like it.'

'Jesus. So what are the police doing about it?'

'That's the thing. There's only so much they can do. We've got our own contacts on the ground, and all we've picked up is that he was taken by three guys as he left his apartment.'

'Three guys? What three guys? You mean people you were watching?'

'I don't know, Kerry. We work undercover. We watch our backs all the time, but we run the risk of something like this happening. Someone must have got inside information that Vinny was a cop.'

'Jesus!' Kerry said. 'You have to find him, John. I mean the cops. They can't just leave a guy to go missing. To ... to ...' The words 'To die' were on the tip of her tongue, but she couldn't say it. Vinny couldn't be dead. He wouldn't be. She had to believe that.

'That's why I wanted to talk to you. There's only so much the police will do. *Can* do. I wanted to ask if you could help. Christ! If my bosses knew I was talking to you I'd be in all sorts of shit. But sometimes it takes people ... well, like your organisation to make something happen. Someone who can go to places we can't. Someone who can maybe get access to people we can't.'

She knew exactly what he was getting at.

'When can I see you?' Kerry said, without even considering if what he was asking was viable. 'Can you come here to my house?'

'Best not to. I can meet you in Glasgow. In a café or something.'

'Fine. Tell me where and when.'

'Tomorrow morning. Bridgeton Cross. There's a café under the bridge. I'll meet you there at ten. Can you do that?'

'I'll be there.'

He hung up, and Kerry stood for a second looking out at the guards patrolling the ground. She always felt so safe and protected in this house. But suddenly she was filled with cold dread. Vinny was missing. If she did nothing else in this world, she would find him. She had to. She thought of Marty Kane and how he must have felt when his grandson was taken. But this wasn't a kidnapped child they could barter with in the hope that the Colombians wouldn't kill a child. If an undercover cop had gone missing in Spain, he was probably already dead.

ACKNOWLEDGEMENTS

When I'm writing, I need to be alone, isolated and living like a hermit. But after a while I go stir crazy, and have to get back to the busy mayhem that is my other life. I'm grateful for all it brings to me, and I'm blessed to have so many people by my side. Here's a few I want to thank for their support.

My sister Sadie who has always been my rock, through laughter and kids, and sometimes tears.

Katrina, Matthew and Christopher, who are an inspiration with their brightness and humour. Wee Jude, who amazes me every day, and Ruairi who makes me laugh, and the adorable, almost new, Cillian, who's bewildered by them both! Thanks also to my brother Des who always takes a great interest in my work.

My cousins, the Motherwell Smiths, and the Timmonses, who have been a huge support, as well as Alice and Debbie and all their family in London. And my cousins Annmarie and Anne, Helen and Irene.

I am lucky to have so many close friends; Mags, Eileen, Liz, Annie, Mary, Phil, Francie, and journalists Simon, Lynn, Mark, Maureen, Keith, Annie, and Thomas in Australia. Also, Helen and Bruce, Mairi, Barbara, Jan, Donna, Louise, Gordon and Janetta, Brian and Jimmy, Ian, David, Ramsay, and Brian Steel.

In Ireland, I am grateful to Mary and Paud, for their support, and Sean Brendain at TPs – the best pub in the West. And in La Cala de Mijas, great friends, Yvonne, Mara, Wendy, Jean, Maggie, Patricia, Sarah and Fran – all of them who help promote my books on the Costa del Sol.

Thanks also to my publisher Jane Wood for all her encouragement and keeping me on my toes! And to Therese Keating, my editor, for her brilliant work, Ella Patel in publicity, and all the top team at Quercus.

Last but not least, I'm so lucky to have a growing army of readers, and want to thank every one of them. Without you, I wouldn't be writing this.